The Face of Another

BOOKS BY KOBO ABE

Secret Rendevous (1979) *
The Box Man (1974) *
Inter Ice Age 4 (1970)
The Ruined Map (1969) *
The Face of Another (1966) *
The Woman in the Dunes (1964)

* AVAILABLE IN PERIGEE BOOKS EDITIONS

Translated from the Japanese by
E. DALE SAUNDERS

The Face

of Another

BY KOBO ABÉ

A Perigee Book

Perigee Books
are published by
G. P. Putnam's Sons
200 Madison Avenue
New York, New York 10016

Originally published in Japanese by Kodansha, Tokyo, as
Tanin No Kao. Copyright © 1964 by Kobo Abe.

This is an authorized reprint of a hardcover edition originally
published by Alfred A. Knopf, Inc.

Library of Congress Cataloging in Publication Data
Abe, Kōbō, 1924–
    The face of another.

    Translation of Tanin no kao.
    Reprint of the ed. published by Knopf, New York.
I. Title.
PZ4.A13Fac 1980 [Pl845.B4] 895.6'35 80-15074
ISBN 0-399-50484-2

First Perigee Printing, 1980

PRINTED IN THE UNITED STATES OF AMERICA

NOTE

The forty-four drawings in this volume are by ROBERT STEELE WALLACE

The Face of Another

AT LAST you have come, threading your way through the endless passages of the maze. With the map you got from *him*, you have finally found your way to my hideaway—the first room at the top of the creaking, harmonium-pedal stairs. You've mounted with somewhat shaky steps. You hold your breath and knock. Why is there no answer? Instead, only a young girl comes running like a kitten. She is supposed to open the door for you. You ask if there isn't a message; the girl doesn't answer but smiles and runs away.

You peep in, looking for *him*. But he isn't there, not a trace is left; and an odor of ruin floats in the air. A dead room. Expressionless walls look back at you; you shudder. As you are about to go, though with a feeling of guilt, the three notebooks on the table, together with the letter, catch your eye, and you realize that you too are trapped at last. No matter how loathesome the thoughts that well up in you, you cannot resist the temptation. You have torn open the envelope with trembling hands, and now you are beginning to read the letter.

You are probably humiliated and angry. But I should like you to fix your eyes on the paper, though you don't want to, and go on reading. I want so desperately for you to come safely through this moment and make a step toward me. Have I lost to *him* or has *he* lost to me? Either way, my masked play is over. I have murdered him, and I proclaim myself the criminal. I shall confess everything, entirely. Whether you act out of generosity or selfishness, I want you to go on reading. He who has the right to sit in judgment also has the obligation to listen to the defendant's statement.

You may be suspected, of course, of false complicity if you simply abandon me as I kneel here. Well, sit down; relax. If the air in the room is bad, open the window at once. A teapot and cups are in the kitchen if you want them. As soon as you settle down, the place will change instantaneously from a hideaway at the end of a maze into a court of law. To make the end of my masked play more real, I have decided to go on waiting, while you look through the deposition. For the time being, just remembering *him* keeps me from boredom.

Well then, let's trace back the skein of my hours. Perhaps it was some time during the morning, about three days ago from *your* "now." That night a sticky, rain-laden wind kept badgering the window in its frame. Though it had been too warm during the day, we missed the heat when evening came. According to the papers it was supposed to turn cold again, but the days had obviously grown longer. Soon, when the rains let up, it would be summer. I was worried as I thought about it. In my present state I was like wax, limp from the heat. Just thinking of the ceaselessly shining sun made my skin break out in blisters.

Then I thought I would like to settle the matter somehow before summer came. According to the long-term forecast, a continental high-pressure system would begin to spread, and apparently for the next three or four days there would be summery weather. In short, it would be perfect if, within three days, I could finish my preparations for meeting you and run the story right on after this letter. But three days could scarcely be considered enough. For, as you can see, the statement is a record stretching over a whole year and filling three notebooks the size of folios. It will be a big job to finish up a notebook a day to my satisfaction—rewriting, deleting, and revising. I had braced myself for the task and come directly back today two or three hours earlier than usual, bringing a midnight snack of meat dumplings liberally spiced with garlic.

But vexingly enough, the result was simply that I was again made aware of the utter insufficiency of time. Actually, when I skimmed through the notebooks, I was dissatisfied with the tone, which smacked too much of apology. It was extraordinary for me to be so irked by this soaking night, although it would make anyone gloomy. I did not intend to deny that the final act was rather wretched, but I continued confident that at least I was always alert in my own way. Without that confidence, how could I possibly go on tirelessly writing such notebooks, which might constitute either support for my alibi or proof of my guilt? I didn't mean I would not admit defeat. But I still firmly believe that the maze in which I was caught is the ultimate, the logical tribulation. Yet, contrary to expectations, the notebooks continued to bawl piteously, like some penned-up tomcat. I wondered if I should work them over until I was satisfied with their smoothness, forgetting the three-day limit.

No. That is enough. I can't stand the feeling of having a piece of half-chewed gristle stick in my throat at the very moment I'm resigned to confess everything. The sections that seem to shriek are all trivial, so I shall be satisfied if I can just get you to read them. Your main irritations are electric drills, the sound of scraping on plate glass, and cockroaches; but you can hardly say that these are the essentials of life. You associate electric drills with the dentist, I imagine; but the other two are strange items which I cannot describe other than as psychological hives. I have never yet heard of hives being fatal.

Well, let's drop it for now and wind things up. It serves no purpose to pile justifications on justifications. It is more important that you should go on reading the letter—my time quite overlaps with your present—that you should keep on reading the notebooks . . . without giving up . . . to the last page, when I will catch up with your time.

(Now you're relaxed, aren't you? Yes, yes. The tea's in the squat green can. The water's already boiled and now in the thermos jug, so go ahead and use it.)

THE BLACK
NOTEBOOK

By the way, the order of the notebooks is by color: black, white, and grey. There is no relationship, of course, between colors and content. I chose haphazardly, merely to distinguish among notebooks.

First of all, I wonder if I should start with the hideaway. It makes little difference where I do start. But it's easy to begin talking about that day. It was then, about two weeks ago, that I was to leave the city for a week on business. It was the first trip I had planned since leaving the hospital; perhaps it was also a day that greatly impressed you. Ostensibly, the purpose of the trip was to inspect progress in constructing a printing-ink factory in Osaka. But this was a pretext. Actually on that day, I shut myself up in my room at the S— Apartments, putting the finishing touches to my plans. Here is a sample from the diary entry for that day:

May 26. Raining. I went to visit the S— Apartments I
located through a newspaper advertisement. A child,
playing in the front garden, broke out crying as soon as
she saw my face. But geographically the location is good
and the arrangement of the rooms almost ideal, so I shall
settle on this one. There is a piercing, pungent smell of
new wood and fresh paint. The room next door seems to
be vacant. Something tells me I could probably rent that
one too....

But at the S— Apartments I did not use another name, nor
did I try to conceal my identity. Perhaps this appears in-
discreet, but I had my own scheme. Having gone this far with
the deception about my face, there was nothing to be done
about it. Actually, some little girl about primary-school age,
playing in front of the entryway, had taken one look at me—
I must have appeared like something out of a nightmare—and
begun sobbing. Of course, the superintendent was stupidly
affable, doubtless because it was his business. . . .
No, the affability wasn't confined to the superintendent.
. . . Unfortunately, almost everybody I met gave me, un-
grudging, only affability. As long as things did not go any
further, everyone put up a fine show. And that was to be
expected. If they did not want to look me square in the face,
at least they had to be affable, I suppose. Anyway thanks to
that, I was able to avoid unnecessary inquisitiveness. Shut off
by a wall of affability, I was always completely alone.
Perhaps because the S— Apartments had been so recently
constructed almost half the eighteen units were still empty.
Although I did not request it, the superintendent showed
me to the farthest room on the second floor, next to an
emergency stairway. That's the long and short of it. Of
course, his picking out that particular unit for me was in-
contestably valuable. The bathroom was ordinary, not first-

class; a desk was provided along with two chairs; and there was a terrace-like bay window which the other rooms did not have. Furthermore, a parking lot with four or five places was located at the bottom of the emergency stairway, and from there one could get out directly by a side driveway. This was quite useful too. I had to be prepared from the start, so I immediately paid a three-months' deposit. At the same time, I told the superintendent to buy bedding from a near-by shop and have it delivered. The man was increasingly less able to conceal his delight and kept on prattling endlessly about the sunniness of the place and the excellence of the ventilation. When those subjects of conversation were exhausted, he would go on jabbering about himself. But when he held out the key to me, it slipped from his grasp—luckily—and fell to the floor, making a sharp clatter. With an abashed expression, he hastily tore the seal from the gas-inlet valve and departed. Thank God! If false veneer always came off so easily, what a relief it would be.

IT HAD already become so dark I could not count the fingers on the hand I held before my face. The room, unused to human habitation, was cold and unaffable. But this was better than an affable man. I had grown terribly familiar with darkness since the event in question. How wonderful it would be, frankly, if everybody in the world

would suddenly lose his sight or forget the existence of light.
Immediately, there would be agreement about *form*. Everybody would accept the fact that a loaf of bread is a loaf of
bread whether triangular or round. The girl a little while ago
would have kept her eyes shut and listened to my voice. If
she had, perhaps we could have become friendly and I could
have taken her to the playground and we could have eaten
ice cream together. Just because there was light, she heed-
lessly thought that a triangular loaf of bread was not bread
but a triangle. This thing called light is itself transparent, but
it apparently changes into something nontransparent.

But there is light, actually, and darkness is at most a stay
of execution with a definite time limit. When I opened the
window, a rain-drenched wind blew in, like black vapor. Without thinking, I inhaled it; I took off my sunglasses and wiped
away the tears, whereupon the tops of telephone poles and
the wires to the shops set back along the main street and the
line of the eaves caught the light from the passing cars and
shone dimly like traces of chalk left on a blackboard.

There was a sound of footsteps approaching along the hallway. With a gesture that had become habit, I readjusted my
glasses. It was a man delivering the bedding I had ordered.
I stuck the money under the door and asked him to leave the
bedding in the hallway.

Somehow it seemed that everything was ready for the start.
When I took off my coat and opened the closet, I found a
mirror attached to the back of the door. I took off my glasses
again, removed my mask, and, looking in the mirror, began to
undo the bandages. The three layers of cloth were swollen
with sweat and felt twice as heavy as when I had put them on
in the morning.

As I removed the bandages, a leech-like mass crept out
across my face . . . the keloid scars, swollen and distended, red

and black intertwining. . . . How repulsive! Since this was daily routine, I should be used to it soon. . . .

I was vexed even more by my unwarranted surprise. When I thought about my feeling, it seemed baseless, irrational. Why did one have to put up a hue and cry about anything so trifling as the skin on one's face, which, after all, was only a small part of the human capsule? Such prejudice and set ideas, of course, are not especially strange. For example, belief in magic . . . racial prejudice . . . groundless fear of snakes (or the morbid terror of cockroaches that I mentioned in my letter). . . .

While such a situation would be understandable in a pimply adolescent who lives in visions, it was ridiculous for me, the section head of a respectable laboratory, moored securely to this world by an anchor-like weight, to be afflicted by psychological hives. I realized there was no particular reason for my abhorrence of the leech-like scars, but I was unable to stop my suffering, although fed up with the whole thing.

Of course, I intended to try. Rather than run aimlessly away, it would be best, I suppose, to face the situation squarely and get used to it once and for all. If I made nothing of it, then surely no one else would either. With this thought in mind, and of my own accord, I had made my face the subject of conversation at the Institute. I had compared myself, for example, to the masked monsters of television, deliberately exaggerated. I had stressed the advantages of seeing-without-being-seen—since my expression was inscrutable to others—and appeared amused by the whole thing. To accustom others to my face was the best short cut to getting used to it myself.

The stratagem seemed to work. I was then able to get along at the laboratory with no sense of constraint. There is more to those popular masked monsters, too, than appears; I began to understand why they turn up over and over again in comic books and on television. My mask itself—were it not for the scars underneath, spreading like webs—was comfortable enough. If covering our bodies with clothes represents a cultural step forward, there is no guarantee that in the future masks will not be taken equally for granted. Even now they are often used in important ceremonies and festivals. I do not quite know how to put it, but I wonder if a mask, being universal, enhances our relations with others more than does the naked face.

Sometimes I believed I was on the way to recovery. But I did not yet truly realize the repulsiveness of my face. Meanwhile, the leech-like corrosion continued its steady progress under the bandage. Despite the doctor's assurance that chilblains caused by liquid air were not as deep as fire burns and that accordingly recovery should be rapid, the leech scars overcame one line of defense after another in spite of every possible countermeasure: X-ray treatments, cortisone shots, and antibiotics taken internally. The scar army called out its reinforcements, one after the other, to occupy new areas of my face.

For example, one day—it was the noon break, and I had just returned from a liaison meeting between my colleagues and another department—a young assistant, a girl, graduated just this year, approached me with a mischievous expression, turning over the pages of some book.

"Look, Doctor. This is a fascinating picture." Under her slim, teasing finger lay a line drawing by Klee entitled *False Face*.

The features were divided horizontally by parallel lines and, depending on how the picture was viewed, could be conceived of as a bandage wrapped round and round. Slight, narrow apertures revealed only the eyes and the mouth, and the expression was expressionless to the point of cruelty. Suddenly I was overcome by an indescribable feeling of humiliation. Of course, the girl hadn't intended malice. What had given her the idea was basically the result of my own conscious provocation. Easy does it! If I were to get angry at this point, all my efforts would fail. Although I admonished myself thus, I was so upset that the picture appeared to be my very own face seen through the girl's eyes. A false face, seen but unable to look back. It was intolerable to think that I appeared to the girl like this.

Suddenly, I ripped the book in two. And with it my heart. From the tear my insides came running out like a rotten egg. I became an empty, cast-off skin. Piling the torn pages together, I regretfully handed them back to the girl. But it was too late. The thermostat of the isothermic tank, which in normal circumstances was inaudible, made a tremendous noise like the bending of a zinc plate. The girl's knees knocked together with such force under her skirt that they might well have fused.

IT SEEMED that I could not yet really comprehend the meaning behind my confusion at that time. I was so ashamed I writhed in anguish, still I did not rightly grasp what I had to be ashamed about. No, if I had tried I might have been able to understand, but perhaps I was taking refuge in what is commonly called "childish behavior," instinctively avoiding a deeper search. I can hardly believe that the face is so important to a man's existence. A man's worth should be gauged by the content of his work; possibly the convolutions of the surface of the brain have something to do with it, but his face certainly does not. If the loss of a face can cause conspicuous change in the scale of evaluation, it may well be owing to a fundamental emptiness of content.

But soon afterwards—several days after the incident of the picture—I was forced to realize to my dismay that the relative importance of a face far exceeds such wishful thinking. The warning came from the inside, stealthily. Absorbed in my defences against the outside, I was taken by surprise and easily overcome. The attack was so sharp and sudden that even while I was being overcome I was unable to grasp it at once.

That evening when I returned home I had an unusual longing to listen to Bach. It did not have to be Bach necessarily, but in my hangnail, wound-up mood, I wanted no jazz, no Mozart—Bach was indeed the most appropriate. I have never been a connoisseur of music, but perhaps I use it well. Sometimes, when my work was not making much headway, I chose music in keeping with my needs. If I chose to interrupt my thinking for a while there was piquant jazz; when I wanted impetus for a spurt there was the speculative Bartok; if I desired a feeling of freedom, there was the Beethoven of the quartets; when I wished to concentrate on a point, there were the spiral movements of Mozart; and then, Bach. He was the best for times when I needed spiritual balance.

But, for a moment, I suspected I had mistaken the record. If not, certainly the machine was out of kilter. The music sounded insane. I had never heard such Bach. If you suppose Bach to be balm for the soul, imagine it as nothing but a lump of clay, neither poison nor balm. It was meaningless and stupid; every phrase played seemed to me quite like a dusty, sticky lollipop.

At precisely that moment you filled two cups with black

tea and brought them into the room. When I said nothing, you must have thought I was absorbed in my listening, and you left, keeping your footsteps as quiet as possible. Then, it appeared that *I* was the one who was mad! Even so, I could not believe it. How should a wound on the face have any effect on one's sense of hearing? But the deformed Bach, no matter how I listened, would not go back to normal again; I could only assume the wound had produced this effect. I stuck a cigarette through the slit in the bandage and asked myself with a nervous fidget what I had lost along with my face. Apparently my philosophy about faces stood in need of fundamental revision.

Then, suddenly, as if the floor of time had slipped away, I found myself in a memory of thirty years ago. The event I had thought of not even once since then abruptly and vividly came back. It concerned my elder sister's false hair. I don't quite know how to put it, but I felt the wig to be unspeakably indecent and immoral. One time I sneaked it away and burned it up. My mother discovered this. She was strangely insistent. She questioned me, and although my action had been intended to do right, when it came to being examined I did not know what to answer and just stammered and blushed. No, if I had tried perhaps I might have been able to answer. But such things are sullied by being spoken aloud; I think my very strict moral sense made me be silent. . . . And if I replaced *false hair* with the word *face* the same unbearable feeling of frustration would fit in perfectly with the crumbling and empty sounds of the Bach.

When I stopped the record and came out of the study, as if impelled, you were just in the act of polishing some glasses lined up before you in the dining room. I cannot trace back what happened to me. But coming up against your resistance, I was at last able to grasp the meaning of my own position. I bore down on your shoulder with my right hand and tried to thrust my left hand up under your skirt. You gave a shriek and, suddenly straightening your legs, jumped up. The chair fell over and a glass crashed to the floor.

We stood transfixed, breathless, with the fallen chair between us. Admittedly my action must have been too headstrong. But I also had some excuse. It was a desperate effort to regain all at once what I was beginning to lose because of my ravaged face. Since the accident, the two of us had completely stopped sexual relations. In theory, I conceded that my face was an incidental reason, but in reality perhaps I was sneaking around trying a direct test of your response. I had been driven into a corner, and there was nothing to do but launch a frontal counterattack. Apparently I had tried to convince you by my action that the face was a mere screen, an illusion of no importance.

The feel of your inner thigh still glowed like powdered alabaster on my finger tips. A cry stuck in my throat like a bundle of thorns. How much I wanted to say . . . but I could not form a single word. Excuses? Consolation? Blame? If we had talked about it, we would have had to decide on one or the other, and such a decision would hardly have been enough. If it were a question of excuses and consolation, I would have preferred to melt away like smoke. Supposing I chose to attack. . . . Well, if I tore your face off, at least you would be the same as I . . . or some even more horrible goblin. Suddenly you began to sob. It was an unnerving sound, like air escaping from a faucet when the water stops.

Suddenly, a deep hole popped open in my face. It seemed gouged out so deep that with my whole body in it there would still have been more room. A liquid, like pus from a decayed tooth, dribbled down. Terrific stenches in the room, catching the sound, came swarming out like cockroaches—from inside the chair, from the corner of the cabinet, from the drain of the sink, from the lampshade discolored with the dead bodies of insects. I wanted a stopper for the hole in my face—anything would do. How I longed to put an end to this anguish, this game of blindman's buff with no blindman.

IT WAS a mere hair's breadth from this point to making plans for a mask. Basically, the idea was not at all extraordinary; like some windblown seed, it needed only a speck of ground and a drop of water to grow. And so the next day, without much enthusiasm or seriousness, as if the whole thing had been predetermined, I began looking through the indices of old scientific journals. It must have been the year before last, sometime in the summer, that there had been an article on artificial organs made of plastic. I would cover up the holes in my face with a plastic mask. Of course, according to one theory a mask is apparently the expression of an extremely metaphysical aspiration to give oneself a kind of transcendental disguise, for the mask is not simply something compensatory. Even I did not regard it as anything like a shirt or a pair of pants that I could change at will. However, I really don't know about the ancients, who believed in idols, and about adolescents who imitate them, but for me, at this point it is probably useless to decorate the altars of my next life with masks. No matter how many faces I have, there is no changing the fact that I am me. I was just attempting to fill in a too-long intermission in my life with a trivial "masked play."

I soon found the periodical I was looking for. According to the literature, it was apparently possible to construct a mask that would simulate real skin, at least outwardly. But there were a number of unresolved points such as mobility. If I were somehow to make it, most certainly I had to achieve expression, presumably by linking the mask to the muscles governing expression. I wanted something that could expand and contract freely, something that could laugh and cry. Even supposing the project were feasible at the present-day level of high-molecular chemistry, it did not seem within reach of a mere amateur's capacities. Yet at that time the mere possibility of the venture was a wonderful tranquilizer for me. If I could not have the tooth taken care of, I could at least take a temporary pain-killer.

At once, I decided to look up Doctor K, the author of the article on artificial organs, to hear what he had to say.

K's response on the telephone, however, was extremely rude; he seemed unenthusiastic, to say the least. Perhaps he felt some resentment at my being engaged in the same high-molecular work as he, But he agreed to see me, some time after four.

I handed over the switch inspection to the man in charge of the overtime shift, and when I had disposed of two or three remaining chits, I immediately left. The street was as bright as if it had been polished, and the breeze was laden with the scent of fragrant olive. I was unreasonably jealous of the smell and the light. As I waited for a taxi, I had the impression of being stared at from all sides, as if I were some interloper. All this was merely a negative image, with black and white reversed, and I stoically bore the too brilliant sunlight, thinking that if I could just get my hands on a mask, I should at once be able to recover the positive.

The building I went to was situated on a residential street somewhat difficult of access, near a station on the inner belt of the transit system. A rather unimposing sign, *K's High-Molecular Chemistry Institute*, hung outside the commonplace house. Just inside the gateway stood three rabbit hutches carelessly piled on top of each other.

In the narrow waiting room, along with an ashtray stand and a shabby wooden bench, lay a number of old magazines. Vaguely, I began to regret having come. *Institute* sounded respectable enough, but this was the kind of setup some neighborhood practitioner might choose. I wondered if K weren't merely some quack who was taking advantage of the uncertainty of his patients. As I looked around, I saw two photographs in slightly dirty frames decorating the walls. One showed a side view of a girl's face. She looked like a chinless field mouse. The other, doubtless after plastic surgery, showed a much better face over which hovered a faint smile.

My accumulated sleeplessness, turned into a heavy stiffness, began to spread to my forehead. The hard bench was beginning to make me restless, when finally the nurse showed me into the next room. The light filtering through the blinds lay in white, milk-like pools. On the table by the window a variety of unusual instruments, like hypodermic equipment, was menacingly laid out; beside the table stood a cabinet for medical charts and a swivel chair with arms; opposite was a waist-high dressing cubicle on rollers and a single-paneled screen with a metal frame—standard accouterments that made me feel increasingly disconsolate.

I lit a cigarette. As I arose to find an ashtray, I was suddenly startled by the contents of an enameled tray on the table. An ear, three fingers, an arm, and the side of a cheek from the eyelids to the lips lay there, casually arranged, with a freshness that bespoke their recent removal. I felt nauseous. They looked more real than genuine organs. I would never have supposed a replica could produce such a brutal impression. Although I could see the cut edges, and knew that the objects were unmistakably nothing more than molded plactic, I had the illusion that I could smell the stench of dead flesh.

Suddenly K appeared from behind the screen. I heaved a sigh of relief at his surprisingly mild appearance. Frizzy hair, thick, rimless spectacles like the bottom of tumblers, fleshy jowls. . . . A medicinal odor to which I was long accustomed gave me a feeling of intimacy with him.

Now it was his turn to be flustered. He studied my face with an expression of amazement, my card in his hand, and for a while said nothing.

"Well, then. . . . You . . . ," he stammered, glancing again at the card. His tone was considerably more temperate than the one he had used on the telephone. "Have you come as a patient?"

How was I to answer him? No matter how good K's technique was supposed to be, he could not possibly satisfy my ambitions. What I expected at most was his advice. But it was not my intention to hurt him by saying it to his face. K apparently took my silence for timidity and added sympathetically, "Please sit down. . . . What seems to be the trouble?"

"Well, you see . . . there was an explosion of liquid oxygen during an experiment I was performing. Perhaps because I was always accustomed to using liquid nitrogen—anyway, I was careless. . . ."

"Are they keloid scars?"

"On the whole face. I apparently have a predisposition to keloids. The doctor who diagnosed it fumbled and only irritated the scars, and there was a relapse; he just gave it up."

"But it appears to be all right around the lips."

Meanwhile I took off my sunglasses. "My eyes are intact too, thanks to my glasses. Perhaps it was fortunate I had to wear them for my myopia. . . ."

"That was lucky!" he exclaimed, as if it were he who was scarred. And then he added eagerly, "At least, you have your eyes and lips. If you couldn't move them, it would be really bad. Camouflage would be worthless, no matter how much form you constructed...."

K appeared enthusiastic about his work. He stared intently into my face, and in his mind he already seemed to be drawing a rough sketch. I suddenly changed the subject so as not to disappoint him.

"I read your article. It must have been last year, in the summer as I recall...."

"That's right. It was last year."

"And you know, I was amazed. I hadn't dreamed anything so elaborate could be done."

K picked up a shriveled finger with apparent satisfaction, and as he gently let it fall on his palm said: "You've got to have perseverance in this work, you know. Don't you think these fingerprints are quite the same as the real thing? They are so much so, actually, that the police department asked to register them."

"Do you use plaster of Paris for making the mold?"

"No, I use a silicon paste. Because plaster of Paris always skips the details. Look, see how clearly even the cuticle of the nail comes out."

I gingerly picked it up with the tips of my fingers; it had the soft feel of a living thing, and while I realized it was a fabrication, I had the weird sensation that it could infect me with— well, with death.

"It's something of a profane feeling, isn't it?"

"I expect a human body is...." K triumphantly took up another finger and stood it vertically on the surface of the table, with the cut edge down. A dead man seemed to be thrusting his finger upward through the boards of the table. "The trick is to deliberately make them slightly dirty like this.

If you went along with the patients' ideas to prettify them, you would get something very strange. For example, this is a middle finger, so on the back side of the first joint, I tried applying this brownish spot. It looks a little like a tobacco stain, doesn't it."

"Do you put it on with a brush or something?"

"Not at all. . . ." For the first time, K laughed out loud. "If you painted it on, it would come right off, wouldn't it? I build up different color elements from underneath. For example, for the nail, acetic acid vinyl . . . at the joints, the shadows of wrinkles . . . in places along the veins, a faint bluish green."

"Isn't this simply handicraft? Probably anyone could do it."

"That's true," he said, jiggling his leg. "But such stuff as this is elementary compared to work on the face. Whatever you say, it's the face that's hardest. First of all, there's the expression. As soon as you put on a bump or a wrinkle, even no more than a tenth of a millimeter, it takes on a profound meaning."

"But you can't make it move at all, I suppose, can you?"

"That's expecting too much." K spread his legs and directly faced me. "I've put all my efforts into making the outside of the face; I haven't come to movement. Of course, you can partially make up for this deficiency by choosing an area where there's little motion. But there's another problem—ventilation. In your case, I wouldn't know until I looked, but judging from what I see, you are perspiring even through the bandage. The sweat glands must still be alive. Because with the sweat glands alive, you can't cover the whole face with something that allows no ventilation. It's not only physiologically bad, but it would be so stifling I doubt you could stand it even half a day. It's best to be moderate about this kind of thing. An extreme change would be as laughable as an old man's fitting himself up with baby teeth. Any modification that doesn't call attention to itself is by far the most effective. . . . Can you take off the bandage yourself?"

"I can . . . but. . . ." Musing how best to tell him I was not a patient, as K seemed to think, I said: "To tell the truth, I'm in something of a fix, since I haven't completely made up my mind. I suppose there's no particular need at this point to be so fussy about my facial injury, to the extent of making such stopgap substitutes as these."

"Indeed there is!" K spoke emphatically, as if to encourage me. "Injuries to the body, especially the face, are not treated simply as problems of form. We should rather speak of them as belonging in the province of mental hygiene. Otherwise, who would willingly devote his efforts to cosmetic work? As a doctor, I have my pride. I should never be satisfied to be only a craftsman making imitations."

"Yes, I understand."

"Do you, really?" he asked. "You're the one who said my work was only on the level of handicraft."

"I didn't particularly mean it that way."

"Don't worry about it . . . please," K rejoined with the generosity of an understanding schoolmaster. "When it comes right down to it, you're not the only one who vacillates. No, it's common enough to feel resistance to having one's face manufactured. Perhaps, since modern times. . . . Even now, primitive men make false faces as a matter of course. . . . I'm unfortunately not enough of a specialist to understand why attitudes have changed. But there's statistical proof. For example, if you consider exterior wounds, facial injuries are about one and a half times as numerous as injuries to the four extremities. And yet the number of people who request treatment for the loss of a limb or even a finger is eighty percent higher. There's clearly some taboo about the face. On this point even doctors are in agreement. There are only a few opinionated men who treat my work as that of a high-class, money-grubbing beautician."

"But it isn't particularly strange to respect content more than appearance, is it?"

"Do you mean respecting contents that have no container? I have no faith in that. As far as I'm concerned I firmly believe that man's soul is housed in his skin."

"Metaphorically speaking, of course. . . ."

"It's no metaphor . . . ," he continued soothingly, but in a conclusive tone. "Man's soul is in his skin. I believe that to the letter. During the war when I was in the Army as a doctor, I learned that through intense experience. It was routine on the battlefield for men to have their arms and legs shot off and their faces smashed to pieces. But what do you think the wounded appreciated most? It wasn't their lives, nor even the recovery of their faculties; what concerned men more than anything else was whether or not their looks would be the same as before. At first, I too would laugh them down. Because on the battlefield any value outside of bodily health and the number of stars on your insignia did not signify. However, one time I came across a soldier who didn't seem to be badly hurt, outside of a horribly disfigured face; but just when he was on the point of leaving the hospital, he committed suicide. He had been in a state of shock. Since then, I have come to observe with the greatest care the appearance of soldiers who have been wounded. And, ultimately, I have come to one conclusion. And it's a distressing one: serious exterior injuries, especially to the face, leave definite mental trauma."

"Well. . . . I suppose there are such cases. But, as long as there's not exactly any basis in theory for the idea, I should not think of it as a general law no matter how many instances there were." Suddenly an intolerable anger welled up in me. I had not come to talk about myself.

"Actually, I myself don't feel so keenly about it yet," I went on. "I beg your pardon. I'm terribly sorry I've been wasting your valuable time when I'm so undecided."

"Please, just a minute." He chuckled confidently. "Perhaps I have imposed on you, but I'm quite certain of what I'm saying. If you let things go as they are, most assuredly you'll spend your whole life in bandages. The very fact of your wearing them at present is proof you think them infinitely better than what's underneath. Well, for the present the face you had before you were hurt is still more or less living in the memories of the people around you. But time doesn't wait. Gradually that memory will grow faint. People who never saw your original face will come to know you. In the end, you will be sentenced for nonpayment on the promissory note of your bandage. Although you're alive, you'll be consigned to oblivion."

"You're exaggerating! What do you mean by that?"

"You can see any number among the injured who have lost the use of their arms and legs. Even blind men and deaf mutes are not so extraordinary. But where have you ever seen a man without a face? You probably haven't. Do you think they have all evaporated into thin air?"

"I don't know. I'm not interested in other people."

Inadvertently, my voice had become strident. It was like being severely lectured and forced to buy a lock after one has gone to the police station to report a theft. But K had not given up.

"I'm sorry, but apparently you don't really understand. The face, in the final analysis, is the expression. The expression—how shall I put it?—well, the expression is something like an equation by which we show our relationship with others. It's a roadway between oneself and others. If it's blocked by a landslide, even those who have been at pains to travel it will think you are now some uninhabited, dilapidated house and perhaps pass by."

"That's quite all right. There's no need for them to force themselves to stop in."

"In short, you mean you're going your own way, don't you?"

"Is that wrong?"

"It's an established theory in infant psychology that the human animal can validate his ego only through the eyes of others. Have you ever seen the expressions of imbeciles or schizophrenics? If the roadway is left blocked too long, one ultimately quite forgets there is one."

To avoid being cornered, I tried to strike back at random.

"Yes, indeed. So let's suppose that expression is precisely what you say. Isn't it all rather contradictory, though? How in the world will you restore expression with your way of doing things, which is to put a makeshift cover over only a certain part of the face?"

"Don't worry. If you're concerned, please leave that to me. That's my specialty. At least, I have confidence that I can offer you something better than your bandages. Well, now, shall we take them off? I'd like you to let me take a few pictures, and with them as a basis, we'll make a graduated selection, by a process of elimination, of the elements necessary for the restoration of expression. We'll pick some stable places with little mobility and...."

"I beg your pardon, but...." I wanted only to get away. I forgot all about keeping up appearances and began to entreat and implore him. "Rather than that, I wonder if you wouldn't just sell me that one finger."

As I anticipated, K was struck dumb with amazement, and rubbing his wrist along his thigh, said: "A finger.... This one, do you mean?"

"If you won't sell a finger, an ear or anything else will do very well."

"But. . . . It's a question of the keloid scars on your face, I thought."

"I'm sorry. If it's impossible, I'll get along without it, but. . . ."

"I don't understand. It's not particularly that I can't sell you a finger, but . . . but, even that is surprisingly expensive. Anyhow, for each one, I have to make an antimony cast, you see. The cost of materials alone comes to about fifty dollars. And that's a low estimate. . . ."

"Fine."

"I really don't understand . . . what you're thinking of."

He didn't have to understand. The whole exchange between us seemed to be proceeding on two quite divergent rails. I took out my wallet and, as I counted out the money, I repeated my earnest apologies.

I left, holding the artificial finger in my pocket like a dangerous weapon. The shadows and light of evening were extremely distinct, but seemed more artificial than the finger. When some young boys who were playing catch in a narrow lane saw me, they changed color and pressed away from me against the fence. Their faces looked as though they were dangling by their ears on clothespins. If I took off the bandage and showed them the real thing, they'd be a lot more surprised! I was seized with an impulse to rip off my bandages in earnest and to jump into the midst of this landscape that seemed like pasted bits of paper. But without a face, it was impossible for me to take a single step away from my bandages. The picture of brandishing the fake finger in my pocket with all my might and ripping that landscape to pieces floated into my mind. I was no more affected by K's disagreeable remark about being buried alive than by the filling of a molar. Well, look, if I could cover my face with an imitation completely indistinguishable from the real thing, however fake the landscape might be, it couldn't make me an outcast.

THAT evening, I stood the artificial finger on the table like a candle and spent a sleepless night endlessly pondering one aspect and then another of the "fake" which appeared more genuine than the real thing.

Perhaps beyond that, I was imagining the masked ball of the fairy tale in which I would before long appear. But wasn't it actually symbolic that even in idle fancy I could not help but add a "fairy-tale" commentary? I have written about this before, but I made my plans lightheartedly, as if I were skipping over some narrow ditch. Of course, I had thought out no final solution. Was it because I strove in my subconscious to consider the mask itself simply the extension of an entirely consistent attitude of self-defense, according to which the loss of my face was not the loss of anything particularly essential? From one point of view, the problem was not the mask itself; there seemed rather to be at work here a challenge to the face and to the authority of the face. If I had not come to feel cornered, because of the collapsed Bach and your rebuff, perhaps I should have felt considerably more nonchalant and glib about my face.

Yet, a deep black shadow grew in my heart, like India ink dropped in a glass of water. It was K's idea that faces were a roadway between men. When I reflected on it now, if I had been struck with a rather unfortunate impression of K, it was not because of his complacency nor his insistence on medical treatment, but apparently because of this thought. If one accepted such reasoning, I who had lost my face was destined

to be shut up forever in a solitary cell ... with no roadway ...
and so a mask became invested with a terribly profound meaning. My plan was to attempt to break out of my jail—on that
I would stake my very being—and accordingly my present
condition was a suitably desperate state. Indeed, what we
mean when we say "terrible conditions" is conditions which
we are aware of as being terrible. It was this awareness that
I could not possibly accept.

Even I recognize that a roadway between people is a necessity. I keep on writing these sentences to you precisely because
I do fully recognize this. But I wonder if the face alone is the
one and only roadway. I cannot believe it. My doctoral dis-
sertation, which was on rheology, was properly understood
by people who had never seen my face. Of course, with a
mere scientific thesis one could not pretend to dispose of the
matter of intercourse between people. Actually, what I ask
of you is quite something else again. I want some sign of a
completely meaningful human relationship—the lines are in-
distinct—call it heart or soul. Because this association is far
more complex than a relationship between animals, who express themselves by their odors alone, I suppose facial expression is an adequate communicating roadway. Just as currency
is a more evolved system of exchange than barter. But even
currency is after all simply a means; it's not almighty in every
single situation. In some cases checks or money orders are
more convenient; in others, jewels or precious metals.

Isn't it a preconception derived from habit to suppose that
the soul and the heart are in the same category and can be
negotiated only through the face? Isn't it common to find a
single poem or book or record that communicates with the
heart far more profoundly than a hundred years of scanning
faces. If a face were indispensable, a blind man couldn't know
such things as human characteristics, could he? I am more
concerned about intercourse between human beings narrow-
ing and stereotyped by too much dependence on the habit of

faces. Actually, a good example is the stupid prejudice about the color of skin. To judge the soul's roadway according to the color of a face is something describable only as an attitude which disregards the soul.

EXCURSUS: *When I read this over now, I suppose I did not want to be bound by my face, but I had apparently been making transparent self-justifications. For example, I was first attracted to you through your face. And even now, when I think of the distance between us, the measure of it is the remoteness of your expression and nothing else. Yes, for quite some time I should have frankly imagined that our positions were reversed and that you were the one who had lost your face. Undervaluation and overvaluation of the face are equally artificial. So it would seem that I referred before to my sister's wig in order to explain my feelings of not wanting to cling to my face, but I am dubious about the suitability of that reference. In short, isn't my concern about my face simply a common adolescent interest in, and antagonism to, cosmetics? Or perhaps I was beginning to feel slightly jealous of the fact that my sister was trying to make herself attractive.*

Incidentally, one more thing—I read once in some news-paper or review a strangely thought-provoking article about a Korean with Japanese blood, who in order to look more like a Korean went to the trouble of undergoing plastic surgery. This was clearly a stress on facial restoration, but it could never be said the man was implicated in prejudice. In the final analysis, I realized I hadn't comprehended a single thing. If the opportunity presented itself, I should really like very much to hear what kind of advice the Korean would give someone like me who had lost his face.

Finally, I tired of this soliloquy about a face, this soliloquy that made no progress. But there was no particular reason, either, to abandon the plans that I had been at pains to begin. I began to devote close attention to technical observations.

The artificial finger had extremely interesting aspects. The more I looked at it, the more I appreciated the fine points of its construction. It expressed as much as an actual finger to me. From the tension of the skin, I should suppose it was the finger of a person aged about thirty. A flat nail, squashed areas on the sides, deep wrinkles in the joints, four small cuts in a row like shark's gills. It probably belonged to a person engaged in light handwork.

Yet, why was it so ugly? Repulsive! A kind of special un-savoriness, neither of the dead nor of the living. No, appar-ently nothing had gone wrong. Was it rather that the recon-struction was too faithful? (If so, that would be true of my mask too.) So, it could be that if one clung too closely to reality, the result might well be far from realistic. It may be all right to be particular about faces, but first take a look at this ugliness!

It is quite true, of course, that an accurate copy may ac-tually be unrealistic. However, could you conceive of a form-less finger? A snake without length, a pot without volume, a triangle without angles? Unless such things exist on another planet, they are not to be seen with one's eyes. If they were, even a face without expression wouldn't be exceptional. Even if such a face did sometimes occur, it could hardly be a face. Indeed, masks have this much *raison d'être*.

Then, the problem may lie in the physical element. First of all, it would be curious to speak of a form that couldn't move as one's person. If this finger could only move, it would look much better. As an experiment, I picked it up and tried working it. It did in fact seem more realistic than when it had been standing on the table. So there was no need worry-ing over that point. Thus I insisted from the beginning that mine must be a mask that moved.

But I was still somehow dissatisfied. What in heaven's name could be the cause of such concern? I focused all my attention, comparing the artificial member with my own finger. There definitely was a difference, but. . . . Suppose it was not the fault of its being severed, nor the problem of movement. Could it be the quality of the skin? I wonder. Perhaps. There was a characteristic difference that could not be masked simply by form or color.

MARGINALIA I: *On the feel of skin. Human skin seems to be protected by a transparent matter having no pigmentation. Is not the look of skin, accordingly, one of complex interaction between the light rays reflected from the surface and those which, having passed through this surface, are again reflected from the pigment? This effect was not obtained in the case of the molded finger, since the pigment was directly on the surface.*

Inquire of a specialist about the composition and optical properties of this transparent matter in the skin.

MARGINALIA II: *Important subjects for investigation: wear of the material, elasticity and flexibility, fixing process, procedure with the edge line, ventilation, procurement of the model, and general procedure.*

To BE SURE, the very fact that I have tried to put these things down faithfully will bore you, and thus I shall lose everything in the end. But I should like to have you at least sense the atmosphere surrounding the early days of the mask, which had come into being almost unperceived by me, regardless of my ideas about it.

First of all, the transparent substance in the skin is a type of horny albumen called ceratin, which contains very small fluorescent bodies. For the handling of the edge line I decided that I should have to make the thickness of the flange no larger, if possible, than a small wrinkle; later I hoped somehow to be able to overcome any remaining artificiality by devising a suitable beard. Moreover, even the problem of flexibility, which I foresaw as the greatest obstacle, was not at all insurmountable physiologically.

Quite obviously the facial muscles are the basis of expression. Each muscle pulls in a fixed direction, and contraction and expansion occur along these lines. The skin tissue, which has a fixed directional mobility, lies over them, and the cellular fibers of both apparently join at approximately right angles. According to the medical books I borrowed from the Institute library, the groupings of fibers in the skin are called "Langer lines." Fortunately, a certain type of plastic showed great flexibility when subjected to directional stress. If I didn't begrudge the time it would take, I could resolve the problem with about this much information.

And so I decided to begin tests, in a corner of the laboratory, on the elasticity of flat epithelial cells. Here, too, my colleagues were most tolerant. I aroused almost no suspicions and was able to make constant use of the equipment.

However, the procurement of a model and general procedure seemed impossible to manage technically. For the model —that is, the taking of a first impression, to reproduce skin details—I should have to borrow someone else's face, no matter how disagreeable this might be. Of course just a little skin surface with some oil and sweat glands would do. Since I would transform it in accordance with my own facial structure, I would not be walking around dangling the face of another. There would be no need to worry about infringing on someone else's copyright.

However, even if that were the case—extremely serious doubts welled up in me—wouldn't the mask be similar to my original face after all? By basing his model on the skull structure, a skilled craftsman could reproduce a completely lifelike appearance. If that were true, then it was the underlying frame that ultimately determined one's looks. I should be absolutely incapable of leaving the face I was born with except by shaving down the bones or disregarding the anatomical basis of expression, which in itself could hardly be called expression.

The thought confused me. After all, wouldn't the meaning of the mask be completely negated, no matter how skillfully it was constructed, if I wore one identical to myself?

Fortunately I remembered a friend of mine from high-school days who was specializing in paleontology. It might well be that reconstructing animals from fossils that he dug up formed a part of his work. I consulted the directory and learned that, as luck would have it, he had remained at the university. I intended to discuss the matter by telephone, but as it was some time since our graduation, he was eager to see me and suggested we meet, refusing to take no for an answer. Perhaps in resistance to my shyness over the bandages on my face, I was unable to turn him down, and I accepted. However, I was immediately tormented by regrets. How meaningless to persist in this scheme out of foolish pride. The bandage alone would be enough to excite considerable curiosity, and since the bandaged man was beginning to delve into details of modeling techniques and facial anatomy, which were not his professional specialty, I would seem like some sneak thief in disguise. To avoid such discomfiture, I should have refused categorically from the very first. What's more, I hated the streets. In all the diffident, casual glances there were hidden needles bearing a corrosive poison, though those who had never been targets could not be expected to understand. The streets quite exhausted me. I felt like an oily dustcloth, spotted with shame, yet there was nothing to do but go to the appointed place, however reluctantly.

The café we had agreed upon was on a street corner at the university which I knew well. I took a taxi and was able to get as far as the door of the place almost unnoticed. However, my friend's confusion, greater than my own, was such that I pitied him. Damn it. . . . I regained my ill-tempered self-possession. No, "self-possession" is misleading. Anyway I'd like you, however inadequately, to imagine my wretchedness at making people around me uncomfortable just by my existence, like some stray mongrel. It was the desperate feeling of loneliness one sees in the eyes of a decrepit old cur on the verge of death. It was an emptiness like the sound of track construction deep in the night when the pinging sings down the rails. Feeling that any expression I carried behind my bandage and my sunglasses would not get out had made me perverse.

"I suppose you're surprised," I said in a neutral voice. "I was covered with liquid air. I'm apparently predisposed to keloids. Hmm . . . rather bad . . . the whole face is a regular web of scar tissue. You probably don't exactly fancy the bandage, but it's still better than letting people see what's underneath."

With a perplexed expression, my companion muttered something, but I could hardly catch what he said. The reunion —how stridently had he insisted just thirty minutes ago that as soon as we met we should go where we could get something to drink—was sticking in my throat like a fishbone. But the point was not to say disagreeable things, so I immediately changed the subject and broached the business at hand. Needless to say, he lost no time in grabbing at this life preserver.

His explanation boiled down to this. A faithful reproduction of an original biological form is not possible by modeling upon the bone, no matter how experienced the modeler may be; what can be correctly judged from the anatomical structure of the bones is at best merely the placing of the tendons. Thus, for example, if you tried to reconstruct a whale, which has especially developed subcutaneous tissue and fatty layers, on the basis of the skeleton alone, you would get a monster not in the slightest like a whale—something between a dog and a seal.

"Well. I suppose one's right in assuming that there would be considerable error possible in modeling the face too, wouldn't there?"

"If the trick were possible, there wouldn't be such things as unidentifiable skeletons. You don't have to go so far as a whale; a human face is a delicate thing, isn't it? It's not easily imitated even by montage photography. Yet, if it were absolutely impossible to get away from the bony structure, plastic surgery couldn't exist to start with."

Whereupon, he took a quick glance at my bandages, mumbled embarrassedly, and then fell silent. I didn't have to ask what worried him. No, let him think what he wanted. What was disagreeable was his quite inexcusable blushing without making any attempt to hide his discomfort.

Excursus: *I wonder what this shyness of mine is, fundamentally. Perhaps, at this point, I should bring up the incident of the wig burning once again. The present situation is just the opposite; by having my wig discovered I have discountenanced my companion, which worries me even more. Is that the hidden key to solve the riddle of my face?*

Yet he was a bungling fellow. Although I tried my best to muddle through with inoffensive, ordinary conversation, he couldn't help stumbling and blushing. I had extracted from him most of what was directly pertinent to my plans; I should have left him then with the uncomfortable memory of our meeting. Those things which evoked shame in me could easily become the source of gossip. But I was tempted to let rumors fly, like keyhole whisperings. His feeling of embarrassment was beginning to infect me too. I started in on justifications that were better left unsaid.

"I can just about imagine what you're thinking. You get ideas when you relate my questions to this bandage, don't you? But that would be a big mistake. It's too late for me at my age to begin worrying over an injured face."

"You're the one who's mistaken. What in heaven's name am I supposed to imagine?"

"If I'm wrong, let it go. But even you unconsciously judge people by their faces, don't you? I think it's rather natural for you to be concerned about me. But if you really think about it, does an identity card fully identify the man it represents? My experience has made me do a lot of thinking. Don't we actually cling too much to our identity cards? Because of them we produce freaks that devote themselves to forgery and alteration."

"I agree . . . completely . . . alteration is the right word . . . quite . . . they say that women who wear heavy make-up are frequently hysterical, but. . . ."

"Incidentally, what would it be like if a man's face were as expressionless as an egg, with no eyes, or nose, or mouth?"

"Hmm. You couldn't distinguish among people, I suppose."

"Between thieves and policemen . . . assailants and victims. . . ."

"And *my* wife and my neighbor's wife. . . ."—as if wanting help. He put a match to his cigarette and gave a short, soft laugh. "That's interesting. Interesting, but there's still something of a problem. For heaven's sake, would human life be easier or not?"

And I too laughed with him; perhaps I should have stopped at this point. But my thoughts had already taken on an uncontrollable momentum, circling constantly around my face. They could only go on circling, aware of the danger, until the centrifugal force broke them free.

"Life wouldn't be easier or not easier. Aren't both generalizations logically impossible? Since there's no correlation, there can be no comparison."

"When there is no correlation, that's retrogression."

"Well, then. Are you trying to say that the difference in skin color has yielded a profit for history? I absolutely can't accept such a meaning for correlation."

"Good heavens! Were you discussing the race problem? But isn't that something of an overblown interpretation?"

"If it were possible, I should like to blow it up as much as I could. To every single face in the world. Only, with a mug like mine the more I talk about it the more it becomes a prisoner's lament."

"If you allow me to talk only about the race problem . . . but that's too unreasonable . . . putting all responsibility on the face is. . . ."

"But I'm asking you, every time I daydream about people on other planets I wonder why in heaven I always start with speculating on what they look like."

"We're getting off the track again," he said, vigorously stubbing out his cigarette after scarcely three puffs. "It would suffice, I should imagine, if you simply explained it as being due to curiosity."

I sensed keenly the sudden change of his tone, but just as abruptly as the plate stops spinning in a game of spin-the-plate, my façade fell away.

"Just take a little look at that picture," I said, still not having learned from experience and pointing to what was apparently a reproduction of a European Renaissance portrait. "What do you think of that?"

"Well, if I answer casually, you look as though you would snap me up, but . . . well, it's stupid, isn't it?"

"I suppose it is. Putting a halo back of the face like that is a false, deceptive idea. Because of it, the face is instilled with lies."

There was a strange smile on my companion's face. It was a remote smile, as if he were looking at something far away, but his constraint had disappeared.

"It won't work. No matter how you exaggerate I can't feel anything without first understanding. Is it because there aren't any common words between us? I specialize in extinct plants and animals, but in art, I lean toward the modern."

No, IT WAS useless to complain. Better get used to such looks right now. To expect better results was only pampering myself. I had been able to get hold of necessary information, and my first plan was to try to overcome my basic humiliation.

I began to hate the paleontologist when I realized that the catch I had brought back from my visit was in reality merely inedible bait. Rather, it was apparently foodstuff, but unfortunately I didn't know anything about the art of cooking.

Miserably, I recognized that the large margin of error in

modeling, even when one began with the same bone structure, forced the plan for the mask another step further. I could choose any face I wanted, but I did have to pick one—anyone. But wouldn't any face at all be to my satisfaction? I should have to decide after sifting through numberless possibilities. What in heaven's name was the scale of measurement for faces?

If you didn't intend special meaning to a face, then any would do. When you went to the trouble of making it, you didn't choose a cardiac's puffiness. Yet it probably wouldn't do at all to take a movie star as the model. This freedom, at first comforting, was in fact a terribly bothersome problem.

I don't mean to insist unduly on an ideal face. Besides, such a thing probably doesn't exist. However, since I was going to make a selection, I had to have some standard or other. Even an inappropriate facial guide, however awkward, would somehow be all right—I hadn't the faintest notion whether to be subjective or objective—but when all was said and done I dragged out the decision for close to half a year.

MARGINAL NOTE: *It would be a mistake to settle this whole thing with vague standards. Rather I should doubtless take into consideration my inner impulse to reject standards. Choosing a standard, in other words, is to commit oneself to others. However, at the same time, men have the opposite desire of trying to distinguish themselves from others. Perhaps the two could be related thus:*

$$\frac{A}{B} = f\left(\frac{1}{n}\right)$$

A = the factor of commitment to others; B = the factor of resistance to others; n = age; f = one's degree of viscosity [its decrease is the hardening of the self and at the same time the forming of the self; generally it stands in inverse proportion to age, but in a locus curve one can observe a number of in-

dividual differences among people according to sex, personality, work, etc.].

In short, with age the degree of my viscosity was decreasing very much, and I felt strong opposition to changing faces at this late date. I must doubtless admit that the paleontologist's view that heavily made-up women are prone to hysteria is an extremely astute theory. Psychoanalytically speaking, hysteria is an infantile phenomenon.

In the meantime, of course, I was not idle. I had a mountain of largely technical work, such as tests of material for the flat epidermis, and my engrossment provided me with a fine excuse to postpone the showdown.

The flat epidermis took up an unimaginable amount of time. Quantitatively, it formed the most important part of the skin; but, more than that, the success or failure of producing the feeling of mobile skin was at stake. I profited by my colleagues' distance from me in the laboratory and quite openly made use of the equipment and materials, but even so it took more than three full months. I considered it a comical contradiction that, while my plans for the mask advanced, I had taken no decision concerning the form of the face, but that did not worry me very much. Yet I could not forever take shelter from the rain under another's eaves. This period passed. Then, the work began to make progress, and I was gradually cornered.

For the ceratin layer of the skin surface, I made a simple, very suitable discovery in the family of acrylic resins. And for the subcutaneous tissue, it would apparently be enough to spray something of the same quality as the skin itself into a sponge and let it harden. The fatty layer was easy: I would simply saturate a sponge with liquid silicon and make it airtight by enclosing it in a membrane. Thus, by the second week in the new year I had completed my preparations as far as the materials were concerned.

With things as they now stood, I could no longer make excuses. If I did not come to some decision about what sort of face to make, I could not advance a step further. But no matter how much I thought about it, my head, like a museum storeroom, was in utter confusion with a thousand sample faces. Yet, if I kept shrinking from making a choice, I would never come to any decision. I borrowed a warehouse storage list, deciding there was no other course open to me except to gather my courage and check the faces off one by one. However, on the first page of the list appeared some unexpectedly obliging instructions, "rules for classification," which I read with pounding heart:

1. The standard of value for faces is definitely objective. If one is involved in personal feelings, one makes the error of being taken in by imitations.
2. There is no such thing as a standard of value for faces. There are only pleasure and displeasure, and the standard of selection is continually cultivated through refinement of taste.

It was as I had anticipated. When one is advised that something is black and white at the same time, it would be better to have no advice at all. Moreover, as I read along, comparing each face, I had the feeling that every one could be equally justified, and thus the degree of complication deepened. At last I was sick at the thought of so many faces, and I still wonder why I didn't decide to put a stop to my plans at that time.

AGAIN about portraits. The paleontologist had made light of my ideas, but I could not help clinging to them. I think that the concept of portraiture, be what it may artistically, embodies a philosophy worthy of deeper inquiry.

For example, in order for a portrait to be a universal representation you have to accept as a premise the universality of the human expression. That is, it is necessary for the majority of people to be in general agreement that certain identical traits are to be seen behind a given expression. What supports this belief, of course, is doubtless the empirical understanding that face and heart stand in a fixed relation to each other. Of course, there is no proof that experience is always reality. Yet it is likewise impossible to conclude that experience is always a pack of lies. Rather, isn't it more correct to assume that the more earthy the experience the greater the degree of truth it contains? Within these limits, I think it is impossible to deny completely that there is some good in an objective standard of values.

On the other hand, we cannot disregard the fact that the same portrait changes its personality with the centuries. Our vision shifts from the classical harmony of heart and face to the representation of character devoid of harmony, completely collapsing into Picasso's eight-sided faces and Klee's *False Face*.

Which in God's name should one believe, then? If I may express my own personal preference, of course, it would be the latter standpoint. I think that applying objective standards to the face is, at all events, too naïve; this isn't a dog show. When I was young, even I used to associate a given face with the ideal personality I wanted to be.

MARGINAL NOTE: *That is, this demonstrated a high degree of inclination toward others, stemming from my high degree of viscosity.*

Naturally, a romantic, unordinary face comes into focus through a blurred lens. However, it would never do to be forever addicted to such dreams. Indeed, hard cash is worth more than any kind of promissory note. There was nothing to do but pay what I could with the face I actually had. Don't men shun cosmetics because they believe in taking responsibility for their own faces? (Of course, with women—that is, women's make-up—it seems to me they use it because their cash has reached rock bottom, hasn't it?)

I COULD not come to any decision at all— I felt queasy, as if I was about to catch a cold—but nevertheless I continued to make progress in technical areas, where my concern was only with the surface of the face.

After the materials came the casting of the back of the mask. No matter how permissive my colleagues were I could not do that in the laboratory, and I decided to take my equipment home with me and set up a workshop in my study. (Ah!

You seemed to think that my enthusiasm for work was in compensation for my face, and, moved to tears, you tried to help me. Indeed, it was compensation, but it was not the kind of enthusiasm you thought it was. I closed the door of the study and went so far as to turn the key; I shut out even your affection when you tried to bring me my evening snack.)

The work in which I immersed myself on the other side of the closed door was this.

First, I prepared a basin large enough to contain my whole face and poured into it potassium alginate, plaster of Paris, sodium phosphate, and silicon. Then, with all my facial muscles completely relaxed, I quickly thrust my face into the mixture. Within three to five minutes the solution changed into calcium alginate in a plastic state. Since I could not be expected to hold my breath all this time, I had inserted in my mouth a slender rubber tube that led out of the basin. However, just imagine having to immobilize your expression for a time exposure. That is difficult enough. With repeated failures—a twitching under the eyes or an itchy nose—I was at it four days before I got anything satisfactory.

When I had finished, I began work on vacuum plating the inner side with nickel. Since obviously I couldn't do that at home, I surreptitiously took the die to the laboratory and, keeping it out of sight, completed the plating there.

At length, I came to the finishing touches. One evening, after making certain you had gone to bed, I placed an iron crucible filled with an alloy of lead and antimony over a propane flame. The melted antimony took on the color of cocoa mixed with too much milk. When I poured it carefully into the hollow of the mold plated with potassium alginate, drops of white steam gently eddied up. A transparent blue smoke first spurt forcefully from the hole of the rubber breathing tube, then rose from all around the circumference of the mask. Perhaps the potassium alginate was scorching.

There was a terrible stench; I opened the window, and the chill January wind suddenly snapped at my nostrils with its claws. I turned the mold upside down and shook it, separating the hardened antimony cast, and extinguished the still-smoking potassium alginate base by submerging it in water. Silvery white scar webs, gleaming dully, flickered back at my own flesh-colored ones.

Somehow I could not believe that this was my face. It was different . . . too different. . . . These could not possibly be the webs so familiar to me that I could scream, the ones I always saw in my mirror. Of course, since the left and right of the antimony cast were the reverse of my face reflected in a mirror, some feeling of difference was unavoidable. Yet, I had already experienced this much variation with photographs without acutely sensing a difference.

Was it a question of color then? According to Henri Boulan's *Le Visage*, which I had found in the library, a surprisingly intimate relationship apparently exists between facial color and expression. For example, a plaster-of-Paris death mask of a man will become that of a woman simply by the control of color. Again, one can detect the disguise of a man dressed as a woman if his photograph is taken in black and white. When I thought about this, color seemed a plausible answer. The ridges in the antimony cast were so slight as to be imperceptible if not held to the light; such faint unevenness would probably be nothing to fuss about in a mask. For an instant I again started at the imprint of my scars, but wasn't I unnecessarily wrestling with myself? Even these metal scar webs would have their own fine repulsiveness, I suppose, if they were tinted a flesh color. Perhaps. It's a shame man isn't made of metal.

If color was that important, tinting at the time of the final flesh modeling would have to be done with the utmost care. As I passed my hand, almost in consolation, over the surface of the still-warm antimony of the molded face, with the pleasure of a blind man in his sense of touch, I was awed by the complexities in the manufacture of this mask. The completion of one operation immediately prepared the way for another difficult problem. Of course, I had devised an extraordinary challenge. I had already come quite far in amount of time and work, but the essential choice of a facial type was still hanging. And now there was the additional difficulty of coloring. With such problems, I wondered when I would realize my dream of being reborn in another face.

No, certainly all the signs were not bad. The creases of the metallic scar webs made me reflect on the irrational role of the face: one must be sent packing like a mangy mongrel because of extra protuberances of barely two or three millimeters. Suddenly I discovered the really vulnerable spot in my enemy.

These metallic scar webs could exist only as a negative picture for making the back of the mask. How shall I put it: it was a negative existence which was to be covered over by the mask and thus wiped out. But was that all? It was indeed a negative existence, but even a mask that would wipe out the scar webs could not possibly exist without using them as a base. In short, this metal base was the point of departure for constructing the mask, and at the same time the mask's objective was to obliterate the base.

Let's try thinking a little more concretely. For example, I could simply use the eyes as they were, making no change in position, shape, or size. Suppose I went about it boldly; should I make a jutting forehead; or should I make the lower part of the face project; or, if neither of the two, should I make the whole thing bulge out, with goggle eyes? The same went for the nose and the mouth. Indeed, the choice of a facial type was apparently not the ambiguous thing I had imagined until now. Perhaps this manner of thinking was limiting, compared

to a slapdash, grab-bag freedom in choosing, but it was far
more suited to my nature. In any event, this way I could see
what had to be done. Even though I might take the long road
of trial and error, first I had to try actually modeling and
studying what facial type was possible with the finished mask.
This way of doing things really suited me. (Apparently my
colleagues' criticism of me—that I was more of a technician
than a scientist—was not altogether off the mark.)

Unawares, I became totally absorbed, plotting the metal
base from every angle with my finger, holding my two hands
over it, covering and shading it. The molded face was such a
delicate thing . . . with the touch of a finger it turned into a
different person, more strange than a brother or a cousin . . .
with a turn of the palm, an utter stranger.

I dare say this was the first time I was able to have such a
positive feeling since I had started making the mask.

YES, I guess I could say that my experi-
ence that night was indeed one of the important and crucial
points. It wasn't all that impressive, but I considered it a
decisive landmark, much like the point at which the water of
a catchment basin takes a determined direction that leads at
last into the river.

For the experience of that night was at least a turning point;
and it was a fact that something like a channel, however

uncertain, opened between the problem of the technical realization and the selection of a face, which until then had been nothing more than parallel lines. Even though I had no method in view for making the mask, I actually felt encouraged and confident that one way or another the possibility was there, precisely because I was accumulating concrete data.

I decided the following morning to purchase some clay and begin to practice modeling. I had not determined my goal, but I groped my way along fumblingly. Guided by an anatomical chart of the facial muscles, the work of carefully building up the thin clay layer by layer was dramatic, quite as if I were assisting at the birth of an adult, sentient human; and I felt that the rather pointless standard of choice itself was beginning to jell, gradually assuming palpable form. Some detective geniuses track their man from an armchair; others gather their evidence by laborious footwork: being on the move seemed to suit me best, too.

About that time, I began to take renewed interest in Henri Boulan's *Le Visage*, which I mentioned before. Previously, I had the impression that his plausible analysis smacked rather of the scholar's habit of classification, and I, driven by purely concrete motives, was plagued by the irritating question of just what use such explanations could be. However, when I came down to the manual task of fashioning the face, I discovered more in Boulan than classifications. There seemed to be quite a difference between the map of a country one knew and that of some unknown foreign land.

The following is a general summary of Boulan's classification:

First, trace a large circle, using the nose as the center, and making the radius the distance between the nose and the tip of the chin. Next, on the same center make a small circle, taking as radius the distance between the nose and the lips. There are two types of face, depending on the relationship between these two circles: concave and convex. Further, one may obtain a total of four basic facial types by differentiating between bony and fatty types of each:

1. Concave type, bony: strong projection of the flesh in forehead, cheeks, and chin.
2. Concave type, fatty: slight swelling of the fatty tissue in forehead, cheeks, and chin.
3. Convex type, bony: sharply pointed face, centering around the nose.
4. Convex type, fatty: slight frontal projection, centering around the nose.

Of course, these do not cover all facial types. The four basic types may be further ramified into any number of secondary types, depending on a synthesis of contradictory factors, on sectional emphasis, or on the shading of details. However, as far as I was concerned, there was no need to trouble myself with such subtleties. Since I would build up the tissue from the bottom, layer on layer, things could not be expected to go according to calculation. As long as I did not forget the base itself, I could well let the rest take whatever course it would.

A Jungian analysis of the four basic facial types would suggest that the first two types are introversial, and the second two are extroversial. Also, numbers one and three tend to be antagonistic to the outside world, while numbers two and four tend to be conciliatory. It is possible to make up a personality combining the two odds and the two evens.

Even more order is brought to the problem if you link to this method of classification Boulan's ideas in *Les Eléments de l'expression*, a work that shows quantitatively the respective influences exerted on expression by over thirty muscles controlling nineteen areas of movement by order of their degree of mobility. The method of calculation is also interesting. By continuously photographing, from about 1,200 models, expressions ranging from laughter to perplexity, and dividing them up with contour lines as in a map, Boulan seems to have obtained the mean value of the function of the various points of movement. His conclusions may be summarized thus: The density of expressive factors is greatest in the triangular area extending from the nostrils to the sides of the lips, gradually lessening around the eyes and the central forehead, which is the least dense area of all. In short, the faculty of expression is concentrated in the lower part of the face, more precisely in the area around the lips.

The distribution of factors by area is furthermore influened and modified by the state of the subcutaneous tissues. The density of factors decreases in proportion to the thickness of these tissues. But sparseness of factors doesn't necessarily mean lack of expression. There is sometimes no expression even when the density is great, and there are frequent instances of expression where the density is low. In short, lack of expression exists with both high and low density of factors.

EXCURSUS: *Shall I try applying Boulan's law of classification to our faces just as an experiment? Your face first. I suppose, if I had to put you in one category, you would be considered a convex type. Subcutaneous tissues slightly fatty. Therefore, you tend toward type four: weak frontal projection centering around the nose. From the standpoint of Jungian psychology, you are extroverted and pacific. The expressive factor is rather low and your expression is stable, with little fluctuation.*

What do you think? I've hit the nail on the head, I believe. I seem to remember your saying you used to be nicknamed "saint" during your school days. The first time I heard that, I broke out laughing. But . . . what was so funny? I seemed to have had a very wrong idea either about saints or about you. Of course, judging only from the outside, I suppose you could even be said to have very individual, sensuous features. Yet, considering the inside, too, you did indeed have the face of a saint, according to Boulan's classification. An outgoing and peaceable disposition is like a three-foot wall of crude rubber. Infinitely pliant, but inviolable. Such a face does have the half-closed eyes and the faint smile of a saintly image, it's true, but those very elements compose the features of someone who wins without weapons. When I looked at you from a distance you would smile invitingly, but when I approached, the smile would change into mist and obstruct my view. I should like now to express my heartfelt respect for the one who invented your nickname—"saint."

Was it sarcasm? I wonder. If there was a thorn in it somewhere, it was surely my fault alone, not yours. It may be that someone else's tenderness can be experienced only as pain.

Well, next, my face. . . . No, let it go. There's nothing to be gained at this point by discussing a face that's completely gone. How should one consider those whose faces are so completely transformed that they do not fit into any classification, like, for example, the Tazarawa tribe with their huge, saucerlike lips? I should like to hear what Boulan would have to say about that.

And, as I had expected, my fingers were considerably more successful than my head alone would have been. As a result of my brief tests on each of the four basic types over a period of about ten days, I had decided to eliminate two of them, and then choose which of the remaining two would be the better.

The one I disqualified first was type four—slight frontal projection; centering around the nose. This type of face had the area of highest density of factors enveloped by fatty layers, so it was highly stable and, once completed, would be quite devoid of expression. I would be obliged to plan the work all the more carefully from the beginning, and the construction would be quite troublesome. I decided to shelve it for the time being. EXCURSUS TO AN EXCURSUS: *In the excursus just before this account I may have appeared to have something in the back of my mind, but I positively intended only one meaning. For, to begin with, there was a time lapse of about three months between the text and the excursus. . . .*

Next to be disqualified was number one, the concave, bony type—a strong projection of the flesh in the forehead, cheeks, and chin. From the standpoint of Jungian psychology it had, in short, an introverted, antagonistic character, and was unstable to boot. At best, that type was the face of a usurer who had never lost a penny. It couldn't be the mask of a seducer. Though this was merely an impression, the type did not appeal to me and I decided to drop it.

Having disposed of two in this fashion I now come to the remaining two. . . .

"A slight swelling of the fatty tissue in forehead, cheeks, and chin. . . ." According to Jungian psychology, this would be an introspective, self-controlled, peaceable face.

"Sharply pointed face, centering around the nose. . . ." According to Jungian psychology, this would be an ambitious face, capable of action, or a hostile, extroverted one.

I had the feeling I could foresee the future. There was a big difference in choosing between types four and two. Four was not simply two times two but contained six combinations for comparison. In short, I was able to reduce the work of choosing by one-sixth. Moreover, the remaining two were contrasting types with rather striking differences; there could be no possibility of confusing them and thus complicating my decision. I should necessarily arrive at the face I was aiming for by just continuing my modeling.

I abandoned myself for some time to a comparative investigation of the two types. However, I had only one face mold, and it was really inconvenient to have to destroy and reconstruct it with every trial. I hit upon the idea of purchasing a polaroid camera. You snap the shutter and the film is developed on the spot. It was convenient to be able to line up the pictures for immediate comparison, and also I could keep a minute-by-minute record of production.

Yes, my heart, singing then like a cicada, for the first time experienced a feeling of the nymph emerging from the earth. I was heedless of the fact that everything might again be brought to a standstill.

ONE day, the sky was smoldering in a south wind, and the central heating, which had been left on, was stiflingly oppressive. When I looked at the calendar, February had more than half gone by. Naturally, I was disturbed. I should have liked to complete my work while the weather was still cool. As far as mobility and texture were concerned, my mask was nearly perfect, but I had not yet figured out ventilation. I would perspire; the mask would be difficult to attach—I could foresee physiologically harmful

effects. Yet there were three more months of detours until I
came to the opening scene of finding my hideaway at the S—
Apartments.

Why in heaven's name did I take such a roundabout way?
At first blush, the work seemed to be going very smoothly. I
had become so proficient as to be able to draw by heart each
of the types I favored; and whenever I saw a face that belonged
to one of them, I immediately analyzed its factors, going so
far as to revise them in my imagination. Well, since the
materials were all at hand, I might as well choose the one I
liked best. But there was no question of choosing one of the
two, unless I could apply some standard. No matter how
much one is pressed to choose between red and white, there
is no sense in choosing without knowing whether it's to be the
color of tickets or of flags. Ah, once again the blindman's buff
of standards! Indeed, is any mystery not soluble by simple
footwork? Of course, my standards now have come to mean
something different from what they once did. However, my
irritation became all the greater as my choice grew clearer.
The peaceable type had the merit of peaceableness, but the
unpeaceable type had its own virtue. There was no room
here for value judgment. The more I knew, the more I was
interested in each type. Hard-pressed and despairing, I thought
many times how much better it would be to settle the whole
thing with a throw of the dice. But as long as there was even
a slight metaphysical significance to the face, I could not possibly commit such an irresponsible act. From the results of
my investigations alone I could not help but accept the fact,
however disagreeable, that facial features had considerable
relationship to the psyche and the personality.

But, as soon as I thought of the corpse of my own face
covered by scar tissue, I wanted to reject all meaning for the
face. Suddenly I was seized by a violent shaking, like some
soaking-wet dog. What in heaven's name were psyche and

personality anyway? Had such things ever been of any help in my work at the Institute? No matter what a man's personality, one and one are always two. So long as an individual is not engaged in a profession in which the face is the measure by which he is judged—people such as actors, diplomats, hotel and restaurant employees, private secretaries, swindlers—the personality signifies no more than the serrations of tree leaves.

I resolved to flip a coin. I tossed many times; heads and tails came out a tie.

FORTUNATELY or unfortunately, before coming to a decision on the facial type, there was the task of obtaining a face to use in the finished product. There was nothing to do but buy one from a complete stranger whom I would never see again; but it was a great responsibility psychologically, and I could not bring myself to attempt it until I was cornered. For this, the situation was quite favorable; I *was* cornered.

I was quite aware that an inevitable ultimatum would be thrust upon me as soon as I finished the work, yet procrastination gave temporary peace of mind, the two poisons cancelling each other. On the first Sunday morning in March I decided at last to go out into the city. I put the equipment for making casts in my briefcase and got on a streetcar.

The cars to the suburbs were rather crowded, but those that

were headed downtown were still comparatively empty. Even so, after several months of not exposing myself to strangers, it was torture. Although I thought I was prepared for it, I stood facing the door, unable to turn around to look inside the streetcar. I reflected how absurd it was for me to be buried in my coat collar despite the stifling heat, unable to make the slightest physical movement, like an insect playing dead. How could I strike up a conversation with a stranger in such circumstances? Each time the car stopped I clung to the door handle, fighting my faintheartedness, wanting to return home.

Yet why in heaven's name was I so frightened? I had not been accused by anyone, yet I shrank back with almost a guilty conscience, as if I were a criminal. If the facial expression were so essential a mask of identity, wouldn't it be impossible to recognize a voice on the telephone? Couldn't one say then that in the dark all men fear, suspect, and hate each other? Nonsense! A face that had properly functioning eyes, mouth, nose, and ears would be enough! A face is not something to show off to others, but something that serves one's self! (No, there was no reason to get upset—a different I began to apologize shamefacedly—I only hesitated to disturb strangers by deliberately showing by expressionless face.) But I wondered if that were really all. With my prescription sunglasses, which were darker than ordinary ones, there was not the slightest reason to worry that someone might feel I was looking at him.

The streetcar turned a corner, and the side where I was standing was struck by the light in such a way that a couple with a child behind me were reflected in the glass of the door. The child, about five, was seated between his two young parents (they were animatedly talking together, pointing to some sort of poster—as I realized later, an advertisement for installment-plan bathtubs) and was just then staring apprehensively at me from under the brim of a navy-blue woolen hat with a ribbon on it. Wonder, fear, discovery, suspicion, hesitation, fascination, curiosity—all were crammed into his little eyes, and he seemed almost to be slipping into some ecstatic transport. I gradually began to lose my composure. The parents were typical, I thought, saying nothing to him nor even admonishing him to behave properly. I suddenly turned my full face toward the child, who clutched his mother's sleeve; the mother, poking him with her elbow, replied with a scolding.

How would it be if, not saying a word, I were to plant myself in front of the parents and child and, contemptuous of their perplexity, remove my glasses and surgical mask and begin to undo my bandages? Their perplexity would turn to panic and then to entreaty. I would go on, regardless. To heighten the effect, I would rip off the last folds with a flourish. I would put my fingers under the upper edge of the bandage and in a single movement rip it down. But, as I imagined it, the face I displayed would be a completely different thing from my face since the accident. No, it would not only be different from my face; it would be quite unlike any human face. Bronze color, or gold, or a pure, waxy, transparent white would be fitting. But they would have no time to ascertain anything more. There would be no time in their fleeting impression to know whether it was the face of a god or a devil; the three of them would be transformed into stones, or lumps of lead, or even insects. And the other passengers who had witnessed the scene would be transformed with them. . . .

Suddenly I came to myself—the car had arrived at my station. I felt fatigued and debilitated as I hurried off onto the platform. There was a bench at one end, and I sat down. I wondered if I were being shunned, for not a soul tried to sit down beside me; the bench seemed reserved for me alone.

Overcome with contrition, I felt like crying as I vaguely watched the eddying current of travelers.

Apparently I had been too optimistic. In such a cruel, self-centered crowd would there ever be some soft-hearted fellow who would sell me his face? There was little hope. If I did single out one man, the crowd would probably turn its collective glare accusingly upon me. The clock that graced the wall of the station told a time common for all men . . . what was this lack of concern in people who had faces? Could having a face be such an important requirement? Was being seen the cost of the right to see? No, the worst of it was that my fate was too personal, too special. Unlike hunger, unrequited love, unemployment, sickness, bankruptcy, natural calamity, criminal exposure, my suffering was nothing I endured in common with other men. My misfortune was forever mine alone. Anyone at all could disregard me completely without feeling the slightest twinge of conscience. And I was not even permitted to protest that disregard.

I wondered if I weren't becoming a kind of monster. Carlyle said that the robe makes the priest and the uniform the soldier; perhaps the face makes the monster. A monster's face brings loneliness, and the loneliness informs his heart. If the temperature of my freezing loneliness were to drop even slightly, I should become a monster, indifferent to my appearance, and break with a crash all the bonds which bind me to this world. In heaven's name what kind of monster would I be, what would I do? Just trying to imagine it was so frightful I wanted to scream.

MARGINALIA: *The novel about Frankenstein is interesting. When a monster breaks dishes, it is usually laid to the destructive instinct of monsters; but this author explains it otherwise—dishes have the quality of being easily broken. Being a monster, he merely wished to assuage his loneliness, but the brittleness of the object necessarily made him an*

assailant. And so, as long as there exist such violable things—
breakable, crushable, burnable objects, or objects that can
bleed and die—the monster can only go on endlessly assault-
ing them. Basically, there is nothing new in the behavior of
monsters, for the monster himself is nothing more than an
invention of his victims.

No, I hadn't screamed, though I thought I had already
begun to. Help! Stop looking at me that way! If I'm to be
forever stared at like that, I really will end up a monster! At
length, unable to stand it, I brushed aside the forest of human-
ity and, as if taking shelter in some cave, rushed headlong
into a nearby movie house, a "market place of darkness"—
the only safe place for a monster.

I do not remember what movie was playing. I took an aisle
seat in the balcony. The artificial darkness with its lingering
warmth crept about me like a muffler. I gradually began to
recover my composure, like a mole that has gone to ground.
The movie house was an endless tunnel. I imagined that my
seat was some speeding vehicle. I dashed along, cutting
through the darkness. If I could fly at this speed, I couldn't
be followed by people. I'd give them the slip. I would arrive
before them in the world of eternal night. And I'd call myself
the king of the land where there are only drops of mist and
phosphorescent animalcules and starlight. I took secret pleasure in such fancies, which were like children's scribblings in
public places. It was as if I were secretly eating something. It
would not do to ridicule it, no matter how tiny a piece of
darkness it was. Considered on a universal scale, this very
darkness was an essential element that occupied a greater part
of the actual world.

Suddenly the seats in the row in front of me began to shake
unnaturally. The suppressed, cynical laugh of a woman rose

to me from out of the darkness immediately in front and to the side. A man shushed her, and the shaking stopped. Perhaps no one else noticed, for the music at full volume made the hall tremble, and the spectators were few. Although it was none of my business, I drew a long sigh of relief. I stared fixedly in the direction of the voices, unable to take my eyes away, try as I might. The screen brightened, and the outlines of two people were distinctly revealed. The fringe of the girl's hair, turned under in back, in the fashion of a child's, fell over the collar of her white mohair coat, and a man's head was lying on her shoulder. But both of them were completely enveloped from the shoulders down in a man's black overcoat. However were they interlaced together beneath it?

The conspicuous thing was the white nape of the woman's neck. The white area seemed to melt into the coat collar, which was the same white, and yet it also seemed to come floating out of it. Actually, the woman may have been moving up and down, but it may well have been that my own eyes were giddy and unfocused. However, the man's form was even more equivocal. The position of his head was such that he seemed to be looking straight at the woman—if he could move his left arm, which was pressed against her, around under her armpit, he would be able to reach her buttocks, I suppose—her free right shoulder dipped sharply down. They could be doing anything. I concentrated my gaze on the right shoulder until my eyes watered. But it was like a picture drawn in India ink on a blackboard. If the shoulder appeared to be undulating, it was because I wanted it to be so; and if it seemed to be doing it rhythmically, it was definitely because I wished it. In short I was apparently infatuated with my own eagerness.

Suddenly the woman gave a loud laugh. I started as if I had been slapped and was seized by the illusion that it was I who was responsible for the unexpected outburst. But actually it was not the woman who had laughed but the loud-speaker behind the screen. An exciting, voluptuous scene was being enacted on the screen, as if in collusion.

A close-up of a woman's white throat filled the screen. The picture gradually shifted as she violently twisted her neck to the right and left as if in pain, and at length her lips appeared, like piping hot sausages; they were vigorously contorted into a terrible, excessive smile. Then nostrils like cross-sections of squashed rubber hose . . . eyelids so tightly closed that they seemed lost in bundles of wrinkles. There was a laugh that changed into the raucous breathing of some frantic wild bird.

I was unhappy. Why show a face to such a degree? Originally movies were supposed to be a show in the dark. Since the person looking at them had no face, the one being looked at wouldn't need one either, I should think, but. . . .

Actually, however, though actors do take off their clothes, not a single one tries to take off his face. On the contrary, they even appear to consider that a performance centers on the face. Isn't it much the same as fraud if they deliberately entice spectators into the darkness? Moreover, peeping is a shameful thing, and can you call it wholesome to act out peeping? I wish they would put a stop to such absurd affectation and hypocrisy! (Isn't it comic for a cripple who has lost his face to be so self-assertive on such a point? Still, the one who best understands the significance of light is not the electrician, not the painter, not the photographer, but the man who has lost his sight in adulthood. There must be the wisdom of deficiency in deficiency, just as there is the widsom of plenty in plenty.)

As if asking for help, I brought my gaze back to the pair in front of me. This time both of them were absolutely quiet and motionless. Why? Had the voluptuous commotion been nothing but my fancy? A sticky perspiration, crawling like a swarm of insects, began to creep out of the gaps in my bandages. Apparently it was not due simply to the excessive warmth. Something like pepper pricked and tingled in the pores of my whole body. (The deception was perhaps not the darkness but rather my own face!) If at this instant the lights in the hall were suddenly to be turned on, doubtless I would at once be ridiculed and sneered at by the spectators as an intruder....

Screwing up my courage, I decided to go outside. Yet I couldn't positively say that seeking this refuge had been completely futile. I had come to feel more defiant than before; in other words, I had to this extent reconciled myself to the world.

AT LENGTH the morning drew to an end. The street in front of the station took on its usual holiday animation, and an almost unbroken stream of people swarmed by. Swallowed up in the current, I continued to walk for about an hour, battling the stares that pestered me like flies. Walking is sometimes considered to have a spiritual effect. For example, military marching is done in formation, columns of two or four, each soldier supplying two legs to maintain that formation. Although the men despair at having lost face and heart, they seem to get an innocent sense of peace in the rhythm of marching. Actually, during long marches it is not at all uncommon for men to experience erections.

Forever chasing the flies away was not going to be much help. Rather, I would have flit covetously among the crowd with the many-faceted eyes of a bluebottle. I would have to find some person who looked as if he might sell me the surface of his face. Sex: male. . . . Possessor of a smooth skin, as much as possible without characteristic markings. . . . Since it will be flexible, size or looks are unimportant. . . . Age: thirty to forty. . . . A forty-year-old man who would agree to such a requirement for money might possibly have rather pocked and unacceptable skin. Actually I was looking for someone around thirty, I suppose.

I tried to pull myself together, but the effort flickered like a light bulb beginning to burn out: it was difficult to keep up the resolve. Furthermore, although the people walking along the streets were strangers to each other, they formed a tight chain, like some organic composition, and I could not squeeze in. Could sharing ordinary, normal faces forge such a strong bond among them? Moreover, even the things they wore matched. The mass-produced patterns of today called fashion. Is that a negation of the uniform, for heaven's sake, or simply a new kind of uniform? From the standpoint of continuous change, it probably is the negation of the uniform, I suppose; but considering that this negation is brought about collectively, it may indeed be considered very much a uniform. Perhaps it's the spirit of today. And because I am against this spirit, I am a heretic. Although my researches bolstered the part of this fashion made with synthetic fibers, not even that would permit me to associate with the crowd; perhaps they thought that a man without a face would be without a heart, too. It was as much as I could do just to keep walking.

If I were stupid enough to try addressing someone among them, even my remote contact with those around me would be sundered at once as easily as a piece of shoji paper. I would be drawn into the midst of the unrelenting crowd and pressed to answer questions about the grotesqueness of my mask. A half-dozen times I crossed and recrossed the street in front of the station, constantly being warned. No, I was not imagining things. In spite of the congestion, pockets of space opened around me, like quarantined areas; not once had I rubbed shoulders with anyone.

It was like being in prison, I thought. A prison's oppressive, constraining walls, its iron bars, all become burnished and pellucid mirrors reflecting the inmate. The torment of imprisonment lies in not being able to escape from oneself at any time. I too was wretchedly floundering around, tightly closed into the bag of myself. My impatience became irritation, irritation became a dark anger; then suddenly it occurred to me to try a public restaurant in a department store. It seemed about time to eat . . . perhaps because I was hungry. But the idea had far more challenging implications. With the intuition of a cornered man, I had succeeded in finding the tear in the bag that confined me. Don't we reveal our weaknesses—solitude, loneliness, defenselessness—and aren't we most particularly vulnerable when we are engaged in sleep, or evacuation, or eating? Department store restaurants are famous for their menu of solitude.

I stepped off the elevator, into an exhibition area behind which lay the restaurant. The words of a huge sign suddenly leapt out at me: EXHIBITION OF NOH MASKS. I stood for an instant rooted to the spot and then began to back away in confusion. This must have been a coincidence. I immediately thought that if I were to back out now I would be much teased for it, and so, though there was a roundabout way to the restaurant, I walked straight into the exhibition area.

I felt as tense as a coiled spring as I headed for the restaurant. Perhaps I wanted to take a preliminary look around before the challenge. Even so, a masked man looking at Noh masks was an unusual combination. If necessary, I was prepared to jump through a hoop of fire.

But unfortunately so few people were going into the exhibition that my enthusiasm was dampened. As a result, I decided lukewarmly to make a round of the exhibit as if I were interested. I anticipated nothing special. There was a big difference between a Noh mask and the mask I sought. I needed something to clear the obstruction of the scars and restore the roadway to other people, while the Noh mask rather seemed bent on rejecting life. The moldy smell that filled the exhibition room, for example, a sort of atmosphere of decadence, was good proof of that.

Of course, it wasn't that I was incapable of understanding that there was a kind of refined beauty in the Noh mask. What we call beauty is perhaps the strength of our feeling of resistance to destructibility. Difficulty of reproduction is the yardstick of the degree of beauty. Thus thin plate glass, if it could not be mass produced, would surely be considered the most beautiful thing in the world today. Even so, the mystery is that man has to seek such rare refinement. The demand for a mask, practically speaking, stems from a desire on the part of those who are not satisfied with, who want something more than, a mere living actor's expression. If this were true, what would be the need of deliberately stifling expression?

Suddenly I halted in front of a woman's mask. It was displayed against the surface of a pleated partition connecting two walls. Hung on a background of black cloth, in a wooden frame painted white like a railing, it suddenly raised its face as if answering my gaze. Quite as if it had been waiting for me, a smile seemed to break out over the whole face, and. . . .

No, of course it was an illusion. It was not the mask that was moving, but the lights which illuminated it. A number of miniature light bulbs, imbedded in a line on the back of the wooden frame, switched on and off in a regular, progressive movement, producing a unique effect. It was a clever device. But even after I realized that it was a device, my initial surprise lingered on. I abandoned once and for all the simple pre-conception that there was no expression in Noh masks.

Not only was the design of this mask very elaborate, but its effect too, compared to the others, was striking.

Its difference was irritating; I don't know why. I made an-other round of the exhibition hall, and when I came again to where the mask hung, everything suddenly came into focus, and the enigma was resolved. This wasn't a face. What pro-fessed to be a face was in fact nothing more than a simple skull to which a thin membrane had been applied. Some masks representing old people were indeed more clearly skeletal, but actually the woman's mask, though it seemed fleshy, on closer inspection revealed the basic skull. The seams of the bones in the brow, forehead, cheeks, and lower jaw stood out in relief with an exactness that made one think of an anatomical chart; and the shadows of the bones, following the movement of the lights, emerged as expression. The mud-diness of the glue, recalling the texture of old porcelain . . . the network of fine crackle covering the surface . . . the white-ness and warmth as of driftwood bleached by the wind and the rain . . . basically, the beginnings of the Noh mask were the skull.

However, any woman's mask was not necessarily like that. With the passage of the centuries, they have changed simply into expressionless faces like peeled muskmelons. Perhaps in order to get the essential lines mask makers today have mis-read the intentions of the makers from the period when Noh began and stress only the expressionlessness.

Then suddenly I had to face a dreadful hypothesis. Why in heaven's name did early Noh mask makers, trying to go beyond the limits of expression, end up with the skull? It was doubtless not simply to suppress expression. So far as escaping from ordinary expression was concerned, any mask would do that. If I really wanted to name a difference, I suppose it was that the Noh mask aimed in a negative direction, in contrast to the ordinary mask which attempts escape in a positive direction. I could give the mask any expression I wanted, but it would still be an empty container, a reflection in a mirror, transfigurable according to the person peering in.

At this point there was no reason for reducing my face, already thick with leech scars, to the skull. But wasn't there in the radical method of the Noh mask some fundamental principle which made the face an empty container, some law applicable to every mask, every expression, every face? The face is made by someone else; one doesn't make it oneself . . . the expression is chosen by someone else; it is not oneself that chooses it . . . yes, that may be right. A monster is a creation, so we can call man a monster too. And the Creator seems not to be the sender but somehow the receiver of this letter we call expression.

Did this describe my inability to make up my mind, to decide on a facial type? A letter with no address is simply returned, no matter how many stamps one puts on it. Well, that was a thought. How would it be to show someone a reference album of established facial types and get him to make the selection for me? Someone? But who? But isn't it decided . . . ? You, of course. The receiver of my letter can be no one but you.

AT FIRST I modestly thought this a very small discovery, but gradually the wave lengths of the light around me began to change, and a rosiness, like a gradually welling laugh, suffused my heart. Gently shading the glow with my two hands so that it would not die away, I went on through the exhibition, leaving it with the exhilaration of running downhill.

Yes, actually, I had made no small discovery. From the standpoint of procedure, there were still many problems—there were bound to be—but having come this far, perhaps everything could be solved. Unhesitantly, I hurried into the restaurant. I entered abruptly, without trepidation, into the heated atmosphere of a large restaurant that included in its mere two-page menu every conceivable aid to gluttony, in contrast to the atmosphere of the Noh mask exhibit. It was not sudden courage on my part. It was rather cowardice with the dawning of hope.

And then, as if by chance, the man stood directly in front of me, blocking my path. His coolness as he stood looking lingeringly at the showcase containing artificial samples of food was somehow appropriate for the person I was seeking. Ascertaining immediately that his age was right and that there were no scars on his face, I made my decision.

At length, having made up his mind, the man bought a token from the cashier for Chinese noodles in broth. Following him, I too got tokens for a sandwich and coffee. Then, with an innocent face—no, I didn't have a face—I sat down casually at the same table, across from him. Since there were other empty seats, the man clearly showed his displeasure but did not actually say anything. The young waitress punched our tickets, brought water, and left. I took off my surgical mask, drew out a cigarette, and aware of the shyness of my companion, gently began to speak.

"I'm sorry. If I am disturbing you . . ."

"No. No."

"But the child over there's staring at my bandaged face. He's quite forgotten the ice cream he was so absorbed in. Perhaps he's thinking you're a friend of mine."

"Well . . . go get another seat!"

"Yes, I suppose I could. But before I do, I just want to ask one thing in all frankness. Would you like a hundred dollars? If you don't, I'll change my seat right away."

There appeared in my companion's expression a wretchedly opportunistic reaction, and without a moment's delay I began to pull in my net.

"It's not really an especially troublesome request. It's not at all dangerous, and with little bother to you the hundred dollars are yours. What about it? Will you listen to what I have to say, or shall I change my seat?"

The man passed the tip of his tongue over his yellowed teeth, and a nerve below his eye twitched. If I classified him according to the Boulan system he would be a concave type, slightly fleshy. In short, he was the introverted, antagonistic type I had excluded. However, since I needed only the quality of the skin texture, I wasn't interested in the type. One had to be imperious with this sort of person, but I would be careful not to hurt his feelings.

EXCURSUS: *While I vigorously rejected the face as a yardstick for myself, it was quite sufficient for others. I realize it was self-centered of me, but treating him this way was a*

*luxury from my viewpoint. People like me who lack something
are liable to become spiteful critics.*

"Even so . . ." he said, staring at the entrance to the roof,
where gift balloons were being distributed to children. Turning the upper part of his body, he looped one elbow over the
back of his chair, as if he could finish the business without
looking at my face. "Well . . . let's talk. . . ."

"That's a weight off my mind. I can still move my seat, but
these waitresses are so sullen. However, before I do, I've just
one promise I'd like you to make. Since I'll not ask you anything about you or your work, you're not to ask about me."

"There's no work to ask about," he said, "and if I don't
know anything I can save the trouble of excuses later."

"After we're done, I want you to forget the whole thing . . .
that we ever even met."

"That's all right by me. Anyway, it doesn't look like something I'll want to remember."

"I wonder. Even now, you can't look me straight in the
face. Isn't that proof you're disturbed? Surely you're itching
to know what's under my bandages."

"That's absurd!"

"Well, then. Afraid?"

"Certainly I'm not afraid."

"Then, why are you avoiding me like that?"

"What do you mean 'why'? Do I have to answer these
questions one by one? Or is this a part of the hundred-dollar
deal?"

"You don't have to force yourself to answer if you don't
want to. I know all the answers even if I don't hear them. I
just thought I could make the load a little lighter for you,
that's all."

"All right. What do I have to do then?"

The man ill-humoredly stuck out his lower lip and drew
from the pocket of his coat a battered package of cigarettes.

All at once the muscles around his mouth began to twitch, like the underside of an insect, jerking the flesh around his thin cheeks. His expression was that of a cornered victim. But could that be? I knew from experience that a child could be thrown into considerable panic by his own fancies, but this fellow was a full-grown man. My colleagues averted their eyes from me doubtless out of the usual feeling of discomfort in front of a superior. Precisely because I knew that, I was only trying to establish a pseudo-equality at best with my hundred-dollar bait.

"Well, let's get down to business right away." I carefully sent out a feeler in a deliberately unpleasant manner. "The fact is . . . I've been wondering if you wouldn't sell me your face...."

Instead of answering, he vigorously struck a match with a grave expression. He broke the matchstick, and the broken part, still burning, flew onto the table. Hastily he blew it out and with his fingernail flicked it to the floor; snorting in exasperation, he struck a new match. It was as I expected. It had been simply a question of a few seconds, but in that interval he had focused all his attention and was engrossed in trying to discover the meaning of the words "sell me your face."

Surely, any number of explanations were possible—starting with extremely feasible ones like wanting a stand-in for a murderer, blackmailer or swindler to fanciful cases like wanting to buy and sell actual faces. Such a request would never arouse innocent speculation. If he had any presence of mind, he would weigh the very real item of the hundred dollars. You can't get much for a hundred dollars. Wouldn't it be common sense to ask at once what I meant, without brooding over it? Overcome by my bandage, he had assumed this stiff attitude as if tormented by irrational arguments in a dream. I had been unerring about the restaurant. And what pleased me more than anything else was that he was concerned about the bandage itself rather than about what lay underneath, as if stopped by the barbed-wire entanglement surrounding a camp.

As soon as I realized this, an amazing transformation took place within me, as if some master sleight-of-hand artist had waved his handkerchief. I was changed into a merciless assailant, aiming my polished, shining fangs straight at my opponent's neck, like a bat that suddenly darts from an invisible hole.

"Well, even though I did say the face, just a little bit of the skin will do. I'm thinking of using it in place of the bandages...."

The man's expression grew darker and darker, and he puffed restlessly on his cigarette; he had apparently quite forgotten the original business. I had at first intended to tell him, and only him, something of the real facts in order to allay his opposition as much as possible, but there was apparently no longer any need to. Under my bandage I involuntarily smiled a secret, bitter smile. Once in a while it's good to give vent to one's anger.

"No. You don't need to worry. I'm not going to peel your skin off. I want just a little skin surface ... some wrinkles, or sweat glands, or pores, or.... In short all I want is a sample of skin."

"Ah ... a sample ...?"

The man's tenseness relaxed and he sighed with relief. Working his Adam's apple up and down, he nodded his head in a number of short jerks; but he did not yet seem to have completely dismissed his doubts. I did not have to ask what was bothering him. He was probably worried about what in heaven's name I was up to, putting on a face exactly the same as his. Yet I didn't try to dispel his suspicions at once. While I was eating my food, which had at last been brought, I deliberately let him stew in uncertainty, adding now and then an ill-tempered thrust. I didn't bear him any personal grudge. I was doubtless only trying to take my revenge against the convention of faces.

Surely, if I were not afflicted with these keloid scars there would be some good in these bandages. For example, I thought that the basic significance of the face could actually be well summed up in the effect of the bandages, that is, the disguising effect. A disguise is a spiteful game where the convention of the face is turned upside down; I suppose one might well think of it as a kind of art of concealment, by which one ultimately suppresses the heart by wiping out the face. In the case of executioners, strolling flute players, religious judges, primitive medicine men, priests of secret societies, and sneak thieves, a disguising mask was indispensable. It had not only the negative aim of concealing the man's face, but also the positive objective of cutting off the connection between face and heart by concealing the expression, thus liberating him from ordinary, earthly ties. Take a more common example: disguise is part of the psychology of the dandy, who wants to wear his sunglasses even though there is no glare. Being released from any mental restraint, he can be utterly free and accordingly infinitely cruel.

However, this is not the first time I have thought about the disguising effect of my bandage. Yes—the first time was before the incident of the Klee picture—I recall being pretty self-complacent, comparing myself with a transparent man, for I alone could see and yet not be seen by others. Then there was also the time I went to visit K of the artificial organs. K stressed the anesthetic nature of disguise and earnestly advised me that I would ultimately be poisoned by my bandages; and now was the third time. Over half a year had gone by. Could it be that I was still plodding around the same circle? No, there seemed to be a slight difference among them. For indeed I was now actually experiencing the hidden pleasure of the disguised spy—the first time had been mere bluff, and the second time I had just been advised by someone else. My thinking seemed to move in a spiral. Of course, I was not without apprehension as to whether the direction of the movement was following a rising curve, or whether it had begun to fall.

Therefore I lured the man out of the department store, maintaining an aggressive attitude all the while; and taking a room in a nearby hotel, I succeeded two hours later in obtaining an impression of the skin of his face by the method I had used in making the mold of the scar webs, but. . . . The man, having finished the job, thrust the hundred-dollar bill into his pocket. He left as though furtively escaping, and as I saw him off I was suddenly overcome with an unbearable feeling of loneliness, as if all my strength had been drained from me. If the convention of the face were empty, perhaps a disguise too was just as empty.

EXCURSUS: *No, such thinking was wrong. Perhaps I felt this way because I imagined the change in my thinking that would come with the completion of the mask would be something like the reaction to wearing a disguise. It was thus no doubt natural for me to be uneasy, since I had deviated from my aim to restore the roadway between myself and others. But my original analogy had been unreasonably fanciful. Since the mask was not my real face, treating it as a disguise was like talking black into white. If the mask was an enlargement of the roadway, then a disguise would be a blocking of it, and the two conflicted with each other. If this were not true, I who was so avidly reaching out for the mask, so eagerly trying to escape from the disguise of my bandages, was a stupid clown.*

Finally, I shall put down one more thing that occurs to me now: isn't the mask something required mainly by the victim and the disguise, on the contrary, by the assailant?

THE WHITE
NOTEBOOK

I HAVE at length changed to a new note-
book, but my state has not altered so abruptly. Actually,
several weeks passed without incident before I could go on
to a new page, and I remained unable to move ahead. There
followed several uneventful weeks, quite suited to my anonymous face, which had neither eyes, nose, or mouth. Two
things did happen, though: I sold a patent to raise funds, and
I received some unexpected criticism from the younger men
in the Institute about this year's budget. The patent was still
far from being of practical use and was extremely specialized;
it was doubtless unnecessary to consider it too seriously. However, the budget question—even though it had no direct relationship with the plans for my mask—was an important one,
and I had to give it some thought. When my colleagues
spoke about it, they apparently seemed to think of it as a
political move on my part. Some time ago I had agreed to
the formation of a special section incorporating the hopes
of the Young Members Group, but when it came down to the
essential budgeting, I simply went back on my word. As they
said, it was nothing so complicated as intrigue, or jealousy, or
the stifling of ambitions. It was nothing but a lapse of memory. I thought I must accept meekly the criticism that I was
deficient in zeal for my work. I was scarcely aware of it before,
but when they spoke up I did indeed realize that for some
time my enthusiasm for my work had been ebbing. I did not
want to recognize the fact, but I wondered if perhaps it was

the influence of the scars. Of course, aside from the more or less underhandedness involved, to tell the truth I actually felt a sort of exhilaration at their protests. Instead of constrained smiles directed at a cripple, I was now being treated on an equal footing.

Now, what in heaven's name was to become of the discovery made at the Noh mask exhibition when I thought I had at last resolved the central problem of the choice of a face?

How painful it is to write about it. The expression is not some hidden door, unlikely to be seen; it is like a front door, constructed and decorated to be the first thing to greet the visitor's eyes. Or like a letter, it apparently cannot exist without an addressee in mind; it is not some advertising handbill to be passed out indiscriminately. Recognizing the validity of this comparison, I at once decided to entrust the right of choice to you, and although I felt I had shifted a heavy burden of responsibility from my own shoulders, the problem was not so easily resolved.

That evening . . . a dirty fog, welling up like muddy water, shut out the sky about an hour earlier than usual . . . an evening the color of earthenware where the crude light of the street lamps committed its showy act of violence, spurring the advance of time. . . . As I walked along in the crowd, which became more dense near the station, I again attempted to play the role of assailant, trying to dispel the unbearable feeling of loneliness which had beset me from the moment of separating from the man. But this failed me, for I had no one to confront as in the department-store restaurant. Once the crowd had gathered—it was a conscience-stricken, end-of-Sunday throng—its faces formed a chain, like amoebae extending their pseudopodia toward each other; there was no place at all for me to wedge in. Still, I was not so irritated as before. I was relaxed enough to take in the brilliance of the tangled mass of neon signs which breathed and streamed through the fog. Perhaps because I now had my plan. The potassium alginate mold of the face I had finally purchased weighed heavily in the briefcase at my side—not to be outdone, my face bandages, equally cumbersome with the moisture they had absorbed from the fog, counterpointed the weight of the briefcase—but anyway I had my plan to try. And I reflected that this expectant waiting for the place to materialize had bolstered me up considerably.

Yes, that evening, my heart was open to you, quite as if the front of it had been sliced away. It was not only the passive expectation of shifting the burden of choice onto your shoulders, nor, of course, was it only the utilitarian motivation of entering the final stage when I would actually produce the mask. How shall I put it . . . I was continually shortening the distance between us—softly, like running barefoot over grass.

It was perhaps relief and confidence stemming from the opportunity to tempt you into being my accomplice, however indirectly, in the lonely work of producing the mask. For me, whatever you may say, you are the most important "other person." No, I do not mean it in a negative sense. I mean that the one who must first restore the roadway, the one whose name I had to write on the first letter, was first on my list of "others." (Under any circumstances, I simply did not want to lose you. To lose you would be symbolic of losing the world.)

HOWEVER, as soon as I confronted you, my hopes changed into a heap of shapeless rags, like seaweed pulled out of the water. No, don't misunderstand. I do not mean to find fault with your manner when you greeted me. Far from that, you always sympathized with me—too generously, as far as that goes. The one exception is when you refused me that time I ran my hand under your skirt. I, and only I, am to blame for that incident. For it is not true that one has the right to be loved by the person one loves, as the poets say.

That day too you greeted me with your usual unobtrusive consideration, or better, unobtrusive pity. Our silence, of course, was quite routine too. . . .

How long would this silence, like some broken instrument, go on between us? Even the everyday exchange of pleasantries and gossip had petered out, leaving at best an elementary, sign-like conversation, absolutely minimal. But even in this instance I did not blame you. Moreover, I was amply prepared to look upon it as a part of your pity for me. A broken instrument is liable to produce cacophony; better let it remain mute. The silence was painful for me, but how much more distressing it must have been for you. How fervently I hoped we could somehow use this opportunity to resume talking once again.

Even so, you should have at least asked me why I was going out. Although it was an exceptional event for me to go out bright and early on a Sunday for the whole day, you did not show the slightest surprise.

You quickly regulated the fire in the stove and at once withdrew to the kitchen, and as soon as you had brought a hot towel you went to check on the hot water in the bath. You had not abandoned me, but neither did you stay close to me. I wondered whether all housewives were like that—I am talking about your excessive impersonality. Indeed you acted cleverly. You manipulated time beautifully, with the precision of electric scales, attaching no unnaturalness to our silence.

To overcome this silence, I tried to put on a show of anger, but that did not work. When I saw your heroic efforts to remain calm I at once backed down, quite aware of my own willful self-conceit. The icy lump of silence that lay between us was apparently too deeply frozen to melt under just any pretext. The questions I had prepared as I walked along— possible opportunities for conversation—were so many matches held against an iceberg.

Of course, I was not so optimistic as to imagine I could succeed, like a wily salesman, by showing you two specimens of face models and asking which you preferred. The first requirement was that my mask should not appear to be a mask; thus, it would not do to reveal to you the real motive of my question. To do so would be malicious sarcasm. From now on, unless I took up hypnotism, my questions would have to be indirect. But I had no further ideas. I had been optimistic, thinking that I could adapt myself to circumstances, as I had fortunately been able to do so far. For example, I went through various of my friends' faces with your tastes in mind.

However, you were not a fish living by nature in silence. Silence was an ordeal for you. I myself would be the first to be hurt by any rash mention of faces; you were concerned about this and were trying to shield me. I blamed my own frivolity, but, saying not a word, I by-passed the silence, returned to my study, and locked up today's booty and my instruments for mold-casting in a cabinet. Then, as usual, I began to take off my bandage in order to cream my face and perform my daily massage. But my fingers stopped unexpectedly in mid-air; I was lost in another dialogue with no one.

—Only my lost face knew how many hundreds of thousands of degrees it would take to melt this silence. And perhaps the mask was the answer. But I could not make it without your advice. Hadn't I been checked into complete inactivity? If I did not break the vicious circle somewhere, it would end in a stupid impasse, repeating the same sequence. I could not give up the whole thing as useless now. Even if I couldn't melt away the whole silence, as least I had to try to light a flame.

I rewound my bandage with the determination of a diver putting on his equipment. When my scar webs were exposed I had no confidence of ever overcoming the pressure of the silence.

I returned to the light room, concealing the strain I was under with feline detachment. I surreptitiously watched your comings and goings between the living room and the kitchen from the corner of my eye, as I pretended to read the evening paper. You were not smiling, but you moved about ceaselessly from one activity to another with that strangely light expression that comes just before smiling. Perhaps you were unaware of it, but it was indeed a curious expression. I believe I proposed marriage to you precisely because I was unexpectedly taken by that look.

(I wonder if I wrote about this before. Well, it doesn't make any difference if I repeat myself. Because for me who sought the meaning of expression your expression was like the beacon of some lighthouse. Even as I write this, I try to think of you, and your expression comes to me first. The instant that expression becomes a smile something suddenly

shines forth, and everyone who receives its light has his existence reaffirmed.)

Yet while you shed this expression generously on everything—windows, walls, lights, pillars—I was the only one on
whom you did not seem to be able to turn it. Though I
thought it natural, I was unable to control my irritation, and
being without definite hope of success, I came to feel it would
be enough if only I could get you to direct the look on me.

"Let's talk."

But when your face turned toward me, the expression had
already disappeared.

"I went to see a movie today."

Looking into the slits in my bandages with such care that
it could not be recognized as care, you awaited my next words.

"No, I don't mean I really wanted to see a movie. I really
wanted the darkness. Walking the streets with a face like this
was like a burden, as if I were doing something bad. A strange
thing, the face. I never felt anything about it at any given
time, but when I found I didn't have one, I felt as if half the
world had been torn away from me."

"What movie was it?"

"I don't remember. Perhaps because I was so upset. Actually, I was suddenly possessed with a feeling of persecution. I
dashed into the nearest movie, quite as if I were taking shelter
from the rain...."

"Where was the movie house?"

"It doesn't make any difference where it was. I wanted the
dark."

You pursed your lips as if in reproval. But your eyes nar-
rowed sadly, as if to show you did not blame me. I was overcome by a terrible sense of remorse. I should not have been.
I meant to talk about something quite different.

"But then, it just occurred to me . . . it's probably a good
thing to go to the movies occasionally. The whole audience

puts on the actor's face. No one needs his own. A movie's a place where you pay your money to exchange faces for a while."

"That's true. Maybe it is good to go to the movies once in a while."

"It definitely is, I think. Because at least it's dark, isn't it? But I wonder, wouldn't it be awful if you didn't like the actor's face? You put on his face, so half the fun would be gone if it didn't fit perfectly, wouldn't it?"

"Can't there be movies without actors? For example, something like a documentary...?"

"That wouldn't work. Everything has a face; it's not limited to actors. Even a fish, or an insect—they all have faces. Even chairs and tables have something corresponding to a face, and you either like them or you don't."

"But I wonder if anybody would watch a movie, wearing a fish's face."

Butterfly-like, you tried to shift the conversation with a joke. Of course, you were right. Any silence must still be preferable to bringing up the subject of a fish's face.

"No, you misunderstand. It's not a question of my face at all. Anyway, since I don't have a face I can't say I like it or dislike it. But you're different. In your case, you can't help being concerned about what actor you want to see in a movie."

"Even so, I really would like one without an actor. I don't seem to be interested in tragedies or comedies now."

"Come on. Why do you always defer to me?"

Without realizing it, my voice had taken on a strident tone, and displeased with myself, I scowled invisibly beneath my bandages. Perhaps it was because the heat had come back, but the scars had begun to squirm like leeches, and in the flesh around them I felt a creepy, burning sensation.

I could not overcome the silence with such conversation.

Wherever we began, the destination of our dialogue was always the same. I lost all power to say more, and of course you fell silent too. Our silence was not the vacuum that comes from having said all there is to say. Whatever conversation we had fell naturally to pieces and crumbled in bitter silence.

THEN for several weeks I continued to walk through the silence, mechanically, as if I were moving on borrowed joints. Suddenly one day I looked up and saw that it was early summer. Outside my window the wind was teasing the slender, soft-green branches of the pine tree. My decision was equally abrupt. I wonder if you remember. I have quite forgotten what the motive was, but it was the night I suddenly exploded in the middle of dinner.

"Why in God's name are you living with me?" I knew that no matter how I shouted, the silence persisted; unable to look you straight in the face, I fixed my eyes in the vicinity of the yellowish-brown darned spot around the little green button at your breast. Trying not to yield to my own voice, I continued to scream. "Well, come on! What about answering? Why do you go on being married to me? It's best for the both of us to clear the air right now. Is it simple force of habit? Well, speak up. Don't mince words. You can't force yourself into something you can't understand, you know."

Withdrawing to my study after these harsh and condescending words, I felt miserable, like a paper kite beaten by the rain. I wondered what connection there could be between the me who was acting out this mad affair about a face and the me who was the acting head of the Institute, with a monthly salary of 850 dollars. The more I thought about it the more my kite filled with holes until at length the paper tore away, leaving only the skeleton.

Down to the skeleton, I suddenly came to myself. I was aware that the abuse I had spewed out at you a moment ago should in fact have been addressed to myself. Yes, we had been married eight years. Eight years was not a short time. It should be long enough at least to know what the other liked and didn't like in foods. If we could tell each other's tastes in what we ate, wouldn't it be the same with our tastes in faces? There was no need to struggle for a subject of conversation.

I groped confusedly among my memories. Surely somewhere there must be a document certifying that I could act for you. There must be. If we had been far apart even before the accident, what was I trying to recapture at this late date with all the fuss about the mask? Nothing was worth the trouble of getting back. There wasn't a single thing to hide from the eight uneventful years we had spent together; since I was enclosed by a wall of nonexpression thicker than my bandages, I had lost all right to complain. One cannot request payment for what one had not lost. Shouldn't I ultimately reconcile myself to the idea that my original real face too was a kind of disguise and, without struggling, be content with the present state of things?

The problem was quite profound. That I thought it profound was itself most profound. Thus, I should probably persevere in the attempt to be your stand-in. It wasn't work I liked, but mobilizing all my memories of your impressions and conversations, I attempted to conjure up various men's expressions, that you might like. It gave me a weird, indecent feeling, as if a caterpillar were crawling down my collar. But far from conjuring up a definite image of the man, I was at my wits' end trying first to define *you*. The lens had to be focused. I couldn't see you, no matter how I tried, if you moved around like a jellyfish. Yet when I forced my concentration, you seemed to become a dot, a line, a face, at last changing into profileless space, slipping through the net of my senses.

I was terribly confused. What in heaven's name had I seen, what had I talked to, what had I felt during all the time we lived together? Was I that ignorant of you? I stood in blank amazement before the unknown territory of you, which was enveloped in an endlessly spreading milky mist. I was so desperately ashamed I could have wrapped my head with another two bandages.

However, perhaps it was just as well I was again cornered. Sweeping the caterpillar from my collar and assuming a defiant attitude, I returned to the living room, where I found you sitting with your face buried in your two hands in front of the television screen, from which you had cut off the sound. Perhaps you were weeping silently to yourself. As soon as I looked, I discovered the possibility of a completely different explanation for my failing to be your stand-in.

Of course, one couldn't say I was ideal as a stand-in, although I had long lived with you. At least I had been living with you in a self-absorbed way. I did not think you would be particular about men's faces. But did it matter? Why at this point should I have to act the pimp? Isn't it the normal form of marriage that from the very beginning one should be unconcerned with one's wife's tastes in other men's faces, if not in food? The moment a man and a woman decide to get married, both of them should put aside such doubts and concerns. If they can't agree, it is best not to opt for trouble from the very beginning.

Taking care not to be noticed, I came up softly behind you; I caught the unexpected smell of asphalt streets just after rain. Perhaps it was the fragrance of your hair. When you turned to look, you sniffled, wrinkling your nose as if you had caught a cold, and then, as if to dispel my misapprehension, you looked back at me with a clear, penetrating gaze, which seemed painted on. With transparent nonexpression, like rays of sunlight filtering through a forest swept with the cold winds of winter....

It was then it happened. A strange impulse possessed me. Was it jealousy? Perhaps it was. Something prickly, like a pokeweed seed, swelled within me to the size of a hedgehog. Then suddenly the basis of facial expression—that errant child of mine—of which I had lost all trace, was standing by my side. It was unexpectedly sudden. So sudden that I could not grasp just how quickly it had happened. But I do not think I was so very surprised. I felt it illogical not to have realized sooner that this was the only solution.

But before anything else, I shall tell you the conclusion. My mask would be the fourth type according to Boulan's system of classification, that is, the "aggressive, extroverted type"—a sharp face centering around the nose; in terms of Jungian psychology, a strong face, showing ability to act.

I had the feeling of being duped; it was too simple. But on consideration, there was nothing particularly unexplainable. Even with the transformation of a chrysalis, the pupa makes preparation in its own way. Suddenly the face had been forcibly shifted from what I myself would choose to what would be chosen for me; yet I could do nothing but continue looking at you intently, just as, in the dark, one sees only darkness whether one keeps his eyes open or shut, looks right or left. My pride was hurt. I was humiliated, irritated, and impatient that at this point I should have to search for you, but though I was weary of thinking about all this, I could not take my eyes from you for a single instant.

I wanted to get close to you, and at the same time to stay away from you. I wanted to know you, and at the same time I resisted that knowing. I wanted to look at you and at the same time felt ashamed to look. My state of suspension was such that the crevice between us grew deeper and deeper, and holding the broken glass together with my two hands, I barely preserved its form.

And I realized it very well. To say that you were a victim bound and chained to me, who fundamentally had no power over you, was a pack of lies I had made up for my own purposes. You faced this fate unflinchingly of your own volition. Wasn't the brilliance of your smile more effectively used on yourself? If you felt like it you could desert me at any time. I wondered if I could make you understand just how dreadful that would be. Although you had a thousand expressions, I did not even have a single one. When I thought of the living flesh and organs under your dress, having their own temperature, their own elasticity, I seriously thought that the end of my agony would never come if I did not run a spike through your body—though it would mean your death—and make you a specimen in a biologist's collecting box.

Thus both the desire to restore the roadway between us and vengeful craving to destroy you fiercely contended within me. At length I could not distinguish between them, and drawing the bow on you became a common, everyday thing; then suddenly in my heart was graven the face of a hunter.

A hunter's face could not possibly be "introverted and harmonious." With such a face I would end up at best as a friend to little birds, or failing that, bait for wild animals. In this light, my solution, far from sudden, might rather be called inevitable. I was dazzled perhaps by the double aspect of the mask—was it the negation of my real face or actually a new face?—and I had been obliged to take an unavoidably circuitous road because I had forgotten the essential point that even this daze was a form of action.

In mathematics there are "imaginary numbers," strange numbers which, when squared, become minus. They have points of similarity with masks, for putting one mask over another would be the same as not putting on any at all.

ONCE I had decided on the type, the rest was simple. I had already accumulated sixty-eight modeling pictures, and it so happened that more than half of them belonged to the "protruding-center" type. Everything was ready—almost too ready.

I decided to start work at once. I had no special model, but I nevertheless tried to sketch a face, as from some invisible picture, groping my way along from the inside for the expression that might appeal to you. First I applied a spongy resin to the part of the antimony cast with the scar webs and smoothed it down. Over that, I placed layers of a thin plastic tape instead of clay along the Langer lines to provide directional control. From a half year of practice my fingers were as versed in the details of the face as a watchmaker's are in finding the bend of a mainspring. I took the area around my wrist as my standard for skin color and used a greater quantity of titanous oxide to whiten the temples and the point of the chin, adding cadmium red to give a blush to the cheeks. Moreover, I deliberately used conspicuous color blotches as I drew near to the surface and went so far as to apply some grey spots especially around the nostrils, thus contriving to produce a naturalness consonant with my age. Last of all, I applied liquid resin to the transparent layer, that is, the thin fluorescent membrane to which I had transferred the skin surface I had bought and which had a ratio of refraction close to that of ceratin. When I applied compressed steam to it for a very short time, it contracted and set in a perfect fit. Since I had not yet put in the wrinkles, it was too smooth, but one had the feeling of something living, as if it had been a moment ago stripped from a living person. (I had spent a good twenty-two or twenty-three days to bring the mask this far.)

The next problem was the treatment of the edging of the skin. Around the forehead I could devise something with my hair (fortunately it was plentiful and also somewhat curly). Around the eyes I decided to make a number of small wrinkles and to hide the edge by darkening the skin pigmentation and wearing sunglasses. As for the lips, I would insert the flange up underneath and attach it to the gums. I could manage the nostrils by attaching two rather stiff tubes and inserting them into my nose. But the jaw line was a little troublesome. There was only one way. I should have to conceal it with a beard.

I planted each strand, carefully observing the angle and direction, using only the thinner hair from my head and planting some fifty to sixty filaments per square inch. The labor was time-consuming—I spent another twenty days on the beard alone—but even more, I was plagued by a psychological resistance to the device. Fifty years ago beards were all too common, but now they are unusual. When I hear the word

"beard" the first thing I think of, unfortunately, is the police-
man in his police-box in front of the station.

Of course, it doesn't follow that all bearded men are bullies
or heroes. There's the fortuneteller's beard, the Lenin cut, or
again the European aristocrat's. And then there's the Castro
beard and what is apparently the latest style—the beards
sported by youngsters posing as artists, but just what that
is called I don't know. Even though I would inevitably appear
eccentric with my beard and dark glasses, there was no other
way; but at least I could try to devise something that would
not create too bad an impression.

The result is what you are already familiar with, and there
is no need to describe it again. I myself was in no position to
judge the mask, nor did I have specific ideas for improving
it. I suppose I should have been satisfied with what I had.
Indeed, I could not avoid some little regret, but. . . .

No, TO SAY regret is off-handed, for I real-
ized that it implies a profound concern for outward appearance. My feeling was still something vague, unformulated, but
it hurt like a swelling on the tongue each time I opened my
mouth, like an unpleasant premonition, warning against heedless chatter.

That evening, when I finished planting the last hair of
the beard, the tweezers had left black blood-blisters on the

ball of my thumb. A pain that made me clammy with perspiration turned into tiny embers that smoldered flickeringly in the depths of my eyes. The whole surface of my eyes had clouded over like dirty windowpanes with a soft, honey-like secretion, that kept oozing out no matter how much I wiped it away. As I stood up to go to the lavatory and wash my face, I was suddenly aware that day had already come. And the instant I involuntarily averted my face from the brilliance of the morning light spilling over the window ledge, piercing to the core of my head, shame suddenly overcame me.

I recalled a dream of a day when summer had come to an end and autumn had just begun. It was a dream like some old silent movie that began with a most peaceful scene, in which my father, back from his work, was taking off his shoes in the vestibule and I—I was perhaps not quite ten—was at his side absently watching him. But suddenly the peace was broken. Another father came back from work. This one, curiously enough, was identical to the first; the only thing different was the hat he wore on his head. In contrast to the straw hat that my first father was wearing, the second wore a creased soft felt. When the father with the soft hat saw the one with the straw hat, he looked clearly contemptuous and gave an exaggerated shudder in rebuke for such evident bad form. Whereupon the one in the straw hat smiled mournfully in quite unbecoming confusion and left as if he were furtively escaping, the shoe he had removed dangling in his hand. The child that I was looked heartbrokenly after the retreating figure of my straw-hat father . . . when suddenly the film broken with a snap. But for some reason, the painful memory of the incident lingered on.

It might be called a child's feeling about the change of seasons . . . but I wonder whether it would be possible after several decades for the memory of such an insignificant incident to remain so vivid. I can't believe it. The two hats I saw were surely something quite different. Something, for example, like symbols for the unforgivable lies that exist in human relationships. Yes, I can say only one thing for sure: the trust I had had in my father up to then was completely betrayed by the exchange of hats. Perhaps, since then, I have continued to suffer shame in my father's place.

But this time the positions were inverted. It was my turn to have to excuse myself. Looking into a mirror, I stared at the inflamed scar webs, whipping up my desire for the mask. Yet, it was not I who should feel ashamed. If there was anyone who should suffer, was it not rather the world that had buried me alive, that made no attempt to recognize a man's personality without the passport of the face?

With a renewed feeling of defiance, I went back to the mask. I was struck by the insolent look of the bearded face with its prominent nose. I thought the weirdness came perhaps from seeing only separate parts, and I tried hanging it flat against the wall, stepping back several paces and peering at it through my hand held like a spyglass. Yet I was not overjoyed at having finished, and a feeling not unlike sorrow that I might gradually be taken over by this other face came to me.

Perhaps my depression was owing to fatigue. I told myself that for encouragement. It wasn't only the mask; wasn't it always like this when one finished a big job? Only those not responsible for the results can experience the pleasure of having finished a piece of work. Perhaps prejudice about faces functions in the subconscious too. No matter how much I fight against considering the face sacred, the root of the evil may exist in the depths of the subconscious. It is much the same as people who don't believe in ghosts but are afraid of the dark.

I decided then to make myself go on with the work, whatever the price. Anyway, I had up my mind to try on the mask for a final check. First I undid the protuberance under the ear, then when I had loosened the part under the jaw, unfastened the lips, and extracted the nostril tubes, I was able to strip the mask completely from the cast. It had become a soft, gelatinous membrane, like a wet plastic bag. Then, reversing the order I had just followed, I carefully placed it over my face. There seemed to be no technical fault, and it clung to me like a well-fitting shirt; the lump in my throat descended with a gulp into my stomach.

I peered into the mirror. A man I did not know looked coolly back at me. Indeed, not the slightest detail would make one think it was me. The color, the luster, the feeling were all successful—a perfect disguise. Yet, what in heaven's name was this emptiness? Perhaps it was the fault of the mirror—the lighting seemed somewhat unnatural—at once I opened the shutters and let in the daylight.

Keen shafts of sunlight, waving like the antennae of an insect, spread to every crevice of the mask. The pores, the sweat glands, the partial degeneration of some tissues, even the minute capillaries stood out distinctly. I could not discover a single defect. What then was the cause of this feeling that something was wrong? I wondered. Perhaps it was the fixity, the lack of expression? It had the weirdness of the face of a corpse whose make-up has been applied by the undertaker. Should I try moving some muscle as an experiment? Since I had not completed the preparation of the glue with which to stick the mask to my face—I intended to use something like adhesive plaster, but less sticky—I could not possibly make the mask move with the muscles, but the area around the nose and the mouth which were comparatively well set might possibly work.

First I tried the ends of the lips, drawing them slightly to the right and left. The result was very good. The extreme care I had taken from the standpoint of anatomy, fitting the directional fibers onto each other, had apparently not been in vain. Encouraged, I tried to smile. However, the mask simply would not smile. It merely contorted limply. It was so strange a distortion that I thought the mirror was bent. When it smiled it was full of the feeling of death, even more so than when it was immobile. I felt drained, as if the supports of my internal organs had been severed and my whole diaphragm collapsed.

But I don't want you to misunderstand. For this is no over-dramatic plot to trade on my suffering. This was the mask I had chosen, for better or worse. It was the face I had come to after many months of experimentation. If I were dissatisfied with it, I could remake it to my own liking. But if it were not a question of the workmanship, what in heaven's name should I do then? Henceforth, would I be able to accept the mask with good grace, frankly acknowledging it as my own face? Thus I felt that this debilitating sense of collapse, rather than the disorientation brought on by finding oneself with a new face, was the depression accompanying extinction, as if I were witnessing my own shadow fading away under a magic cloak. (Under such circumstances I wondered whether I should be able to carry out my plans for the future.)

Of course, expression comes like the annual growth rings in a tree trunk, and perhaps it would be quite impossible to laugh with no preparation at all. Depending on the life one has led, a tendency to repeat certain expressions causes them to become fixed by sags and wrinkles. A smiling expression becomes naturally engraved in a face that is often smiling. Chronic anger engraves itself on the face, too. But on my mask, which was like the face of a new-born infant, there was not the crease of a single growth-ring as yet. Even with a smile on it, the face of a forty-year-old child would naturally be somewhat monstrous. Indeed, it would have to be. Actually the work of making wrinkles suitable for my face was included in my first plans after I had gone to my hideaway. If only I could succeed, this mask would become natural and easily managed. This was something I had anticipated; there was absolutely no need of losing my head now. The result was that, far from heeding my throbbing shame, by cleverly side-stepping the real problem I inevitably involved myself deeper and deeper.

WELL, it would seem I have come around to the point of my hideaway in the S— Apartments, where I began. But when did I get off the subject? Oh, yes, it must be just about the time when, alone with myself in hy hideaway, I had begun to undo my bandage. Well, I shall try to go on from there without wasting any more time.

The first task, needless to say, was providing the mask with wrinkles. No special technique was necessary, but it was terribly time-consuming work for which I could not have too much determination, perseverance, and attentiveness.

First, I applied glue to my whole face. I put the mask on, starting from the nose. Then I fixed the nostril tubes in place and inserted the part that went over the lips into the gums. Next, I tapped the ridge of the nose, the cheeks, and the chin, taking great care to make a perfect fit with no sags, and pressed the whole surface down. I waited for it to set, and then, warming it with an infra-red lamp maintained at the prescribed degree of heat, I repeated certain specific expressions. The material decreased sharply in flexibility when the prescribed degree of heat was exceeded, and wrinkles fitting the expressions naturally appeared along the Langer lines, that is, following the direction of the fibers I had previously installed. Concerning the content and distribution of the expressions, I drew up the following tentative list as ratios of 100 percent.

1.	Concentration of interest	16 percent
2.	Curiosity	07 percent
3.	Assent	10 percent
4.	Satisfaction	12 percent
5.	Laughter	13 percent
6.	Denial	06 percent
7.	Dissatisfaction	07 percent
8.	Abhorrence	06 percent
9.	Doubt	05 percent
10.	Perplexity	06 percent
11.	Concern	03 percent
12.	Anger	09 percent

It cannot be considered satisfactory to analyze such a complicated and delicate thing as expression into these few components. However, by combining just this many elements on my palette, I should be able to get almost any shade. The percentages, needless to say, indicate the frequency of occurrence of each item. In brief, I postulated a type of man who expressed his emotions in approximately such ratios. I should be hard pressed for a ready answer if I were asked what the standard of judgment was. I weighed these expressions one by one on the scales of my intuition, placing myself in the position of a seducer and imagining the scene when I would confront you who were the symbol of "the others."

Like some fool, I repeated getting angry, crying, and laughing until morning. As a result, it was already drawing toward evening when I awoke the next day. A light like red glass came through the cracks in the shutters, and apparently the rain that had been going on for some time had stopped. However, my disposition had not cleared equally well, and a fatigue like old tea grounds clung to me. The area around my temples throbbed feverishly, but that was not unexpected. I had been moving my facial muscles for over ten hours.

But it was not the movement alone: I had been straining all my nerves, really laughing when I laughed, really angered when I expressed anger.

Anyway, in that time even the most trivial expression became deeply etched on the surface of my face as an un-alterable coat of arms. For example, if I had repeatedly made artificial smiles, then my mask would be forever branded with artificial smiles. So I was obliged to be prudent of even casual imprints when I considered that they would be formally recorded as a part of my life.

I prepared a hot towel and massaged my face. The steam penetrated my skin. As I had stimulated the sweat glands with the infra-red lamp and blocked the openings with adhesive material, the skin was naturally inflamed. It would surely have a bad effect on the keloid scar too. But the condition could not get any worse than it was, and at this point it served no purpose to be concerned about it. It makes no difference to a dead man whether he is buried or cremated.

For three more days I repeated the process in the same order. Since I had corrected what needed correcting and the mask had arrived at a stable state, on the third day I decided to try eating my supper while wearing it. I should have to try it sometime, of course; why put off what could be done now? And I would be prepared when the situation demanded it. After the adhesive had set sufficiently, I tousled my hair to conceal the hairline, put on some amber sunglasses so that the line around my eyes was not obvious, and completed my preparations just as if I were going out.

Avoiding looking into the nearby mirror, I first laid out on the table the dishes of food left over from the evening before and, imagining that I was dining in a restaurant with a lot of people, I slowly raised my face and looked in the mirror.

Of course, my companion raised his face too and looked back. Then adjusting the movements of his features with mine, he began to chew his bread. When I ate my soup, he ate his. Our breathing, exactly coordinated, was most natural. The dullness of the nerves around my lips slightly reduced my sense of taste and made chewing awkward; but when I got accustomed to it, I would certainly be able to forget the feeling of the lips as easily as of a false tooth. Yet drops of saliva and soup tended to escape from the corners of my lips, and I realized I needed to pay constant attention.

Suddenly my companion arose and came to look at me with an expression of suspicion. At that instant I was enveloped by a strange feeling of harmony, sharp yet rapturous, shocking yet smooth, as if too many sleeping pills were all at once beginning to take effect. Perhaps cracks were opening in this husk of mine. For some time we gazed at each other, but my companion laughed first. Drawn in, I too chuckled, and then with no resistance I slipped into his face. At once we fused, and I became him. I wasn't particularly envious of his face, but I did not find it unpleasant; I had apparently begun to feel and to think with it. Everything was going perfectly, so that even I who knew the trick scarcely suspected it.

Surely the glove fitted too well. I wondered if, swallowing the thing whole as I did, some reaction wouldn't occur later. I stepped back five or six steps and shut my eyes, then judging the moment when I looked most cantankerous, I snapped them open. But my face was laughing as before, vibrating like a tuning fork. There seemed to be no mistake. Moreover,

I appeared to have grown, at a conservative estimate, five years younger.

Yet why had I been so worried until yesterday? I had rationalized that one need have no scruples about the skin of the face, because it is unrelated to a man's personality; but this was merely prevarication, bound after all by prejudice. Compared to scar webs or bandages, this plastic mask was a far more living face. The former were *trompe l'œil* doors painted on a wall, but the mask was like a door ajar, through which the fragrance of sunlight is wafted in.

Someone's footsteps, which apparently had been audible for quite some time, gradually grew louder as they approached. They came steadily closer; they were my pulse. The open door was urging me on.

Well, let's go out! Let's go into a new world, someone else's world, through someone else's face.

My heart was throbbing. It was palpitating with the anxiety and anticipation of a child who for the first time is permitted to ride on a train alone. Thanks to the mask, everything would change completely. It was not only me; the world itself would appear in completely new garb. I was exhilarated by the bubble of my anticipation, and the shame that had so distressed me seemed to have vanished.

EXCURSUS: *I expect I should confess: I had taken quite*

a few sleeping pills that day. No, not only that day. I had
begun to do so regularly for some time previously. Yet it was
not in order to deaden my anxiety, as one might imagine. I
was trying to maintain a more rational state and offset my
futile irritation. As I have often repeated, my mask was more
than anything else a challenge to the prejudice surrounding
the face. I must be continually alert to the mask, as one is to
handling complicated machinery.

And one more thing: when I took certain types of sleeping
pills and tranquilizers simultaneously in the right amounts,
for several seconds after the effect of the medicine was apparent I was strangely possessed by a pure, clear stillness, as
if I were peering into myself with a telescopic lens. Of course,
as I had no assurance that it was not some ecstatic narcosis,
I omitted writing about it; but now I have come to feel that a
deeper meaning than I had imagined was concealed in the
experience of those several seconds. Something, for example,
that would bring me closer to the essence of human relations
that are composed of the transitory elements we call the face.

As the drugs began to take effect, I experienced first the
feeling of stumbling over rocks. For an instant my body
floated in air and I was seized with a slight giddiness. Then
a fragrance like crushed grass tickled my nose, and my mind
wandered out into a distant countryside. No, the expression
is perhaps not exact. Suddenly the flow of time seemed to
disappear, and I lost my bearings, drifting away outside the
current. It was not only that I drifted away; all the things
that had flowed along with me, creating the relationship we
had had until now, crumbled to pieces. With a feeling of
release as I was freed from the flow, I became supremely
optimistic, taking a generous view of everything; I repeated
my singularly rash judgment that my own face was identical
to yours in that it resembled a Buddhist saint's. The period

*during which I was quite indifferent to the thing we call face
lingered on for seven or eight minutes.*

*Perhaps then in an eddy of that current, not only was I
indifferent to the scar webs, but also I had gone beyond the
face itself and arrived at the other side of the problem. I may
have glimpsed, if only for a moment, a freedom which was
unimaginable when I relied on human relationships seen
through the window of the face. Perhaps I had stumbled unexpectedly on the terrible truth that anyone closing the window of the soul with a mask of flesh was merely shutting away
scar webs inside. Having lost my face, perhaps I could make
contact with another world of real things, which were not
pictures painted in windows. This pellucid feeling of release
could not ultimately be false—it could not be a temporary
trick of the drugs.*

*But—distressingly enough—my mask might restrict the
freedom of facelessness. And wasn't this the cause, surprisingly, of my shame about the mask? Yet the mask already
screened my face. And the drugs, close to twice the usual
amount, were beginning to make me forget the freedom of
having no face.*

*I remonstrated with myself. After all, wasn't the ugly duck-
ling in the fairytale ultimately granted the right to be transformed into a swan?*

In order to become completely someone else, I had to get
out of my ordinary clothes. But unfortunately I had made no
preparations for such a contingency, and that evening, deciding that mental adjustment made more difference than
clothes, I decided simply to put on a jacket and go out. It
was a commonplace, ready-made one that would surely not
be conspicuous.

Walking on air as I was, it seemed strange that my weight

should make the emergency stairs creak. Fortunately I met
no one until I came out on the front street. However, the
instant I turned the corner of the lane, I almost collided head
on with a woman neighbor carrying a basket of groceries.
Shocked as if I had bitten on a firecracker, I stood stock still
in my tracks, but the woman simply glanced up and hurried
on as if nothing had happened. Good. Wasn't it the best
assurance that nothing at all had happened?

I continued walking. Since for the time being my objective
was just getting used to the mask, I had decided on no particular destination. As I had anticipated, simply walking at
first was rather hard work. The joints of my knees were stiff
as if rusty, and there was considerable looseness in the mask's
breathing apparatus. Although there was no question of the
mask blushing, the muscles of my back were writhing with
worry lest my shame, and my real face, be seen. If my mask
could be penetrated, it was more likely to be due to my awkwardness. Since I was behaving like a suspect, I would *be* suspected. After all, I was merely trying to change the design on
the wrapping-paper a little. All would be well if only I were
not challenged. If I had no deception within me there was
nothing to fear from anyone.

Though I reasoned in that way, my initial enthusiasm was
gone, and I felt more and more dispirited, for my physical
state betrayed my emotions just as my emotions betrayed my
thoughts. I walked for about three hours. If there was a
brightly lit shop window on my side, I would pretend interest
in the store front across the street and cross over. If a street
was glaring with neon street lights, I would pick my way
toward the darker lanes, pretending to seek adventure. At a
trolley stop, when I saw a car pulling up, I consciously hastened my steps to avoid meeting anyone; on the other hand,
when someone overtook me, I deliberately slowed up to let
them pass. I was finally disgusted with myself. I could con-

tinue walking in this fashion for days and never get used to managing the mask.

There was a small tobacconist's that shared a shop front with a bakery. I decided to attempt a little exploit. The expression is exaggerated; all I decided was to purchase some cigarettes. As I approached, I began to experience palpitations in the area between my abdomen and my diaphragm. I began to shed tears. Suddenly the mask increased in weight and seemed about to slide off. My legs were cramped as if I were descending some fathomless precipice on a single rope. For a mere package of cigarettes, I was putting up a struggle as if I were in combat with some monster.

However, for some reason, as soon as my eyes met those of the shop girl, who came indifferently toward me, I instantly became audacious. Was it because the girl did not show any more reaction to me than to an ordinary customer? And was it also because I could feel the cigarette resting lightly in my fingers like a little dead bird? No, the reason seemed rather to lie in the transformation of the mask. I was afraid of my own shadow as long as I *imagined* others to be looking at me, but when I was actually looked at, I seemed to become aware of my real character. Perhaps in my imagination the mask was something that exposed me, but in actuality it was an opaque means of concealment. While beneath the mask the blood vessels expanded and the sweat glands poured out their moisture, the surface didn't shed a single drop of perspiration.

Thus I was easily able to recover from my fear of blushing, but I was already exhausted. I did not have the energy to walk further and, hailing a taxi, I returned directly to the apartment. I felt depressed when I considered that all I had gotten for so much wear and tear was a mere pack of cigarettes, but taking into account my awareness of the mask I realized I had profited to some extent. As proof of it, when I returned to my room, took off the mask, washed away the adhesive material, and again looked at my real face, the merciless scar webs seemed less real. The mask had already become just as real as the webs, and if the mask was a temporary form, so were the webs. Apparently the mask was safely beginning to take root on my face.

THE following day I resolutely decided to increase the scope of testing. Quite early, on getting up, I questioned the superintendent of the apartment house, saying I would like to rent the room next door for my younger brother if it were still free. The "younger brother," of course, was my other self, the one who wore the mask.

Unfortunately, I was too late, for a tenant had been accepted the day before.

However, the contretemps did not change my plans. I had taken the occasion to let it be known I had a "younger brother," and it was more important to have impressed this on the man.

As the "younger brother" lived in a remote suburb and was engaged in work at most irregular hours, he wanted a room to relax in from time to time. However, if the place next door was rented, we had had to bow to circumstances. The two of us were in about the same situation, and so we had decided not to be too demanding and to share my room.

Then without a moment's delay I suggested that I pay an

increase in my rent of thirty percent. The superintendent put on a distressed look, but at heart he was not the least troubled. Finally I succeeded in securing an extra latchkey for my "younger brother."

About ten o'clock I put on my mask and went out. My purpose was to complete the "younger brother" 's attire along with the beard and the glasses. For some while, I was unable to escape the tenseness that came with the first sortie of the day—was it because the roots of the mask's beard, which had seemed to show signs last night of growing, had really begun to sprout like real roots? Or was it because of the increased dose of tranquilizers? Anyway, while waiting for the bus, I calmly began to puff on a cigarette.

But I was really made aware of the stubborn power the mask had over me when I entered a department store to order some clothes. Though it might have been appropriate to chose something quite flashy to match the beard and glasses, I selected a conservative three-button suit with a narrow collar, a style which was the fad of the moment. It was unbelievable. First, the very fact that I had any awareness of fashion was itself beyond comprehension. However, that wasn't all; I deliberately went to the jewelry department and purchased a ring. The mask was apparently beginning to walk on its own and to ignore *my* plans. I didn't consider this particularly bothersome, but it was nevertheless strange. Although there was nothing funny, gasps of incoherent laughter came welling up one after the other as if I were being tickled, and I seemed to be in an unaccountably jovial mood.

After leaving the department store, I decided to attempt another little venture. It was not much . . . just dropping into a small Korean restaurant that was situated in an inner lane away from the busy street. Since I had not had a decent meal for some time, my stomach easily persuaded me; in any case, the tasty barbecued meat had long been a favorite of mine. But was that my only motive for going in?

To what extent I was aware of my motives was another question. But it would be false to say that there was no reason for deliberately choosing a Korean restaurant. I had clearly taken into consideration that the restaurant was Korean and that there would be Korean customers. Of course, I had unconsciously reckoned that even if there still were some crudeness about my mask, Koreans would probably take no notice of it, and moreover I felt it would be easier to associate with them. Or perhaps, seeking points of similarity between myself who had lost my face and Koreans who were frequently the objects of prejudice, I had, without realizing it, come to have a feeling of closeness with them. Of course, I had no prejudice against Koreans personally. Being faceless did not qualify one for having prejudices. Indeed, since racial prejudice generally goes beyond an individual's private ends, and because it decidedly casts its shadow on history, it has unmistakable substance. Thus, subjectively, the very act of seeking refuge among them was theoretically perhaps a form of prejudice, but....

Blue smoke enshrouded the place. An ancient electric fan made a clattering noise. Fortunately the three customers all seemed to be Koreans. At first blush, two of them were indistinguishable from Japanese, but the fluent exchange among them in Korean was unmistakable proof they were the real thing. Although it was mid-day, the three had emptied a good many bottles of beer, which had greatly speeded up their usual hurried manner of speaking.

As I ran my hands over the cheeks of my mask to check it, I was at once infected by their cheerfulness. Perhaps I was predisposing myself to getting drunk, feeling that I could if I really wanted to. Or was my state of mind like that of the beggar, a frequent type in novels, who wants to talk with his rich relatives? Anyway, sitting down at a table, I ordered some barbecued meat, preening like a movie hero.

A cockroach crawled up the wall. Rolling up a newpaper that someone had apparently forgotten, I struck it down. I absently glanced at the headlines; there were the usual columns of Help Wanted advertisements, guides to movies, music halls, and other amusement centers. As I threaded through the columns of the advertisements, a scene characterized by enigmas and whisperings began to unfold, to which the endless chattering of the three men was appropriate accompaniment.

Attached to an ashtray was a fortunetelling device. You put in a coin and pushed a button; out of a hole underneath came a tube of paper rolled to the size of a matchstick. My mask had apparently become so zestful as to want to try such a trivial thing. I opened the roll of paper and read my fortune:

Moderately lucky. If you wait, there will be fair weather for a sea voyage. If you see a "weeping mole," go west.

In spite of myself I let out a suppressed laugh, and one of the three Koreans suddenly broke into Japanese. Turning to the girl who had brought my order, he shouted:

"Hey! Girl! You've got the face of a Korean country girl."

I felt that he had screamed rather than simply raised his voice. Startled as if I myself had been insulted, I looked questioningly at the girl, but as she placed the plate of meat before me, she smiled at the laughter of the three, appearing not the least perturbed. I was confused. Perhaps there was not such a pejorative meaning to the Korean's expression "country girl" as I had thought. Anyway, "rustic" fitted the man who was making the fuss more than it suited the girl, a middle-aged fellow who was the crudest of the three. Judging from their laughter, they had perhaps made a simple joke on themselves. Moreover, it was quite possible that the girl actually was

Korean. It was not uncommon for Koreans of her generation to speak only Japanese. If she were Korean, his remark, far from poking fun, was rather more an affirmative, friendly remark. It must surely be that. In the first place, a Korean wouldn't use the term "Korean" negatively, would he?

As my mind shifted back and forth, I ultimately came to feel unbearable remorse about my superficial self-deception, which contained such an impudent feeling of closeness to the Koreans. Figuratively, my attitude was like that of a white beggar treating a colored emperor as his bosom friend. Even though we were both objects of prejudice there was a difference between their case and mine. They had the right to sneer at people with prejudice; I did not. They had companions who joined with them against prejudice; I did not. If I sincerely wanted to stand on an equal footing with them, I should bravely have to cast aside my mask and lay bare my scars. And who am I to talk about faceless spooks? No, that's a meaningless hypothesis; I wonder how people incapable of loving themselves are able to find companions.

I could only return dejectedly to my hideaway with the feeling that I was again stricken to the core with a sense of shame, that everything was detestable. The enthusiasm I had felt until then had suddenly cooled. However, once again I committed a surprising blunder, out of sheer carelessness, in front of the apartment house. As I was casually turning into the lane I suddenly happened on the superintendent's daughter.

The girl, leaning against the wall, was playing awkwardly with a yoyo, an especially large one that shone with a golden color. Startled, I stopped in my tracks. That was quite stupid. The lane was a blind alley intended only for people using the parking lot in back or the emergency staircase. Until I had introduced myself to the superintendent's family as the "younger brother," I should not have gone in and out through the back entrance wearing the mask. Of course, since it was a brand-new apartment house with new tenants coming in almost every day, it would have been all right if I had just gone on by without paying any attention, but . . . I tried at once to regain my footing, but it was too late. The girl had apparently already become aware of my confusion. How could I muddle through the situation? "I'm in that room up there," I said, thinking how awkward my explanation was but having no other inspiration. "My brother lives there. . . . I wonder if he's in now . . . ? He's the one with the bandages wrapped all round like this. . . . Do you know who it is?"

However, the girl, barely turning her body, neither spoke nor changed her expression. I became even more flustered. I wonder if she could have sensed something. No, she couldn't possibly. If I believed the grumblings of her father, her IQ was too low for elementary school, though from outward appearance she was a grown girl. Apparently from meningitis in childhood she had never developed mentally. Her weak mouth, like insect wings, her childish chin, her narrow, slanting shoulders, and contrasting, her adult thin nose and great, oval, deep-set eyes left little doubt that she was retarded.

But the girl's silence, as I passed on by, somehow gave me the feeling something was wrong. Anyway, I chattered along, forcing her to speak.

"That's a great yoyo. Does it work well?"

The girl's shoulders trembled with fear, and in confusion she hid the toy with her hand, answering me in a defiant tone.

"It's mine!"

All at once I felt like laughing out loud. I was relieved and at the same time wanted to tease her some more. There was also something that worried me, and I was not altogether trifling with the girl, who once before had shrieked at my bandage disguise. In spite of her low IQ, the girl had the charm of a misshapen sprite. If things went well, the situation could go far in helping me recover some little power over the mask, which was beginning to become dangerous.

"Is that true? How can I be sure you're not telling a lie?"

"You better believe it. I won't be any trouble at all for you."

"All right, I believe you. But I think there really is someone else's name written on the yoyo."

"You can't go by that. Once upon a time, a cat said . . . it was a snow-white cat, without a single spot, like our cat. . . ."

"Do let me see it."

"Even I keep some secrets."

"Secrets?"

"Once upon a time, a cat said: 'A mouse wants to put a bell on me . . . now what shall I do?' "

"All right. Shall I buy you one exactly like this?"

I was satisfied with myself just for being able to keep this exchange going, but the effect of my blandishments appeared to exceed by far my expectations.

The girl stopped rubbing her back against the wall after a while and stood still, apparently weighing the significance of my words. Then she retorted with a suspicious look: "A secret from my father?"

"Of course, it's a secret from him."

At length I broke out laughing (I, laughing!), and aware of the effect of the jubilant mask, I duplicated the laughter on both levels of my face. Apparently the girl too at last understood. She relaxed her back, which she had kept stiff as a board, and thrust out her lower lip.

"All right . . . all right," she repeated in a sing-song voice. And rubbing the gold yoyo wistfully on the sleeve of her jacket, she said: "If you'll really buy me another, I'll return this one. But . . . I didn't really steal this one without saying anything. It was promised a long time ago. But I'll return it. I'll go and return it right now. I really love it. Whenever I get any present from anybody I really love it."

She sidled along with her back to the wall and slipped by me. Children were children. Just as I was beginning to feel relief, the girl passed me and whispered: "Let's play secrets!"

Play secrets? What did she mean? There was nothing to worry about. A retarded girl like her would never understand such involved tactics. It would be easy to put it down to a restricted field of vision, yet a dog with a restricted field of vision compensates by a keener sense of smell. In the first place, the very fact that I had to be so worried seemed to prove that my self-confidence had again begun to waver.

I had a terribly bad aftertaste. Just making my face look as if it were new, with my memories and my habits unchanged, was quite like dipping up water with a bottomless dipper. Since I had put a mask over my face, I needed one that would fit my heart. If possible, I wanted to be so perfect in my inventions and my acting as to be undetectable even by a lie detector.

WHEN I took the mask off, the adhesive material, musty with sweat, gave off an odor like overheated grapes. At that very moment an unbearable fatigue flowed over me, eddying in my joints like syrupy tar. But everything depends on how you think of it. For a first trial, things had not gone altogether badly. The pain of giving birth to a child is no ordinary thing. Since a full-grown man was trying to be reborn as a completely different person, I should realize all the more that a certain amount of setback and friction was natural. I should be grateful rather that I hadn't been fatally injured.

I wiped off the back of the mask, replaced it on the antimony cast, washed my face, and rubbed in some ointment. Then I stretched out on the bed with the thought of giving my features the rest they had not had for a time. Perhaps as a reaction to the strain that had lasted too long, I fell into a deep sleep, although the afternoon sun was still bright. When I awakened darkness had already begun to fall.

It was not raining, but a thick fog screened the backs of the stores that cut off my vision of the street itself. It seemed like some gloomy forest. Perhaps because of the fog the sky had taken on a faint rosy-to-purple tint. I opened the window wide, filling my lungs with the air, which was heavy like a salt breeze; this period of seclusion when I had no need to fear the eyes of others was like a seat reserved for me alone. Yes, wasn't the real form of human existence apparent in this very fog? My real face, my mask, my scar webs—all such evanescent adornments were diaphanous as if pierced with light. Substance and essence were cleansed of all affectation. Man's soul became something one could taste directly with the tongue, like a peeled peach. Of course, I doubtless had to pay the price in loneliness. But even that made no difference, did it? Perhaps my companions who had faces were as lonely as I. Whatever signboard of a face I hung out, I certainly had no need to select some shipwrecked castaway for the inside.

Loneliness—since I was trying to escape it—was hell; and yet for the hermit who seeks it, it is apparently happiness. All right then, what about putting an end to acting like some maudlin, tragic hero and give the hermit's role a try? Since I had deliberately put the stamp of loneliness on my face, there was no reason why I should not put it to good use. With advanced nuclear chemistry as my god, rheology as the words of my prayer, and the laboratory as my monastery, I had absolutely no fear that my daily work would be disturbed by loneliness. Far from it, wasn't each day guaranteed more than ever before to be replete with simplicity, correctness, and peace as well?

As I gazed at the sky, which was gradually assuming a rosier tint, my heart grew brighter too. When I thought of the tribulations I had undergone until now, the change was somewhat disappointing . . . rather out of proportion; but rowing out to sea like this had been an unique experience—perhaps I had no warrant for discontent. Giving heartfelt thanks that I had seized the opportunity of heaving to while still in sight of shore, I turned and looked at the mask on the table. I intended to bid it farewell, lightly with generosity and a clear, honest feeling of detachment.

But the brightness of the sky had not reached the mask. This dark countenance, belonging to another person, staring expressionlessly back at me checked any intimacy; it was like something concealing its own independent desires. It was like an evil spirit, I thought, that had come from some legendary country. And suddenly I recalled a fairytale I had read or heard far in the past.

Long ago, a king contracted a strange disease. It was a frightful malady that wasted his body. Neither doctors nor medicines were of any avail. Thereupon the king foreswore doctors and made a new law, which condemned to death anyone who looked upon his face. The law was effective; although the king's nose disintegrated, and his hands disappeared from his wrists, and his legs vanished from the knees down, not a single person doubted that he was enjoying his customary health. The disease worsened, and the king, no longer able even to move, like a candle that had begun to melt, at length decided to seek help. But it was too late; his very mouth had gone. He died, but not a single one of the king's faithful ministers suspected his absence. And since the silent ruler never again committed an error, it is said that for many years hence his people respected and felt affection for their wise sovereign.

I was suddenly irritated and, closing the window, threw myself once again on the bed. Actually I had tried the mask out for scarcely half a day—nothing to boast about. I could draw in my horns any time. Closing my eyes, I conjured up meaningless fragments of scenes one by one, starting with the rain-drenched window: a blade of grass sprouting from a crack in the pavement; a splotch on the wall in the shape of an animal; the bump on the old, scarred trunk of a tree; a spider's web on the point of breaking under the weight of dewdrops. It was my ritual at times when I could not fall asleep.

But now it didn't work. Indeed, for no reason my restlessness grew more and more intense. Suddenly I thought how good it would be if the fog outside were poison gas. Or else, how nice if war erupted, or a volcano exploded, all the world were asphyxiated, the realities of life smashed to pieces. K, of the artificial organs, had told me of soldiers who had lost their faces on the battlefield and had committed suicide; and I knew very well that such incidents had occurred, for I had spent a great part of my youth in battle. It was simply a period when the market in faces was in a slump. How much significance could the roadway to others have when death was closer than one's companions? The charging soldier did not need a face. This, indeed, was the only period when a bandaged face appeared beautiful.

In my imagination, I was a gunner, aiming at anything that came in sight, picking off one thing after the other. At length, in the gun smoke, I fell asleep again.

THE influence which the rays of the sun exert on the mental state is a strange thing. Or was it simply that I had had enough sleep? Anyway, after shifting from side to side in their brilliance, I awoke. It was already past ten, and my twilight musings, like morning dew, had quite evaporated.

On the next day, the period of my sham departure from home would come to an end. If I intended to put my plan into execution, I would have to complete the training with the mask today. I made preparations and put on the mask with an unexpectedly buoyant feeling. I cut quite a stylish figure when, with some embarrassment, I got into the brand-new suit and slipped the ring on my finger, thus completing my disguise. I should never have dreamt it was the same self who spent morning and night in a smock stained with chemicals, brooding over molecular formulas. I was too impatient even to stop and ponder why I could never have imagined it to be me. And not only was it impatience; also I seemed slightly intoxicated with my own gaudy disguise. Deep inside my head was a fitful sound of fireworks, apparently announcing some

grand opening. I was in fact behaving like a young blade
setting off to the fair.

This time I boldly decided to leave by the main entrance.
Since in my mask I had been the "younger brother" all along,
there was no particular need to avoid being seen; and if I met
the superintendent's daughter, I wanted to check on the location of the shop where they sold the yoyo. I had no idea where
such toys might be sold. After our first child had died and
the second had miscarried, I had had nothing to do with the
world of children, which I perhaps consciously avoided. But
unfortunately I saw neither the superintendent nor his daughter.

Having no special goal in mind, I decided to begin my
search for the yoyo. I knew nothing of the specialty shops, so
I first looked in the toy sections of the department stores.
Perhaps it was a fad now, for every store I visited had its showcase of yoyos, and around them the children clustered like
flies. Entering such places was evidently not the most desira-
ble kind of mental therapy, and I hesitated somewhat. But,
well, I wanted to have done with this awkward "playing secrets," and so, gathering myself together, I tried to squeeze in
among the little vermin. But unfortunately I could not find
the type of yoyo I was looking for. Come to think of it, considering its color and shape, it probably wasn't a kind they
would carry in department stores. It gave the feeling of cheap
candies sold in a street stand. I left and walked around for
about an hour, looking for just such a place. Finally, on a
back street behind the station, I found a cramped shop that
specialized in toys.

As I had expected, it was quite different from the toy sections in the department stores. It was not a cheap place, like
a shop that sells inexpensive sweets, but neither did it handle
high-class merchandise. Perhaps aiming at slightly older children who would make their own purchases with their own

small change, it somehow gave a sense of mysterious, innocent evil. In other words, it would frankly appeal to the kind of child who preferred colored sugar water in a triangular carton to bottled fruit juice. And, as I had anticipated, the yoyo was there. Holding the cleft, plastic sphere in my hands, I suddenly thought of its creator, who had been able to express so beautifully an off-beat idea, and I could not resist a bitter smile. There was great subtlety in the overstatement of the basically simple form. If he had not mercilessly sublimated his own tastes, he could not possibly have thought up such a thing. This was not denying his taste; rather it was shedding the utmost light of awareness on his discernment. He had cast his own taste on the ground like a worm and voluntarily smashed it with the heel of his shoe. Was that cruel? Naturally, cruelty exists. However, presuming that he had chosen of his own free will, hadn't he also possibly experienced a feeling of release, as in stripping off one's clothes, or the satisfaction of revenge against the world? For it was not merely a question of the freedom to act according to one's tastes, but of the freedom to escape from one's taste. . . .

Yes, this was undeniably a concept that fitted in with my own viewpoint. I would have to walk along, treading my own tastes underfoot with every step, if I wanted to produce another heart suitable to my new face. The task, however, was not so difficult as I had imagined. My heart had become a withered leaf waiting to fall, as if the mask were possessed of the power to summon autumn, and the slightest help from me—a light shaking of the branch—would suffice to send the leaf drifting down. I wasn't entirely unsentimental, but it was surprising not to feel any more pain than the sting of an insect . . . something like the smart of wintergreen in one's eye. The ego is apparently not what it is said to be.

But what kind of heart, in heaven's name, did I intend painting over this old canvas? Of course, it would be neither the portrait of a child nor of myself. The heart in the cause of tomorrow's plans, of the program of action—even though one could not explain it with terms in dictionaries: yoyo, travel postcards, jewel boxes, patent medicines—was something I could definitely prearrange, like a map drawn from aerial photographs. How many times I have obliquely hinted at it already. However, now that things had really jelled, perhaps I should not stop at mere hints just because of the pain of putting it into words. I shall try and state it clearly here. I, as a complete stranger, planned to seduce you, to violate you—you who were the symbol of the stranger.

No, just a minute. I did not mean to write that. I do not intend to be so remorseful as to attempt to buy time by repeating what you already know without my writing it. What I wanted to write about was my strange behavior after buying the yoyo, which I can scarcely describe.

The innermost third of the toy store was composed of display shelves with toy revolvers. Among them were a number beautifully made, apparently imported, and priced high. Not only were they quite heavy and their muzzles plugged with stoppers, but the trigger and magazine mechanisms were not in the least different from the real thing. I remembered having seen a newspaper article the other day, according to which a model revolver had been rebuilt to shoot actual bullets; I wondered if they had used such ones as these. Can you really imagine me absorbed in toy revolvers? Probably even my closest colleagues at the Institute could not. No, until I myself was actually taking part in the act, it would have been inconceivable even for me.

The storekeeper wrapped up the yoyo. "You like it, don't you?" he murmured with a seductive smile. "May I show you anything else you might care for?" For a moment I began to doubt that I was myself. It might be more precise to say that I was confused at not showing a reaction typical of me. As I became conscious of this fact, my consternation seemed inconsistent, but that was because of the mask. The mask, indifferent to my confusion, nodded back at the storekeeper's unsuspecting face, and as if confirming my own reality, I began to concentrate on the business of the "anything else."

That was a Walther air pistol. It had the power to pierce a half-inch board at three yards. The price at seventy-five dollars was rather high, but—guess what—I talked him down to seventy and bought it. (. . . "You're sure it's all right? It's illegal, you know. An air pistol isn't an air rifle, it's considered a real pistol. The regulations are very strict about illegal possession of pistols. Please be very careful. . . .") Nevertheless I bought it.

It was a strange feeling. My real face tried to murmur quietly in a small voice, slipping deep into inconspicuous belly folds. . . . This shouldn't be. . . . I had wanted to choose the extroverted, aggressive type, a hunter's face, with the very simple motive that it would suit your seducer. . . . Let me change the subject here . . . I only asked the mask to help me recover . . . I never once asked it to do things its own way. . . . What in heaven's name was I to do with this pistol I had acquired?

But as I deliberately tapped the hard object in my pocket, the mask smiled at my perplexity and even appeared pleased. Of course, the mask itself could not really know the answer to my face's questions. The future is merely a function of the past. There could be no plan of action tomorrow for a mask that had been alive not yet twenty-four hours. The human social equation, in short, is, like a child, too unrestricted.

I was unable to make up my mind immediately whether, frankly, to mock or to fear this creature aged zero. However, the creature in dark glasses reflected from the mirror of the station washroom, was wild and defiant, perhaps abetted by an association of ideas with the object concealed in its pocket.

WELL, what to do? Rather than standing
around, arms folded, not knowing what to do, I was overflowing and alert with curiosity. At any rate, I was walking alone
with my mask, and I had no particular plan other than just to
let it walk by itself. The first problem was to get used to the
feel of things. Knowing that inadequate preparation of the
mask could, make me shrink away from my project, I had
intended to nurse it along with the greatest of caution. But
since the occurrence at the toy shop, the tables were turned.
Far from leading, I could only follow in dumb amazement
after this searching spirit like a prisoner just liberated.

Well, what to do? Well, what to do? As I lightly stroked
the jaw of the mask with my fingers, perhaps reacting to my
old bandage disguise, I ostentatiously struck a number of
poses, like a hunter testing decoys—eagerly expecting, lick-
ing of lips, watching, coveting, defying, verifying, desiring,
showing confidence, aiming, searching—rolling, as it were,
some of each into one compound expression, incessantly
sniffing around like a badly behaved dog who has made off
with something from under the shepherd's nose. This was a
sign that the mask was beginning to gain some self-confidence
from others' reactions; and I, in part, could not deny that I
had a feeling of satisfaction in acting this way.

Yet, at the same time, I was terribly anxious. No matter
how different I might be from my real face, I was still myself.
Since I was not under the influence of hypnotism or drugs,

whatever the acts of the mask—even the concealing of an air pistol in my pocket—it was the real I who would have to assume the ultimate responsibility. The personality of the mask was certainly not something that, rabbit-like, popped out of a magician's hat; it must really be a part of me that had come into being without my being aware of it, because the gatekeeper, my real face, had been so severely forbidden access. And while I theoretically understood this to be so, nevertheless, it was as if I were suffering from amnesia; I could not conjure up the whole of the personality. Imagine my irritation at not being able to provide a content consonant with this abstract self. Once I distractedly tried to put on the brakes.

—The failure of that thirty-second experiment: was it because the testing technique was bad or was there something wrong with the hypothesis itself?

I want to recall my viewpoint concerning an important problem in the laboratory just now. I had obtained precisely the experimental results I had anticipated for certain types of high-molecular matter, verifying an hypothesis that a functional relationship apparently existed between the variation in the rate of elasticity under pressure and under temperature. This idea seemed to have been completely upset by the latest, thirty-second experiment, and I found myself in a serious quandary.

The mask, however, merely frowned, apparently but slightly distressed. While I thought it natural, I felt that my self-esteem had been injured, and I became rather defiant.

MARGINAL NOTE: *Originally the mask was nothing more than a means for recovering myself. I mused that it seemed like having the house taken over when one has let but one room; self-respect had little to do with the matter.*

—Well. What in heaven's name do you want? If I felt like it, I could stop you right now.

However, the mask coolly and nonchalantly took no notice.

—You understand, I suppose . . . I'm no one. Since I have had to undergo the anguish of being someone up till now, I shall deliberately take this opportunity to withdraw again from becoming someone. Even you don't really think you would like to make someone of me, do you? As a matter of fact it would be impossible even if you did, so shouldn't we let things go as they are? Ah, I told you so, take this crowd . . . and it's not even a holiday. A crowd isn't formed after people gather; people gather after the crowd forms. It's true . . . students wearing their hair like hoodlums, modest housewives made up like actresses who won their reputation by their indecency, porcine girls wearing the latest fashions designed for bony mannequins. Lost in the crowd, it's all right to pretend for a moment to be no one. Or do you intend to insist that only you and I are different?

I could make no answer. There could be none. For it was the mask itself that had set forth the ideas conceived in my head. (I wonder if you laughed just now? No, it would be too selfish of me to expect that. It was a bad joke. If I could get you to realize that there was a partial truth in the explanation, I should be quite satisfied, but. . . .)

I who had been defeated—or who pretended to have been defeated—decided to let the mask have its way without further opposition. Whereupon the mask set up surprisingly (considering that it was nobody) sensible and bold plans which were in no way inferior to the incident of the pistol I spoke of before. Anyway, when I had finished lunch, I would try going as far as our house and check the looks of things. No, I do not refer to the looks of the house, but to my own. How far could I endure the seducer's ordeal, which had at last been set for the morrow? At least I should try getting a look at the house. I entertained my own inner hopes, but since I was unable to express them, I readily agreed.

EXCURSUS: *I do not mean to praise myself, but I was too kind. It was like arguing the Ptolemaic theory while believing in the Copernican. No, the crime of being too kind should never be thought of as slight. Just thinking of what happened before this was apparently enough to make the worms of shame come wriggling out of all the pores of my body. If I am ashamed to reread this, how much more ashamed I am to imagine you reading it. Even I knew full well that the Copernican theory was the correct one. Surely I have made too much of my loneliness. I thought my loneliness greater than all mankind's combined. As a sign of repentance, in the next notebook at least, I should like to delete any suggestion of tragedy.*

THE GREY
NOTEBOOK

ALTHOUGH a bare five days had passed since I had last taken the suburban streetcar I habitually rode, the experience was as fresh as if five years had gone by. Though it was a ride I knew well, one where I could go with my eyes closed, it was a completely new one for the mask. If it had the feeling it remembered something, that was because this ride was a vision in the womb before the mask was born.

Yes, actually it was that way. Indeed, the very clouds along the way, which I could glimpse from the window of the streetcar, were things I remembered as if they were white-bearded relics of a bygone age. The inside of the mask seemed bathed in soda water and tiny bubbles fizzed around on the surface. . . . I wiped my forehead, which was not even damp, with the back of my hand in a reflex movement, then heaved a sigh of relief as I looked around, for no one had noticed the blunder. I seemed to be permitted a normal relationship with people at a natural, proper distance. Suddenly laughter welled up within me. The feeling of exhilaration, as if I were entering enemy territory, changed imperceptibly into the mellowness of homecoming; the feeling of guilt, as if I were committing some crime, was transformed into the nostalgia of reunion. It was an individual matter. Quite like an invalid who at last is able to leave off dieting, I adjusted myself to the movement of the car, and greedily began to send out tendrils, like a creeping vine, toward your white forehead, toward the faint pink scar a burn had left on the underside of your wrist, toward the lines of your ankles resembling the underside of a snail's shell.

Was it too sudden? I wondered. Even so, there was nothing to be done for it. Though you may say that these are the incoherent mutterings, the intoxicated babblings of the mask, there is no basis for denying them. Surely, this is the first time I have written about you in such a way in these notes. Yet it is not because I set you aside in a holiday savings club until the date of maturity came; rather it is because I considered that I did not have the qualifications. A faceless monster talking about your body is as funny as a frog discussing a canary's song. Hurting myself was hurting you, I expect. But then . . . did that mean the spell was broken by the mask? I wondered. That, of course, was a much bigger, thornier problem. Yet in the future I would be obliged to come to a showdown, no matter how unpleasant it might be for me.

Since it was approaching the time the early-closing stores let their employees out, the streetcar was fairly crowded. I shifted my body a little, and the buttocks of a young woman in a green coat brushed my thigh. When I turned my body, trying to conceal the revolver, the contact with her became much more intimate. Then, since she did not particularly try to draw away, I too decided to stand as I was. The contact increased, following the movement of the streetcar, and our two bodies drew no further apart. As the girl's buttocks stiffened and relaxed, she resolutely feigned sleep. While I was musing lightheartedly what would happen if I were to press the muzzle of the revolver in my pocket against her buttocks, the car came to my stop. I glanced at her as I was about to get off, and from the style of her hair I could see she was *not* young; with a disagreeably serious expression she earnestly continued to scan a sign beyond the station platform. No, there could be no further significance to the incident. All I wanted to say was that I suppose that things would not have gone at all as they had if I had not had my mask on.

EXCURSUS: No, the explanation in this section lacks candor. If candor is lacking, so is honesty. Was this because of my constraint toward you? I wonder. If that were true, I should not have mentioned it at all from the very beginning. If I were just indicating the efficiency of the mask, there was no need to waste ten or twenty lines on such a fake erotic confession. Consequently, I said honesty was lacking. Thanks to having engaged in this makeshift subterfuge, I was not only unable to tell the truth, but I might well have the bitter experience of your misunderstanding me.

I am not particularly interested in trading on honesty. Since it is inevitable that I should touch on the matter, I shall mention it and simply bring the real motive out into the open, concealing nothing. From the standpoint of general morality, it was a quite ordinary shameful act, at best to be repented; but seen from the standpoint of an act by the mask, I consider that it provides an extremely important key to my subsequent actions. To put it bluntly, I had begun to have an erection at the time. Perhaps I cannot go so far as to call this illicit intercourse, but it must at least be considered an act of mental masturbation. I wondered if I would be betraying you. No, I don't want to use the word "betrayal" so cheaply. If I were to say such a thing, then I had been betraying you ever since the webs had begun to form on my face. Furthermore, since I feared that my cutting a ridiculous figure would make you lose the desire to read this, I deliberately refrained from mentioning it, but at least seventy percent of my thinking continued to be possessed by frantic sexual fantasies. They did not appear in my actions, but I was indeed a potential sexual criminal.

It is often said that sex and death have an intimate relationship, but it was about that time that I became aware of the real meaning of the statement. Until then I had shallowly interpreted the ultimate moment of the sexual act to be so much a self-effacement as to suggest death, but having lost *my face and finding myself buried alive, I was made to comprehend for the first time the very real meaning of the words. Just as trees bear their fruit before winter, just as bamboo grass produces its seeds just before it withers, sex is simply a struggle with death on the human level. Thus, an erotic impulse without a definite object can be said to be the hope of man on the verge of death for human recovery. The proof of this is that eroticism flourishes among soldiers. An increase in the number of erotics among townspeople is an indication that in the cities, and in the nation itself, there will be a greater number of deaths. When men can forget death, sex for the first time will change into love that has an object and will be able to insure stable human reproduction.*

The action of the mask in the streetcar, both for me and for the woman, was terribly lonely; but from my standpoint, I felt that I was in a situation of erotic love, as it were, or rather, in a transition from eroticism to love. The mask had not yet achieved life completely; perhaps it had halfway begun to live. In this condition, far from betraying you, it did not yet have even the capability of such betrayal. According to my schedule, the mask's ability to come completely alive was possible only after it had successfully met you.

To conclude what I have been saying, perhaps things would turn out this way. Thanks to the mask, I had somehow been able to avoid the extreme criminal sexual impulse; but that did not change the fact that I was semi-erotic, and these erotic elements did not bring me to you. Rather I was convinced that they were a stimulus to shake me free of you. Thus in some way I had to make you fall in love with the mask.

As I stood urinating in the public toilet of the station, I was thinking that nothing could be better for the mask, in growing up, than having all kinds of experiences. I decided to avoid the commercial streets and go through the back lanes. It would be unfortunate to happen upon you in front of the fishmonger's. I still did not have the confidence to withstand surprise, and furthermore I wanted everything to go as planned, especially the meeting between the mask and you. Even though everything was going well, I was distracted. For no reason at all, my feet became entangled and I almost stumbled on the flat ground. Breathing through my mouth like a dog in order to cool the air which had begun to heat up inside the mask, I panted and panted as if reciting some magic formula.—Listen. This is my first time here. Everything I see, everything I hear is new. From now on, the buildings I see, the people I meet—I shall be seeing all for the first time. Even if I have memories that fit what I see now they are merely mistakes, or strange coincidences, or fantasies. Oh, yes . . . broken manhole covers too . . . and half-painted Police Alert signals . . . and street corners with their year-round pools of waste water that overflowed the gutters . . . and elm trees jutting out into the streets . . . and . . . and. . . .

One by one I endeavored to eject colors and forms from my memory as if spitting out sand from my mouth, but something always remained—you. I earnestly admonished the mask: You're a complete stranger . . . tomorrow's meeting will be the very first confrontation with her . . . you haven't yet seen her, nor heard her . . . well, you had better forget such impressions at once. But the appearance of things around me was crystal-clear in my memory. The further away I got, the more clearly, the more distinctly your face floated before me, and I was at a loss to know what to do.

I—and the mask too, of course—passed the front of our house time after time; with your image as an axis, I kept circling tirelessly around the unequal-sided tetragon that defined the yard, like a moth drawn to the light.

Moreover, there was no fear of being challenged. The

groups of neighborhood women, their shopping baskets on their arms, ignored in their haste the unknown man walking down the street; and the children insatiably played away the few moments that remained before dinner. As I approached the house for the fifth or sixth time, the street lamps came on and suddenly the sun began to set. I slowed down as much as I dared without raising suspicion. From a window I could not see, a faint light fell softly on the garden, telling me that you were there. It was the living-room light. I wondered if you were preparing dinner all by yourself.

Abruptly, I began to feel jealous of the living room light. It was nothing so precise as thinking there was some guest taking my place; I was apparently jealous of the very light burning when evening came, of the living room the same as it had always been. I should be reading the evening paper by that light as I waited for dinner, and apparently I felt it somehow unfair and unacceptable that I should have to loiter outside the window, my face concealed by a mask. The living room light, whose calm brightness remained unchanged even though I was not there . . . just as you did. . . .

Then I suddenly realized the shabbiness and the unreliability of the mask, which until now had given such satisfactory results, on which I had placed so much hope. My big scene, in which I had imagined putting on the mask and becoming someone else, was after all merely a scene; and with the coming of evening, a switch had been turned and the living-room light lit. The mask was a poor weak thing before such everyday certainties. When it saw you smile it would dissolve like unseasonable snow.

In order to get over this feeling of defeat, I decided to let my mask dream as it would for a while. The dreams would be somewhat crude, like the mask, but I could not complain if it was filled with fancies, or delusions—these were its daily fare. In the meantime, pretending to ignore what was going on in the mask, I again began to circle around the house with the air of being there on business.

But these musings, far from emboldening the mask, had the effect of demonstrating the treacherous impassability of the deep channel that separated me from it.

The instant the chains were loosened, the mask would boldly march toward the house. That would place me in the position of a pimp. The gate off its hinges . . . the mud-clogged gravel path . . . the diseased entry door from which the paint had begun to peel . . . the half-rotted rain barrel, beginning to collapse in a corner of the entryway. . . . None of your business, this is somebody else's house! I would strain my ears for your presence as I rang the doorbell and step back, controlling my breathing. At length, the sound of footsteps would draw near, the porch light would go on and then the sound of your voice would ask who was there. . . .

No. No matter in how much detail I tell such a story, it is all quite hopeless. There is no need to tell it, and furthermore, it would be impossible. It might turn into something funny, if by hook or by crook I could apply logical syntax to the wild fancies; but they were like scribblings on a blackboard, all mixed up, disregarding time or sequence, writing and erasing, erasing and writing—their order was like graffiti on the wall of a public toilet. I should like to extract two or three fragments, restricting myself to what is necessary to make you understand the impact these thoughts had on me.

Well, the first one is a scene that follows the point when I hear the murmuring of your voice. Thrusting my foot into the door, which you have cautiously opened halfway, I push my way in and abruptly thrust my pistol in your face, which is blank with amazement as if you had swallowed a sudden gust of wind. I would like you to realize my perplexity. The

act was simply too shameful. Indeed, I have often been
irritated by your imperturbability, but even so it was unnecessary to act like some movie villain. If I were a seducer
couldn't I invent some pretext for approaching you, something more in keeping with a seducer? Since this was fancy,
even a transparent lie would do . . . something like pretending
to be an old classmate of your husband's. Far from being a
seducer, was I not an intimidator really? Furthermore, had
there not been concealed in my mask from the beginning a
scheme of revenge? There was at work here a justifiable feeling of vengeance, of defiance, of abhorrence for the worldly
prejudice that deprived a man of citizenship along with his
face. But with you . . . I don't know . . . with you I think it
doesn't work that way, but I don't know. . . . Then my reasoning powers were completely overwhelmed by the violent
emotion that swept over me.

It was jealousy. Jealousy based on imagination was something I had experienced many times, but this was different.
It was such a vivid physical feeling of excitement that I could
not at once define it. No, it would be doubtless much more
exact to call it a peristaltic movement. Waves of numbing
pain, one after another, crept at regular intervals from my
feet up to my head. You will get the exact picture if you
imagine the movements of a centipede's feet. Indeed, jealousy
is an animal feeling, capable even of rising to murder. There
are apparently two hypotheses about jealousy: that it is a
product of civilization and that it is a basic instinct of animals.
I opted for the latter.

But what in heaven's name did I have to be so jealous of?
Again, it was such a stupid reason that I hesitate to write about
it. It was merely that the mask might lay hands on you and
you might not resist and brush his hands firmly away . . .
colors swirled around me. How funny it was. What you would
do existed only in my imagination, and since these wild ideas

were merely ones my mask had cooked up at its will—how shall I put it?—I had dreamt up a cause for my jealousy by myself and I was jealous because of myself.

If I was so aware of things, I could immediately put a halt to the imaginings or order the mask to make a fresh start, but . . . why did I not do so? Not only did I do nothing, but, as if I had a lingering attachment for this jealousy, I egged the mask on, even tempting it. No, it was not a lingering attachment; it may indeed have been revenge. Perhaps I had fallen into a vicious circle, pouring oil on the fire, as it were, using the agony of jealousy to spur the mask to acts of violence, and then, by these acts of violence, stirring my jealousy even more. If this were so, the motive could be my own desire, lying dormant within me. These seemed to be problems I had to face squarely and resolutely, without blaming only the mask. Yes, possibly . . . these were imaginings I was reluctant about, but—since before I lost my face, from the time when I had planned on leading an ordinary married life—was I not already secretly fostering the sprouts of jealousy against you? I was not unaware of this. What a pathetic discovery! Even though I do realize it now, it is already too late. . . .

It really was too late. The mask that was supposed to mediate between us was only a shameless rogue. Of course, supposing even for the moment that it was a gentle seducer, the situation would be the same. On the contrary, there was every possibility of being afflicted with a malignant jealousy that had no safety valve. And the result would surely be a scene of violence.

At length your fright changed to orgasmic spasms, which I myself had not anticipated . . . No, that's enough . . . granting that I was acting in opposition to ordinary, every-day behavior, even so I had strayed too far from the proper course. If this deviation were a dream, I would take care to dress it in elegant metaphors, but it was merely realistic fantasy, altogether lacking in imagination. Enough of such hackneyed expressions.

I must not camouflage the last scene with such stereotypes. In fact, it was not only the stereotypes; the very ugliness was more than ordinarily suitable for an ending; at the same time it was a turning point that inspired my next actions. Pointing my gun at you, I began to bully you into a confession. Have you been masturbating during my absence, or what? . . . Don't try to conceal anything, for I know what you've been doing, I persisted impatiently . . . And gradually I coiled around you. I would soon be at the end of my endurance. The time had come to put a stop to these filthy, wild fancies. How should I attempt to bring things into the open? Suddenly I was firmly convinced that the best way, the only way, would be to take off the mask and show you my face at the very instant you tried to answer me.

But for whom, in heaven's name, should I bring things into the open? For me? For the mask? Or even for you? Perhaps I had not thought this point through. It was natural not to have thought about it. It was not these things I wanted to bring into the open, but the very concept of "face" that had driven me thus to the wall.

I had begun to feel an intolerable desolation at the great cleavage between the mask and myself. Perhaps I was already anticipating the catastrophe that was to come. The mask, as the name implied, would forever be my false face; and although my true nature could never be controlled by such a thing, once it had seen you it would fly off somewhere far beyond my control, and I could only watch it go in helpless, blank amazement. Thus, contrary to my purpose in making a mask, I had ended by recognizing the victory of the face. In order to consolidate myself into one personality, I must bring this masked play to an end by tearing off the mask.

But as I expected, the mask was not so stubborn. As soon as it perceived my determination, it retreated in haste, smiling bitterly, and I stopped my empty musings there. I inflicted no further chastisement on it. Since I was really not inclined to abandon my plans for tomorrow, however much I discouraged myself from the encounter in my fancies was I not as guilty as the mask—were we not both of the same ilk? No, of course, we were not equally guilty. There was no need to be so obsequious. At least in *my* plans for the next day, flashing the gun was not part of the program. The sexual element was there, to be sure, but such shamelessness was absolutely out of the question. While it might be possible with some unknown person with whom one might be riding in a streetcar, it was quite impossible to be aimlessly erotic about one's wife.

Finally, when I passed in front of the house and peered through a crack in the fence at the living-room window, I saw several strings of bandages suspended like white kelp from the ceiling to dry. I suppose you had been washing the bandages I had been using in expectation of my return the day after tomorrow from my sham business trip. As soon as I saw this, I had the feeling that my heart, thrusting through my diaphragm, had sunk a foot or so. I was indeed in love with you. Though I was perhaps awkward about it, my love was constant. But the unhappy state of affairs was that I could affirm this love through awkwardness alone. I was like a child who cannot go on his school outing; at this point I could only be jealous of others.

Excursus inserted on a separate sheet
of paper: *This may be tedious, but I should like to attempt
here once more a detailed investigation of the shameless
fantasies of the mask. For I feel that concealed in the maneu-
vers surrounding these musings there was a significance beyond
what I had perceived—to express it in detective-story terms—
that the key to putting the finger on the guilty man, that is,
the clue to the outcome of the whole affair, everything, was
obvious.*

*Of course, I intend to write down the actual conclusion
elsewhere. I dare say that within three days from the moment
I am writing this, I shall have shown these notes to you; the
three days are merely a rough estimate of the number probably necessary for getting the outcome into shape. But as it
is my objective here merely to suggest the conclusion without
going into details, it will be enough to include it in my final
statement. I am determined that that is the best way for completing my notes. My goal, properly speaking, is something
quite different. I want at least to add a correction to the
general idea of the erotic—or stress the difference between
the mask and myself—which I intended as a justification,
but which to the contrary resulted in my being plagued by
shackles. Since I have already acknowledged my guilt, there
should be some margin left for justifying myself, as long as
I do not distort the truth.*

One day I casually accompanied the mask out, as if allow-

ing a good child out on its own. A bright, cheerful feeling
spread over me, infecting me with the frolicsomeness of a
dog that has just been let off his leash. However, thanks to the
unexpected role my jealousy was to play, the mask and I were
to fall into an extraordinary dilemma about you, which would
plunge us into a desperate duel. At the same time, of course,
this jealousy made me remember again the affection and love
I had for you—owing to that, the plans, which I had suspended until the following day, inevitably became more and
more pressing—and reluctantly I could do nothing but ask
the mask for a temporary truce.

Of course, the constraint remained a deep-piercing thorn.
The streetcar toward town was empty, and whatever seat I
took, the window glass became a dark mirror, reflecting my
mask: an unknown character, sporting a beard, attired in
strangely affected clothes and, though it was evening, still
wearing his sunglasses. I put an ultimatum to him: he would
either have to observe the truce calmly for a while or I would
rip the mask off. Moreover, the character was concealing a
pistol. He was extremely vigilant. As the mask smiled its
sarcastic smile at me, it seemed to say:

—Well. Don't gripe so. I'm a necessary evil. . . . If you
expect to get something from me, you'd better be prepared
to take the good with the bad.

I tried opening the window a crack. The clear, damp
evening air whistled in. It did not touch my feverish cheeks
but stopped exactly in front of my necessary evil, cooling only
the nape of my neck and my palms. The mask, whose difference from me was distressing psychologically, adhered too
closely and was disagreeable physically. It was like some
botched false tooth.

But—I too, not to be outdone, tried to justify myself—if I
could put up with a few obstacles (the jealousy, for example),
by hook or by crook the cease-fire agreement could be pre-

served, and some way or other I could achieve my immediate goal, which was restoring the roadway to you. It should be impossible for me to entertain such a shameless interest in you, my wife. And furthermore, I became amazingly gentle in my feelings toward you, in inverse proportion to my sentiments toward the mask.

But was that really true? You already know the result, though I do not repeat it here—the problem does not concern the results alone—so what grounds are there to treat myself as different?

Surely one may say that an aimless erotic act is a sexual tangent to the abstract human relationship. As long as the definition of "other people" is confined to abstract relationships, those people are merely something in abstract opposition, one against others, enemies; and their sexual opposition is, in short, the impersonal erotic act. For example, as long as the abstract idea of womanhood exists, free-floating masculine eroticism is an unavoidable necessity. Such eroticism indeed is not the enemy of women, as is usually thought; rather woman herself is the enemy of its impersonality. If that is true, an erotic existence is not deliberately distorted sex, but may be considered a typical form of sex as it exists today.

Anyway, today the line of demarcation between enemy and fellow man, which in other times was easily and clearly distinguishable, has become blurred. When you get on a streetcar, you have innumerable enemies around you rather than fellow men. Some enemies come into your house disguised as letters, and some, against which there is no defense, infiltrate into your very cells in the guise of radio waves. In such circumstances, enemy encirclement becomes custom to which we are already inured, and "fellow man" is as inconspicuous as a needle in a desert. We have coined concepts of succor, such as "All men are brothers," but where is such a vast, imaginary repository of "brothers"? Wouldn't it be more logical to reconcile oneself to the fact that others are enemies and abandon such highflown, misplaced hopes? Wouldn't it be safer to hurry up and produce some antibody for loneliness?

And why shouldn't we men, surfeited with loneliness, become involved in impersonal eroticism even with our wives, not to mention other women? My own case cannot be exceptional. If, as a function of the mask, I acknowledge a considerable abstracting of the human relationship—indeed, I am probably addicted to empty fancies precisely because of this abstracting—I, who am trying to find some solution, had best shelve my own problems and shut up. Yes, no matter how clever I am, the very subject of my plans is perhaps merely erotic fancy.

If that is so, the plans for the mask were not my own special desire alone, but merely the expression of a contemporary, detached man's common craving. Even though it seemed at first blush that I had again lost to the mask, in reality I had not at all.

Just a minute! The plans for the mask were not the only thing. The fate of having lost my face and of being obliged to depend on a mask was in itself not exceptional, but was rather a destiny I shared with contemporary man, wasn't it? A trivial discovery indeed. For my despair lay in my fate, rather than in the loss of my face; it lay in the fact that I did not have the slightest thing in common with other men. I envied even a cancer victim, because he shares something with other men. If this turned out to be untrue, the hole into which I had fallen was not an abandoned well provided with an emergency escape; it was a penitentiary cell, recognized by everyone but me. My uncertainty exerted a tremendous influence on my despair. Even you could probably understand what I wanted to say. Youths whose voices are beginning to change and girls who are beginning to menstruate know that the temptations of masturbation create a lonely despair, for they are convinced that this temptation is their unique sickness. Or their humiliating feeling of desperation at a first little theft (marbles or bits of erasers or pencil leads), which like measles every one of us has experienced once, seems a crime of which they and they alone should be ashamed. If such stupidity extends beyond a given period of time it ultimately produces toxic symptoms, and these people may become either actual sexual criminals or inveterate thieves. No matter how they may try to universalize their feeling of guilt to avoid this trap, it will probably be to no avail. Rather, escaping from loneliness by realizing that everyone is equally guilty is by far the most effective way of settling things.

Perhaps because of this realization, when I later went out to drink saké, to which I was unaccustomed, I had such a feeling of closeness to others that I wanted to embrace all the strangers I saw. (I will write about this episode immediately following this passage and have decided to avoid duplication here.) Was this not because I had dimly felt among them the intimacy of kindred souls who had also lost their faces? Of course, it was not that I felt close to fellow men, but that I recognized the very lonely, abstract relationship in which everyone is an enemy. I could hardly imagine an occasion where we would frolic around together like puppies on some vague electric blanket of good intentions, like the cast of characters in a novel.

But as for me, it was a big discovery just knowing that on the other side of these concrete walls, people with the same destiny as I were prisoners. When I strained my ears, a groaning from the next cell came palpably to me. As time passed, innumerable sighs, murmurings, and sobbing cries swirled up like cumulus clouds, filling the whole jail with the sound of cursing.

—I'm not the only one . . . I'm not the only one . . . I'm not the only one. . . .

Even in the daytime, if luck is with them, they are allotted time for exercise and bathing, and it may be that they will find the opportunity of secretly sharing their fate by looks, and gestures, and whisperings.

—I'm not the only one . . . I'm not the only one . . . I'm not the only one. . . .

When you take all these voices together, the dimensions of the jail are no trifling matter. But that is to be expected. The crimes with which they are charged—the crime of having lost one's face, the crime of shutting off the roadway to others, the crime of having lost understanding of others' agonies and joys, the crime of having lost the fear and joy of discovering unknown things in others, the crime of having forgotten one's duty to create for others, the crime of having lost a music heard together—these are crimes which express contemporary human relations, and thus the whole world assumes the form of a single penal colony. Even so, the anguish at my being a prisoner remains unchanged. Moreover, in contrast to their having lost only their spiritual face, I have undergone a physical loss, and so there is naturally a difference in the degree of our solitude. Nevertheless, I cannot help feeling hope. It is not the same as being buried alive, and surely there is cause for hope. Isn't it true that the liabilities of an incomplete person —not being able, without the mask, to sing, to exchange blows with an enemy, to be a lecher, to dream—have become a common subject between me and others, and I alone am not guilty? Perhaps so. Perhaps so indeed.

Now, I wonder what you think of these points. If there is nothing wrong with my reasoning, even you are no exception, and I presume you cannot but agree, but—of course, you must agree—if you do not, there is no reason for you to force me into a corner like some wounded monkey by brushing my hand off your skirt, nor to ignore the trap of the mask, nor to drive me into a state where I could not help but write these notes. *The fact has been made clear that your face—the mobile, harmonious type—was a mask too. In short, we are two spots of the same ink. It was not solely my responsibility. Indeed, simply writing these notes has been fruitful. It was impossible to be left without any communication at all. You will surely agree with this point.*

I am saying that you must not make fun of my writing. For the act of writing is not simply replacing facts with arrangements of letters; it is a kind of venturesome trip. I am not like a postman on a preordained route. There is danger, and discovery, and satisfaction. I was beginning to feel there was some purpose to the writing itself, so much so that I thought I should like to go on with these notebooks for ever and ever. But I was able to curb the inclination. I should be able to avoid the ridiculous posture of an abominable monster offering gifts to an unattainable maiden. My three-day schedule stretched into four and then into five days. If I can get you to read these notes, the work of restoring the roadway will surely become ours together. Was this the song of a man being led off to prison, singing to bolster his courage? No, I was averse to over-optimism, and I had no intention of flattering myself. I realized that we were fellow casualties and anticipated an attitude of mutual sympathy. Well, let's try bravely putting out the light. When the lights go out, that's the end of the masquerade ball. In the dark, with neither face nor mask, I should like us to try to reestablish relations with each other. I should like to believe the new melody that comes to me from the darkness.

WHEN I got off the streetcar, I at once dashed into a beer parlor. I was strangely grateful for the texture of the glasses, frosted with drops of water. Perhaps it was because the breathing of the skin on my face was hindered by the mask, but the mucous membranes in my throat had dried up right to the back of my nose. I downed a pint of beer in one gulp, as if I were a suction pump.

I had drunk no alcohol for some time, and the effect was more rapid than usual.

Of course, no color appeared on the mask. Instead the scar tissues began to feel creepy, almost to writhe. Not caring, I tossed off two, then three, glasses, as if in a race, and at length the writhing began to subside. Carried away, I followed up the beer with a bottle of saké.

In the meantime, the irritation I had been feeling suddenly vanished, and I became strangely arrogant, defiant. Apparently even the mask was beginning to feel tipsy.—Faces, faces, faces, faces. . . . I rubbed my eyes, wet with tears in place of sweat, and scowled around through the noise and cigarette smoke at the innumerable faces that packed the place.—So what! Just speak up if you've got any complaint! You can't?—I could see no reason why they should. As I drank my saké, my drunken babbling was proof enough of my respect and esteem for the mask. I zestfully abused my superiors and boasted what a big shot a friend of a friend of a friend was; in short, it was as if I had become someone other than my real face. Even so, this was a pretty sloppy way of getting drunk. The real face definitely could not get drunk the way the mask did. The best the real face could do was to put on a drunken face. Even dead drunk, it would be only a fraction of the mask, never like the mask itself. If I wished to wipe away name, occupation, family, even official registration, I had merely to resort to a lethal dose of poison. . . . But the mask was different. . . . It was prodigious the way it got drunk. . . . It could become a completely different person even without alcohol. . . . Like me, as a matter of fact. . . ! Me. . . ? No, this is the mask. . . . Again the mask had become presumptuous, forgetting all about our truce. . . . But I was no less tipsy than it. . . . Could I be responsible for tomorrow's plans in such a state. . . ? These questions were not pressing, and without realizing it, I went along with the mask's demand for autonomy.

The mask was growing thicker and thicker. It had grown at last into a concrete fortress that enveloped me; and I crept out into the night streets wrapped in concrete armor, feeling like a member of a heavily equipped hunting party. Through the peepholes, the streets looked like the haunts of deformed stray cats. There they loitered, their noses suspiciously in the air, looking greedy, seeking their own tattered tails and ears. I hid beneath my mask, which had neither name nor status nor age, elated at the security guaranteed me alone. If their freedom were a freedom of frosted glass, then mine was the freedom of flawlessly transparent glass. In an instant, my craving had reached the boiling point, and very soon I should not be able to help having a try at making this freedom materialize. Yes, what we call the goal of life is doubtless the consumption of freedom. People often treat the preservation of freedom as if it were the goal of human existence; but isn't this merely an illusion, after all, that stems from a chronic lack of freedom? Since people make goals out of such things, they fall into the dilemma of talking beyond the confines of this universe; they become misers, or failing that, religious fanatics—one or the other, at least. Yet even the plans for tomorrow could not themselves be a goal. Since by seducing you I shall try to enlarge the validity of my passport, the plans must rather be thought of as a kind of means to an end. With no regret, I shall use the mask now to its fullest capacity.

EXCURSUS: *Of course, this was merely alcoholic sophism. The instant I revealed my love to you, I did not intend to beg you to accept such irrefutable logic for impudently justifying the illicit intercourse, nor did I myself intend to. Precisely because I did not, I was preparing my farewell address to the mask. But what worried me slightly was that I could not help but want to use exactly the same logic even in a sober state.*

"The goal does not lie in the results of research, the very process of research is itself the goal." Yes . . . words that any researcher would utter as a matter of course. While at first blush they seemed unrelated to my case, I could not help but feel that I was after all saying the same thing as they. The process of research, in short, was merely the expenditure of freedom upon matter. The results of research, on the contrary, by being calculated in terms of value, encourage the preservation of freedom. The point of the words was to warn against the tendency to overemphasize only results and to confuse means and ends. I thought this was a much more enlightened logic, but on reflection what I had put forth was quite like the alcoholic babblings of the mask. I was not at all satisfied with the explanation. Was it not simply that, although I had intended to control the mask, I had actually found it to be unmanageable? Or was freedom like some powerful medicine which, though beneficial in small quantities, produces ill effects as soon as one exceeds the given dosage? I should like to hear what you think. Surely, if I must follow the mask's dictates, then not only the hypothesis of the mask as a prison, which I went to some pains to describe, but the whole body

of these notes could be the product of misunderstanding. I could by no means believe that you would support such arguments to justify illicit relations.

WELL now, how shall I deal with this excessive freedom?

If someone were to view my covetous behavior with dispassion, he would frown upon it. However, the mask had originally been no one, and thus it experienced no pain at all, for it made no difference to it how it was thought of. It had no need to be ashamed, nor to justify itself, and this feeling of release was very comforting. The release from the sense of shame, especially, bathed me in a music that rose bubbling round my ears.

MARGINAL NOTE: *True, I must make special mention of this music. Ornamental neon lights, blanched night skies, girls' legs that expanded and contracted with their stockings, forgotten alleys, corpses of dead cats in trash cans, tobacco ashes, and then . . . and then—I cannot name them all—every one of these scenes made its own particular music, its own particular noise. And for the sake of this music alone, I wanted to believe in the reality of the time I was anticipating. . . .*

EXCURSUS: *It goes without saying that the above "marginal note" took place before the immediately preceding excursus, and was written down immediately after the text.*

From my present feeling, it is difficult to recall just where such
music was. But I do not have the confidence to strike the pas-
sage out.

Though the mask's alibi was flawless, and the freedom it
promised inexhaustible, I wondered if it were not ignoble to
be satisfied with the freedom of behaving covetously; I was
disoriented, like a penniless man who has suddenly acquired
a great sum of money. I knew this already. The saké brought
a tipsy feeling of release, knotting into lumps of craving
throughout my body, and I became like an old tumorous tree.
In addition, the freedom placed right under my nose now,
compared to the "freedom" I had been enjoying, restricted
by age, position, and profession, was exactly like raw meat
dripping blood as opposed to the mere word "meat." Just
looking and saying nothing could do me no good. Far from
being satisfied, my mask opened the roadway wide, like the
mouth of a frogfish gloatingly awaiting the arrival of the bait.

But unfortunately, I did not know if hunting down the
game would be worth the expenditure of freedom. Was I too
accustomed to conserving freedom? If my craving for freedom
were inadequate, even though it left my body cancer-ridden,
humorously enough I could augment my craving only by the
exercise of logic.

I wasn't boasting about fine craving. In any case, my alibi
was guaranteed, and I did not mind a bit how disgusting or
even immoral it might be. Rather, since I had a feeling of
release from my real face, it was tempting to break the law,
to disdain good sense. However, what came in answer to my
demand—perhaps unconsciously induced by the air pistol
in my pocket—were grossly unattractive acts that smacked of
gangsterism: blackmail, extortion, robbery. Of course, if I
could bring even these off successfully, it would be a great
exploit for me. If their real character were to be exposed, the
strangeness of this combination would be first-class news

copy. If I were really inclined to try, I would not hold back. I might make those with real faces—pseudo-masks—who feign ignorance, understand the actual form of abstract human relations, and at least I could express my pent-up revenge on the scars.

I was not being hypocritical, but why was I not inclined to this type of immorality? The reason was extremely simple: for one thing, there was no particular need for a real mask; even a bandage disguise would serve the purpose. And another thing: even if I were to try extortion or blackmail, getting money to redeem my freedom was the only goal. Two hundred dollars left from my business travel expenses were still warming the inside of my pocket. I could certainly manage tonight and all day tomorrow. As for the means of getting more money, I might as well let that go until it became a problem.

But what in heaven's name was a pure goal, uninvolved with the question of means? Interestingly enough, almost all the illegal actions that occurred to me were concerned with money, that is, the illegal transfer of ownership. To give one example, gambling, which is said to be a relatively pure concentration of passion, is termed by psychology an escapist craving. This act attempts to replace a continuous, chronic anxiety with a momentary channeling of that tension—if this is really true, it would surely make no difference at all whether it were escapist or whether it were an expenditure of freedom —however, if one eliminated the give and take of money, gambling would become quite insipid. One gambling experience leads to another, the chain is potentially endless, and the fact that it ultimately becomes habit seems to prove that it is merely the swing of the pendulum between means and ends. Fraud, embezzlement, robbery, counterfeiting—all are inconceivable without the means by which they are committed. Even fellows who appear to disregard the law and behave according to their personal dictates actually belong to a freedomless world surprisingly imbued with wants. Isn't pure purpose simply an illusion?

For example, carrying off whatever materials I wanted from the storeroom at the Institute by intimidating the guard, or stealing the expense sheets and progress charts of experiments by breaking into the locked files of the administration department—these were practical objectives, typical of me. They were amusing daydreams, good for adolescent television serials, not motivated by greed but by my dissatisfaction with a company that provided only provisional independence under the name of an Institute; but the fact remained that they were means to an end, and furthermore, the role I wanted my mask to play above all would perhaps not be realized. Maybe there would be grounds for further consideration after I had let the mask have its way and I had settled down to this life.

MARGINAL NOTE: *Needless to say, as long as no obstacle arose, I intended to go on indefinitely living this double life of the mask and the real face.*

Of course, among the various crimes, there was only one that suggested an exceptional possibility. That was arson. In arson many elements are simply means for preserving freedom: receiving the insurance as beneficiary, or destroying evidence after theft, or scheming by a fireman thirsting for fame. And is not almost all calculated arson based on grudge after all, an attempt to recover freedom which has been frozen or snatched away? But I realize that there are also cases of pure incendiarism, which themselves have no value other than the direct satisfaction of a craving—pure incendiarism, where the billowing flames lick at the walls, twist the pillars, pierce the ceiling, and suddenly shoot up to the clouds, oblivious to the milling crowd of curiosity seekers; where the dramatic destruction, the reduction to ashes, of a bit of history, which until then had been in undeniable existence, was food that

satisfied a spiritual hunger. It seemed by no means a normal
craving. An arsonist is an eccentric by definition. But since
the mask was a mask and not bound by a "right" way of doing
things, if the expenditure of freedom itself were guaranteed,
there was no need to bring normality or abnormality into the
question.

But since I myself had no intention of becoming an arsonist,
there was no point in further discussion. As I threaded my
way through the alleys between the main streets, which were
filled with flashy billboards crowded together edge to edge, I
tried imagining a scene where flames would spurt out suddenly from the crevices in the walls and from under the eaves,
but it had no appeal at all. I wasn't especially frightened, I
think. If you were to try putting on the mask just once, you
too would surely understand; trying to suppress such acts of
violence was meaningless and fatuous. For example, even
the most fainthearted child can enjoy a horror movie calmly
if he covers his face and looks through his fingers. Further, a
heavily made-up woman is more easily seduced than one who
wears no make-up. This is not restricted to sexual seduction;
it is demonstrable, statistically, in cases of habitual shoplifters.
People get excited about upholding discipline, or custom, or
rules, but in the final analysis such things, depressingly, are
merely houses on sand supported by a thin layer of skin, the
real face.

Indeed, I was not frightened. From now on it would serve no
purpose to hold back out of shame. Basically, the mask itself
was the crystallization of shame. It may not be prohibited by
law, but is there another act more reprehensible than disguising oneself with a mask unrecognizable as such? In short,
even though I could imagine what the psychology of an arsonist might be, I myself was simply not one. However, I too
became uneasy when I found that the single, apparently pure
goal I had at last hit upon was unfortunately not what I had

ordered. Since I could decide on no other suitable plan, there was nothing to be done about it. Even so, the plan would be better than doing nothing. But I could not possibly think of all those cravings, those throbbing tumors, as classifiable under "means." It was too pitiful to have become so accustomed to frugality in freedom. Anyway, I shall suppress incendiarism for the time being....

Just a minute. I realize I have made an important omission either deliberately or by accident in what I have written until now. If it were a question of illegal acts, there was another type of criminal I should have mentioned above: the bandit who attacks suddenly. If one accords a pure motive for arsonists, then there should be no question about doing the same for bandits. None at all. On the outside he is not so ostentatious as the arsonist, but in his heart he is no better than a murderer. Even so, could I have forgotten such a representative example? No, I had forgotten it precisely because it was representative. Didn't the bandit escape me because he had more destructive motives than the arsonist, in whom I was not interested anyway?

The extroverted, unpacific type. My mask, which passed itself off as a hunter, drew back on hearing the words "destructive motives," and in so doing could not help but show its origins. It may appear that I am repeating, but not because I am a coward. While cowardice is something to be denied, I do not particularly need to deny it. Looking into myself I could find not the slightest interest in either banditry or arson. The thousand volts of electricity that stimulated the mask was completely different from destruction; it was something that coiled closely round the mask and had a character I might well call the direct opposite of destructive.

Of course, it would be too much to say that I had absolutely no destructive motives in me. In daydreams, I was more than once carried away by impulses such as wanting to tear your skin from your face to make you experience the same agony as I, to release into the air poison gasses that would paralyze the optic nerves and blind the whole world. Indeed, I remember having often used similar harsh language in these notes, but before the mask was made. After it was completed I had the feeling, though still I made similar protests, that a delicate transformation had taken place. Perhaps it had. Precisely because it had, the mask wanted to expend its freedom on something quite different than destruction. It was not a negative something, such as letting the mask help dispose of criminal evidence by destroying it. Oh, come on. What do I really want to say? Do I want such classical harmonies as love, or friendship, or mutual understanding? Or do I want to suck on the suitably sweet, sticky cotton candy they sell in street stalls at fairs, that makes one go all soft inside?

Irritated, like a child that cannot have what it wants, I entered a coffee house and with water and ice cream alternately bathed the tumor of craving that rose in my throat hard as a fist. I wanted to do something, but what would be best I did not know. Would I end up by doing nothing at all or by forcing myself to do something I didn't want to? I regretted having started nothing. It was a wretched feeling, like wearing wet socks. Under the mask my face felt as if it were in a steam bath, and I seemed to be bleeding at the nose. Apparently the time had come for serious action. As I well realized, I had become my own analyst, and was earnestly organizing my own cravings, sifting them out, to discern the real forms pent up in this tumor.

I DON'T mind telling the conclusion of my analysis first. It was sexual desire. I wonder, did you laugh? It was a somewhat commonplace conclusion, considering all the showy thinking leading up to it. Realizing this motive, I had some clue as to what was going on. But since this conclusion was like an elementary algebraic platitude, agreeing too readily without proof was more than I could bear. It would appear that self-respect could live in surprising compatibility with shame, considering their inconsistency.

Well, there is not much left to this third notebook. There was no point in being concerned with only the test run of the mask. But however tedious, I think it would be best to tell you what the grounds were: that the purest expenditure of freedom is actually the satisfaction of sexual desires. The expenditure of freedom, however pure, has no value in itself; value is rather in the production of freedom. I did not claim that my logic was faultless, but my actions on the following day were all inspired by this sexual desire, and I thought I had to be honest with myself, just as I expected fair judgment of you.

Since I was trying not to be unkind, it was not so difficult to understand the mask's feeling, to grasp why it turned its back on arson and murder. In the first place, the mask was itself a serious act of violence against the custom of the world. Whether arson and murder would be more destructive than a mask could not be answered with pure common sense. To put it succinctly, it would be best to begin mass production of an elaborate mask, like the one used for myself, and presuppose a public opinion that in time would be favorable. In all likelihood, masks would attain fantastic popularity, my factory would grow larger and larger, and even working full time it would be unable to meet the demand. Some people would suddenly vanish. Others would be broken up into two or three people. Personal identification would be pointless, police photographs ineffective, and pictures of prospective marriage partners torn up and thrown away. Strangers would be confused with acquaintances, and the very idea of an alibi would collapse. Unable to suspect others, unable to believe in others, one would have to live in a suspended state, a state of bankrupt human relations, as if one were looking into a mirror that reflects nothing.

No, perhaps one would have to be prepared to accept an even more disadvantageous state. Everyone would begin to change masks one after the other, attempting to escape the anxiety of not seeing by becoming less apparent than the invisible. And when it became common practice to constantly seek new masks, the word "stranger" would become obscene, scrawled in public toilets; and identification of strangers—like definitions of family, nation, rights, duties—would become obscure, incomprehensible without copious commentary.

I wonder whether mankind could stand such an orgy of novelty, whether it would discover promise in such a weightless state, whether it would be able to evolve new customs. Of course, I do not intend to declare that it would be absolutely impossible. Indeed, the uncommon depth of man's ability to adapt and his capacity for disguise are already well attested by the history of war and revolution. But before that—before we permit the mask such unbridled diffusion—I think the question is whether we really are broad-minded enough to get along without exercising our instinct to organize sanitary squads. No matter how much we might be fascinated by masks, society would erect stout barricades against individual abuses. For example, the use of the mask in places of employment—public offices, firms, police stations, laboratories—would doubtless be forbidden. Furthermore, as a matter of course popular actors would insist on facial copyrights and start movements against the free production of *their* masks. To take a more common example, the family: husband and wife would both have to promise not to wear dissimulating masks. A new style of manners would probably evolve for business transactions: before negotiations began, one would have to pinch the skin of the other's face. In the case of job interviews, the custom of pricking the applicant's face with a needle and drawing blood to show it was real might well arise. For the police to put a hand on the face in interrogations would be the subject of court cases, to determine whether the act was justified or whether the police had gone too far, and it is conceivable that legal scholars would publish dissertations on the subject.

Day after day, in the "Advice to the Lovelorn" columns of the newspapers, one would read the complaints of women who had been deceived into marriage by a mask—(they would not mention their own). However, the answers would be just as irrelevant and irresponsible: "The insincerity of not once showing his face during the engagement is deplorable. But you are still thinking in terms of a life with a real face. The mask does not deceive and is not deceived. How about putting on a new mask, turning over a new leaf, and starting another life? On these days of masks, we can put on a new look unconcerned with yesterday or tomorrow." No matter how great the deception, it's the inconvenience that would be discussed; the pain of deception would never outweigh the pleasure it provided. While there would be many conflicts, the fascination with masks would be predominant.

On balance, of course, some things would be definitely

negative. The popularity of detective stories would naturally decline to a shadow, and novels of family affairs dealing with double and triple personalities would be popular for a while; but since the purchasing of masks would occur at the rate of five or more different kinds per person, the resultant complexities of plot would exceed the limits of the readers' patience. For some the *raison d'être* of the novel, except for fulfilling the demands of lovers of historical fiction, would possibly disappear. This would not be restricted to novels alone; plays and movies, which fundamentally would be exhibitions of masks, would be peopled with outrageously abstract ciphers that would convey little dramatic interest to the audience. Cosmetic manufacturers would go bankrupt, and one after another the beauty parlors would take down their signs. All the writers' associations would set up a clamor about the destruction of man by the mask, and beauticians and dermatologists would devote themselves to detailed studies of skin damage caused by masks.

Of course it is extremely doubtful that such actions would have much more effect than temperance pamphlets. Furthermore, Mask Makers, Inc., would already have grown into an enormous monopolistic enterprise, extending its network of ordering, processing, and marketing throughout the country, and would have silenced the mere handful of discontented elements as easily as twisting a baby's arm.

Problems would doubtless arise eventually; when the use of masks reached a point of saturation and their curiosity and strangeness faded, masks would come to seem commonplace, and people would long more than ever for the feeling of release from complex human relationships. At this time the smell of crime and vice would suddenly become a piercing stench, like that of overripe cheese, and anxiety would return; when the various masquerades one had thought of as mere holiday exuberance would be seen as noisome, possibly harmful offenses. For example: unlicensed dealers would specialize in plagiarizing other people's faces and members of the Diet would engage in swindling; certain well-known artists would be accused on suspicion of car theft; leaders of the Socialist Party would make Fascist speeches; bank directors would be indicted for bank robbery—all such antics would be frequent occurrences. And while at first I laughed as if at some circus act, I suddenly realized that someone else, my exact image, would be assiduously picking pockets and shoplifting before my very eyes. . . . Realizing this, I was obliged to face facts. Thus, one would have to consider the fabricated alibi as a burden too, preventing proof of guilt as well as substantiation of innocence. The pleasure of deceiving would fade to a shadow before the anxiety of being deceived. Teachers would lose their educational ideals (since the concept of forming the personality would have vanished); mass truancy of students would follow; and parents (that is, nearly everybody) would begin to curse the mask. Immediately newspaper editors, sensitive to the winds of change, would begin to advocate a registration system for masks; but unfortunately masks and registration systems would not be at all compatible—in the same way that a jail without doors would be meaningless. A registered mask could not be a mask for long. Public opinion would reverse itself; people would fling their masks aside and urge the intervention of the government to banish the mask. This movement would take the form, rarely witnessed in history, of cooperation between citizen and police, and in no time at all laws proscribing the mask would be enacted.

However, governmental fear of excesses would be the same as before. Even though officials promised to discipline infringements of the law, they would handle them as minor offenses at best. The weakness here would be that such action would stimulate curiosity and result in the spread of illegal factories and black-market gangs, bringing a period of confusion like the prohibition era in America. Then, although probably too late, the law would be revised: masks would be legal in cases of conspicuous injury to the face or as prescribed by a doctor to treat a patient afflicted with some serious nervous disorder. But the falsification of documents and corrupt practices by mask makers would continue, and soon there would no longer even be special cases. A special Inspector of Masks would be appointed, and the mask submitted to thoroughgoing control. Yet crimes perpetrated by masks would show absolutely no decline. They would fill the newspaper columns, and ultimately right-wing groups would appear, wearing identical masks like uniforms. There would be scandalous assassinations of government officials. Courts too would be able to do nothing but view the mere wearing of a mask as the equivalent of premeditated homicide, and ultimately public opinion would unhesitatingly support this.

EXCURSUS: *Even though these fancies were drunken musings, they were of absorbing interest. The result was highly casuistic: in a hundred-man group, each member would have a ninety-nine percent alibi and a one-percent suspicion of involvement, for even though an act was committed, there would be no single agent. At first blush, the act of wearing a mask would appear to suggest premeditated crime, but why did one sense it to be of an animal-like cruelty? Perhaps it was because of the perfect anonymity of the offence. Perfect anonymity means the sacrificing of one's name to the perfect group. Rather than some intellectual trickery for the purpose of self-defense, this sacrifice is rather the instinctive tendency of individuals face to face with death. Just as various groups— racial, national, trade, social, religious—first attempt to erect altars in the name of loyalty at the time of invasion by the enemy. For the individual, death is fatal; for the perfect group, it is merely an attribute. The perfect group originally had an aggressive character. You will surely understand if I use the army as an example of a perfect group, and a soldier as an example of perfect anonymity. Considered in this light, there seemed to be some contradiction in my musings. Why should a court of law that cannot judge an army uniform as being equivalent to premeditated murder look so stringently on right-wing groups wearing identical masks? Does the nation consider the mask something evil and subversive? I wonder whether the nation itself is not an enormous mask intolerant of the rivalry of individual masks. Then the most harmless thing in the world must be an anarchist. . . .*

I have proved that a mask by its very existence is basically destructive. Equivalent to premeditated murder, the mask can stand shoulder to shoulder, with no feeling of inferiority, with arson or banditry. It was not surprising that the mask, which itself was a form of destruction, was not inspired to such crimes as arson and murder, although it was in the act of walking now through the ruins of human relationships destroyed by its existence. Despite the throbbing cancer of its cravings, it was satisfied simply to be.

THE centripetal, child-like cravings of the forty-hour-old mask . . . cravings of a famished fugitive who had just wrenched free from the scar webs. . . . What kind of freedom could this greedy craw, still carrying the traces of its manacles, possibly have?

Frankly, there was an answer. Basically, its cravings were not something understood by discussion; they had to be felt. Let me put it simply. They were a compulsive urge to become a sacrificial victim of the tribe. I realized this clearly the instant I stepped out into the street. What need had there been until now to be indirect, as if making excuses? Did I think I could perhaps avoid shame by being circuitous? No, I seem to be piling on justifications. But at this point I was not clinging to shame. I was clinging to just one thing: to try to super-impose an affair with you, however disagreeable, onto these cravings.

An affair with you, of course, was the shameless fantasy of the mask. Even though I wanted to feel something, hope for something, attempt something, the poison of jealousy (I had deliberately begun to forget it, though it was the root of all these fancies) recovered its breath and began to check the flow of blood in my veins. My fancies were connected, by an association of ideas, with the plans for the next day. The mask, as might be expected, could only feel ashamed and non-plussed at this. Anyway, the freedom of the mask, even though it lay chiefly in the abstract relationship with others, was like a bird bereft of its wings. The mask that had escaped banishment and was observing its truce could only stammer un-certainly.

Thereupon, the mask soothed me; with my continual worry-ing, it was I, not it, who would end up a means to an end. Even though I did wear a mask on my face, my body was the same as before. Well, I might just as well close my eyes and blot out the light from the world around me. Suddenly the mask and I became one, and there was no "other one" to be jealous of. If it was I myself who was touching you, then it was I too who was being touched by you; and there was no need to falter.

MARGINAL NOTE: *On consideration, this is rather selfish reasoning. If one supposes that for oneself one is a set person and that for others one is an unknown person, half of me is a stranger. Even we yellow-skinned men were not originally a yellow race. We were first called yellow by a race of men whose skin was of a different color. Disregarding the promise of the face and making the lower half of the body the basis of personality are equally deceptive. If I maintain that the lower half of my body is unchanged, then I shall have to assume absolute responsibility for the erotic acts of the mask. In my fancies I accused you of shamelessly betraying me, and my body was wracked with the poison of jealousy; yet as soon as it was a question of myself, I called it a pure expenditure of freedom and was too selfish to think how much it might hurt you. In the final analysis, jealousy itself is something like a pet cat that insists on its rights but does not accept its duties.*

Soothing me thus, blankly, as if it felt nothing at all, the mask had to make me understand that sifting desires through sieves would leave nothing like what was hoped for. Pure desires are surprisingly few and simple, and it is no trouble to spot them, if we leave out the destructive ones. For example, let me enumerate some here as they occur to me.

First, food, sleep, and sex are the three great cravings. After them come general cravings, such as evacuation, thirst, escape, possession, leisure. Coming to rather special cases, we have desires for alcohol, tobacco, drugs, and suicide. And, if we interpret cravings in a wider sense, we can include the desire for work and for fame.

But what I have called "expenditure of freedom" is eliminated with the first sifting. No matter how overpowering drowsiness may be, it is not a goal in itself; it should doubtless be classified as a preserving of freedom. And no matter how you consider it, basically sleep itself is simply a transition to waking up. For the same reason, it would be best to place outside the present investigation such things as evacuation, thirst, possession, escape, fame, and work. One would surely be criticized if one treated the last item, work, in the same category as evacuation. Surely considering the results, work dominates among the desires. If one did not create things, there would be no history, no world either, and perhaps indeed man himself as a thinking being would not have evolved. Moreover, through self-denial, work may become more than simple labor. Though one may make it a personal goal, unlike desire for possessions or fame, it will not make a poor impression. People nod approval and say: "He's a hard worker." And though they may be envious, they will hardly be censorious, as long as the work is gainful and reputable. (Actually, I was sixty percent satisfied with my work at the Institute—if I were deprived of it, I suppose I should experience a ninety-percent affection for it—but I could get along without the mask.) Even if work for the sake of work were somehow to slip through the first sieve, inevitably it would be culled in the second sifting. May I remind you that I am not talking about values, but of the immediate cravings of an escaped prisoner whose alibi is guaranteed.

Among the remaining cravings, the desire for food apparently is also eliminated in the second sifting. Let's exclude the jumping of a restaurant bill, since that is a means rather than a goal; but it seems to me I have heard somewhere about a law that says you can't go on stuffing yourself. Suppression of appetite is conceivable, but not suppression of desire for food. Still, if one ventured to carry this suppression of appetite to the ultimate, couldn't it result in cannibalism? But with cannibalism, the element of killing would seem to be stronger than the desire for food. And I have already decided not to talk about murder.

For the time being suicide was a forbidden escape; I could perform it with my real face, but the mask had just made a heroic escape from being "buried alive." If I were going to commit suicide, it would have been better to have done nothing from the first. Moreover, rather than consider the desire for leisure as an independent unit, I should like to take the view that it is something composite, sometimes a form of escape, sometimes a sort of work that has no object. Further drug addiction like alcoholism is merely a bad copy of the mask—and thus there was no need to discuss the problem again.

So my siftings finally left, most suitably for my condition, these sacrificial compulsions.

By the way, I wonder what you think of this reasoning. Yes, of course I mean reasoning. While that night I intended to expend freedom purely by succeeding in reasoning that there was nothing for me but a sexual crime, actually I committed no act that might possibly be construed as a crime. It was not that I felt no inclination to do so, nor that there was no opportunity, but one way or another I did not translate my thinking into action. So the only thing I am asking you about is my reasoning.

I was not so optimistic as to expect to gain your approval. Perhaps, as you see it, this clearly reflects some foolish deficiency in me. Since I am already in fact experiencing the failure of reasoning, I cannot but accept the existence of a deficiency. At that time it was not apparent to me, however, and I cannot grasp it even now. Didn't all this reasoning mean, perhaps, that while I pretended to submit reluctantly to the forceful persuasions of the mask, I was covering up to myself the fact that the mask's wish was my own.

As far as sex was concerned, from the beginning my inclination to kick over the off-limits sign was as violent as my reticence about doing so. That was as it should be. I had tried not to mention this, but as long as I did not agree to a sexual crime, my plans to let the mask seduce you could not actually come off. If it were a question of a single seduction, perhaps there was no problem. But if I intended to create a new world by continuing the relationship between you and the mask, I should certainly have to live as a sexual lawbreaker. If not, how could I put up with this double life without being eaten away to the marrow of my bones by jealousy? Perhaps, the mask's tedious persuasions were due to my own conscious provocation.

Yes, oddly enough, the instant I was given any reasonable support, I at once completely sympathized with the aspirations of the mask. Remember that I was not famished for sex, as if it were hunger or thirst. What concerned the mask was a transgression of sexual taboos. If I had no consciousness of taboos, it would be doubtful whether I could feel such shuddering fascination. And when I looked at this fascination without blinking, the poison of my jealousy, by which I was most troubled, suddenly seemed to lose its virulence; and I began to wallow in erotic impulses, quite as if I were taking an antidote.

Through my new, lecherous eyes, the whole town appeared like some mysterious fortress composed of sexual off-limit signs. It would have been fine if the fences had been strong, but every one, worm-eaten, nails missing, looked as though it would collapse at any moment. Even though these very fences with their air of preparation against invasion pricked the interest of the people in the streets, when one approached and looked carefully, the worm holes and traces of nail holes were sham, yet no one ventured too close. What in heaven's name were sex and sexual taboo? To think about the meaning of the sham, the origin of the fences, would inevitably make one a lecher. Of course, the lecher himself was only one of the fences. And precisely because of this, he would have to shed tears of remorse and anguish over his own desires. When he broke the sexual taboo he would be pulverizing his own fences at the same time. However, once one has become interested in the existence of the fence one's mind will never be at ease until one has ascertained its real origin. The lecher in general is like an honest, hard-working investigator who, once aware of a mystery, will go to any length to solve it.

I too, a novice investigator, dropped into a bar, anticipating nothing special. As a place that openly displayed its fake wormholes and nail holes, it had a certain interest. Moreover, what they sold in the bar was the fake mask of alcohol. It was just the place for me now.

There was the comfortable feeling I had anticipated. Fake darkness that shut out fake light . . . suspended desires incapable of doing good or of perpetrating evil, dream-like . . . the proper mixture of hypocrisy and evil. . . . When I had taken my seat and ordered a whiskey and water, and the pores of my whole body had begun to open, I began to toy with the finger of a girl in navy blue seated next to me. No, it was not I, but the mask. Although the girl's fingers were sweaty, the sweat was rough, as if starchy. Of course, the girl just let herself be played with. She was neither angry nor not angry. It was the same whether I did something or nothing; nothing or everything, it was all the same.

When I told a lie, so did she. Apparently she began to think of something else at once, and of course I pretended not to notice. Should I make this girl just for this once, tonight, in revenge for the scars, for you, and for my real face? No, no need to worry, for while anything at all *could* happen here, nothing at all would. I told a lie and she told another, and then for some reason she suddenly took me aback by suggesting that I might be an artist.

"Why? Is there something that makes me look as if I painted pictures?"

"But, in general, artists don't want to appear special, do they?"

"True enough . . . but then is make-up something to show oneself off or conceal oneself with?"

"Both," she said, nibbling a pebble-like cocktail cracker, which she held with the tips of her fingers. "Both intentions are sincere, after all, aren't they?"

"Sincere?" Suddenly I felt dispirited, as if I had been shown the secret of a sleight-of-hand trick. "That's all shit!"

The girl wrinkled up her nose: "Disgusting! Must you be so obvious?"

True! Any real thing is a fake here, and any fake passes for the genuine article. Amusing oneself with painting pictures of holes on taboo fences just before getting aroused was apparently what one did in a place like this (if I got any more drunk than I was, my very realization that I had a mask on would be dangerous) and under the palm of my hand the girl's thighs, as if bored, began to yawn. The psychological moment had apparently come for me to leave. Nothing had happened, but it made no difference. I should consider it benefit enough to have approached the forbidden fence and ascertained its strength. However disagreeable, tomorrow I should have to try a desperate assault on my fence.

I felt no distance between this experience and the subsequent events; it was as if I were looking through a telescope. However, I did not make the mistake of giving in to my drunken impulses and tearing off the mask; I told the taxi driver to take me not to my own house, but to my hideaway. It would appear that the distance between my real face and the mask, no matter how precisely I tried to match the surfaces, no matter how strong the adhesive materials I used, could not be filled in simply. All night long I dreamed of you, between short intervals of wakefulness. In the dreams, you seemed to be continually appealing to me for something. I thought you were warning me about how close I was to lechery, but later that seemed mere imagination. Once I dreamt of being in a jail.

THE next day, as I had anticipated, I had a terrible hangover. My whole face was swollen and smarting. Perhaps I had been poisoned by the adhesive materials, for I had not taken the proper care of my face after coming home. When I had vomited and then washed my face, I felt better. But it was still before ten. Since I was not to go out until after three, I decided to lie down for two or three hours more.

What a sorry thing it was to put off even for a few hours the great moment on which I had staked the efforts of a year. Thrashing wretchedly around on the bed, seeking some cool place on the mattress, I couldn't fall asleep. How stupid of me to have poured down the drinks. What in God's name was so enjoyable about tearing around as I had? I felt there was something I had to remember . . . roaming the streets, wearing my mask, trying to be a transparent being . . . fences . . . taboos. . . . Yes, I was on the verge of becoming a lecher. . . . Save for being the acting head of a high-molecular-research institute, I was completely insipid and inexcusably harmless. . . . Yes, come what may, I had to be a lecher in order to get over the fences.

I frantically tried to scrape the remains of my drunkenness out of the back of my cranium by recalling in detail my impressions of the preceding night. But the erotic feelings, so vivid then, would not come back. Was it because I was not wearing my mask? That was it! The instant I put on the mask, the lawbreaker would be resuscitated. There must surely lie concealed in even the most harmless being a criminal capable of responding to a mask.

I am not going so far as to say that all masked actors have criminal tendencies. It is also true that a certain head clerk of a well-known general affairs section, though he actually demonstrates a pre-eminent genius by showing special interest in costumed processions on company excursions, is on the contrary an uncommon optimist, quite satisfied with his present situation. . . . However, if we realize that this law-abiding every-day life is definitely not as safe as the world of crime, we still might have nothing to do with criminals—but it is doubtful. It is unbelievable that there are people who have never once in their lives wanted to be transparent beings, who live in a world where they would be lost if they ever forgot a single one of the many things one has to do: assiduously punching the time clock every day, having personal seals made, ordering calling cards, saving money, measuring collar sizes, collecting autographs, taking out life insurance, registering real estate, writing Christmas cards, pasting photographs on identity papers. . . . Somehow, for a brief moment, I seemed to have dropped off into a doze. A wind had apparently sprung up, and I was awakened by the noise of the shutters. My headache and my nausea seemed better, but I was still not completely recovered.

I wanted to take a bath, but unfortunately the water pressure was low and there would not be enough to rise to the second story. I decided to try the public bath. After hesitating between the mask or my bandages, I finally decided to go out with the mask. I was hesitant about the impression the bandages would make on my fellow bathers. And I also liked trying the mask in all kinds of situations. (When I put it on, my pluck returned at once.) As I was searching through the pockets of my coat for my wallet, my hand touched something hard. The air pistol . . . and the gold yoyo. Thinking that I might see the superintendent's daughter on the way out, I wrapped the yoyo up with my soap and towel and went out.

Unfortunately, I did not meet the girl. I did not anticipate any particular trouble, but I gave the neighborhood public bath a wide berth and set out toward some baths a bus stop away, at the next intersection. Since the place had just opened, there were few bathers and the water was still clean. As I soaked in the pool to rid myself of the last of my hangover, submitting to the steam, I was suddenly aware of a man wearing a black shirt in a corner on the other side. No, it was not a shirt, but tattooing! I could not make out the design very well in that light, but he gave the impression of wearing a fish skin.

At first, I tried as much as possible not to look, but I could not take my eyes away. The pattern did not particularly bother me, but the very idea of tattooing left me at a loss, like a name on tip of the tongue.

Perhaps I felt here a true kinship with my mask. Surely the mask and tattooing have a surprising element in common: they both seek to bring about a transformation by obliterating the real skin. But of course, there were points of difference too. Fundamentally the mask was something removable, but tattooing was assimilated and incorporated into the skin. The mask, moreover, furnished an evasion of reality, but tattooing, of course, was an effort to make oneself obvious and showy. If it were a question of conspicuousness, my scar webs would be second to nothing.

Nevertheless, what I did not understand was why in heaven's name one would go to such lengths to be conspicuous. Of course, the man himself would probably not be able to answer such a question as that—I suppose being conspicuous was meaningful to him, precisely because he could not answer. By and large, there are many monstrous individuals who, liking riddles, pose meaningless problems and make a business of forcing people who are unable to answer to pay a forfeit.... There also appears to be some problematic element in tattooing that forces an answer.

I myself sometimes became frantic trying to find an answer. I tried, for example, to trace how I should feel if I were to be tattooed. And the first thing I thought of were the eyes of others that would descend upon me like thorns. Since I had already gone through the experience of the scar webs, I could understand very well. Then gradually the sky would draw away ... and around me would be the shining brilliance of high noon. The place where I stood would alone be completely dark. Yes, yes, I seem to remember that tattooing is the sign of an exile.... Since it was the sign of vice, it repelled light.... But for some reason I did not feel the slightest bit cornered or regretful—it was natural that I should not—for, by carving a sign of vice on myself, I would be condemning myself to oblivion by my own volition, and then there would be no point in regret.

When the man got out of the bath, the image of a demon covered with cherry blossoms coiled around his body. Amber sweat was pouring from him, and feeling that I was his ac-

complice, I had the most exhilarating sense of his attitude of
rejection. Quite true, the kinship between the mask and the
tattooing depended apparently on which side of the real face
one lived. As long as there were people who could bear to live
with tattooing, there would be those who could put up with
masks too.

However, at the exit of the baths, the tattooed man shocked
me by picking a quarrel. When his tattooing was covered by
his long-sleeved shirt he seemed younger and smaller, much
less impressive. But he was accustomed to taking care of himself and therefore an expert in the art of intimidation.

In a hoarse voice the man demanded an apology for my
impolite staring. Judging from his words, he was quite provoked. It would have been best if I had begged his pardon as
he demanded; but I did the wrong thing at the wrong time,
for underneath my mask I was boiling like soup from my
long stay in the bath and felt dizziness coming on.

"But tatooing's something you want to show off, isn't it?"
The man let fly with his fist before I had even finished
speaking. But my instinct to protect the mask was no less
rapid. The fact that his first blow had missed seemed to
excite him even more. He grappled with me, shaking me
roughly, apparently wanting to land one good blow on my
face. At length, he had me up against a partition, and his arm
or my own—I am not clear which, since we were all entangled
—gouged up from below my jaw, and in an instant my mask
was ripped from my face.

I was as shocked as if my pants had been stripped off in
public. Indeed, my opponent's amazement was no less than
my own. Muttering unintelligibly in a cowardly way, he
hastily departed, indignant as if he himself had been victim-
ized. I wiped away the sweat and readjusted the mask, feeling
half dead. Apparently there was a crowd of bystanders, but
I did not have the courage to look around. Had it been on a

stage, surely everybody would have had a good laugh. The next time I went out, I would definitely not forget my air pistol.

EXCURSUS: *How in the world did my tragicomedy appear to the tattooed fellow, not to speak of the people gathered there? No matter how they might laugh, they could not dismiss the matter so simply. Perhaps it would remain an unforgettable memory for the rest of their lives. But in what form, for heaven's sake? Would it penetrate their hearts like a bullet . . . ? Or would it distort the appearance of the world by its impact on their eyeballs . . . ? Whichever it was, they would never again stare hard at a stranger's face, that I could say for sure. Strangers were transparent, like ghosts, and the world was filled with gaps like a picture painted on glass with thin pigments. The world itself, like the mask, began to seem difficult to believe in, and I was stricken with an unutterable sense of loneliness. I needed to feel no responsibility for strangers. For what they were looking at was the truth. What was visible was only the mask, and those strangers had perceived a truth more profound than eyes could see directly. No matter how bad the truth appeared from without, it had its own reward.*

I had an experience over twenty years ago: I once saw the abandoned corpse of a child. The body was lying face upward in a clump of bushes in back of the school. I think I had gone to retrieve a baseball and had happened to see it by chance. The corpse had swollen up like a rubber ball, and the whole thing had a faint pinkish tinge. There was movement around the mouth, and looking closely, I saw that myriads of maggots were wriggling around, working at the lips. I was terrified, and for many days afterwards could not get my food down. It was at the time a frightful, excruciating impression, but with the passage of the years—perhaps the corpse had grown older with me—all that remained, enveloped in a peaceful sorrow, was the faint flush of the smooth, wax-like skin. And now, I did not even think of avoiding the memory of the body. I had even come to be fond of the memory. Every time I recalled the body, I was taken by a feeling of our being fellow creatures. It reminded me that, outside of plastics, there was a world that could be touched with one's hands. The dead body would go on living with me forever as a symbol of another world.

No, I am not making such excuses only for complete strangers. At this point, these misgivings should concern you too. I want you to believe my words, even though I feel they may cause you much pain. It is not really pain, but a memory of the impression I had when I looked under the mask. Perhaps, indeed, the time will come when these memories will be as dear to you as the corpse is to me.

I DELAYED my departure to take care of my bruises and change the adhesive materials, and then, as I headed directly for the bus stop in front of the station, I made a detour to buy the mask some items for daily use: a lighter, a memorandum book, a wallet. I arrived at the bus stop at precisely four o'clock. I had decided to lie in ambush there, waiting for you to return from your handicraft class that met every Thursday. It was the beginning of the evening rush hour, and a clamor filled the space around me as if I were in an amusement park. Yet I wondered why I was possessed with a strange feeling of quiet, as if I were in a forest where the leaves had started to fall. Perhaps my previous shock remained and was overwhelming my senses from within. When I closed my eyes, innumerable stars flashing light eddied up like swarms of mosquitoes. Perhaps my blood pressure was rising too. Certainly my experience had been traumatic. But apparently it wasn't altogether bad. The humiliation, acting as shock treatment, was spurring me on to lawbreaking.

I decided to wait on a step under the eaves of a bank building that projected slightly into the crowd. A bit higher than the crowd, I could see very well, but I was not conspicuous because many others were waiting too. I had no fear of your seeing me before I saw you. Since your class lasted until four, even if you missed one bus you would surely arrive within ten minutes.

I had never thought that your class would be so useful. Going to such a useless thing, faithfully, year in year out, was, I thought, good proof of woman's unpredictability. Particularly the fact that you had enthusiastically taken up the making of buttons was highly symbolic. How the devil many buttons, big and small, had you cut out, incised, painted, and polished until now? You did not make them to use but persisted in producing these generally practical objects for impractical purposes. No, I do not mean to blame you. Actually, I was never opposed to it. You were really quite addicted, and I was willing to give this innocent pursuit my full blessing.

But, I do not have to explain minute by minute what went on. For you yourself were in the drama too. What is necessary is to expose to broad daylight the shameful face of a hidden parasite by turning my heart inside out. You arrived on the third bus and, getting off, began to walk past the bank where I was standing. I set out after you. From behind, you looked strangely fresh, strangely sleek, and I almost lost my nerve.

I caught up with you at the traffic light on the other side of the station. In the few minutes' time it would take to get from here to the station, I had to win you over somehow. I could not be abrupt, but there was no time to be indirect. As if I had picked it up, I casually held out one of your leather buttons which I had smuggled out of the house in advance, and flung at you the line I had prepared.

"Isn't this something you dropped?"

Without concealing your surprise, you attempted to find out where it had come from, lifting your handbag and looking at the bottom, checking the clasp; and with an uncomprehending expression, you glanced quickly at me. Once I had spoken, I followed up immediately, not wanting to lose the opportunity on which I was determined.

"Wasn't it from your hat?"

"My hat?"

"Even a rabbit comes out of a hat with a pass of the hand, doesn't it?"

But you didn't even smile. Far from that, you nailed my mouth shut with a glance like surgical forceps. You looked at me with an unflinching stare, of which you yourself were perhaps unconscious, as if you had forgotten yourself. If the look had gone on three seconds more I should have concluded that I had been seen through and would have beaten a quick retreat. But that could not be. My mask had already been proved successful in every situation. There was absolutely no fear that I would be suspected as long as you did not tear the mask off by force as the tattooed man did or put your lips directly to it—the difference in temperature could probably not be hidden. Moreover, I had consciously made my voice lower than usual, and even if I hadn't, my labials, the b's, p's, and m's, were quite transformed.

Perhaps, indeed, I had been too worried; at once your gaze fell away, and your usual, far-away expression returned. But my erotic feeling seemed to slip away when I met your look, and if you had left on the spot I too should doubtless have given it up with good grace, thinking that after all it would be best for us both. At any rate, it was broad daylight, and the efficiency and expediency of the mask seemed to be fading. But you too hesitated for an instant. And the crowd, undulating around us like some greedy marine protozoan, sucked up our oozing thoughts from the edges. There was no time to explore in detail the significance of the distortion in the magnetic field that had sprung up between us as a result of your momentary hesitation, and with my sights fixed on this hesitation, I instantly delivered the second prepared line.

MARGINAL NOTE: *The expression "distortion in the magnetic field" is actually quite precise. Perhaps I had had a dim premonition of the grave significance of this instant. I could be neither proud of, nor justified in, the prophecy; but if these few lines were missing I would have had no premonition—I shudder at the very thought—that I would be sentenced to the punishment of being ridiculous, because of the crime of insensitivity. Whatever I did would merely provoke laughter, and these notes would not be the record of the mask, but those of a simple clown. Being a clown would be all right, but I did not want to be a clown unaware that he was one.*

I wonder if you remember. I casually asked, in a tone as if weary from too many inquiries, where buses on a certain line arrived and departed. I did not know whether you knew the answer or not, but choosing that stop was not a plan to kill time; it was a far-sighted, clever trap.

First of all, that stop was the only one at which one could reach the station from an affiliated bus line, and it lay in an inconvenient and inconspicuous location.

Next, it was located on the other side of the station, and

to get to it one had to take a long, circuitous route via the overpass if one did not know the way through the underground passages. Third, the layout of the underground passages was terribly complicated, and it was difficult to explain the several exits in simple words. Finally, if you made good use of the underground passages, the distance to the platform of the bus you would take would not be much different than if you went straight through the station. And, of course, you knew the stop.

I was understandably tense as I awaited your answer. My whole body was stiff and awkward with my efforts to conceal my underlying motive. If I had not put on the mask, though you consented, I would not have had the confidence to walk along with you. More than that, I was even doubtful that I could manage to dissimulate my agitated breathing. I continued to wait with a feeling of being enclosed in a thin glass jar—in a jar of glass thinner than paper, that would fly to pieces at a mere sneeze. I cannot deny that I was also irritated, but it was true too that your answer was slow in coming. Was it something you had to hesitate about? I clung to the fact that you were hesitating. Such a situation was one that required a prompt decision either way. The more you hesitated the more unnatural and false our position would be. If you did not want to, you should say a simple "no"; but by hesitating you implied that your consent was already half given. You would soon have no excuse for refusing, because you had already half consented. Perhaps I should put in another good word to make the decision easier. Just then, a young man in a hurry pushed his way roughly between us. I became aware that the two of us had become a conspicuous obstacle, an eddy in the streaming crowd. Desperately regaining your balance, you gave me a suspicious glance. Then you looked at me as if you were flipping indifferently through the pages of a calendar. Displeased with your expression, I closed the distance be-

tween us, thinking to hasten the decision a little, and just as
I began to speak, you finally answered.

But when I heard your response, while I applauded in my
heart that things had gone well, I wondered why I had the
painful feeling that I had been betrayed. It was all right since
it was I, but what if it had been some complete stranger? Once
you had hesitated, you acquiesced. There was a significance
that you should have had to hesitate in acquiescing. In short,
it suggested something like a sexual barrier. You realized what
it would mean to consent to walk side by side with me for
seven or eight minutes over a distance of several hundred
yards, and I naturally could assume that this was more than
simple kindness. This was too much to do in return for a
button I had picked up for you. To put it bluntly, by your
acquiescence you had consciously aroused my erotic feelings.
And since you consciously provoked them, you too must have
some feeling. . . .

No, things were going all right. How could I dare object
now, since I had originally planned just such a situation. If,
by chance, you had turned me down, all the pains I had taken
would have come to nothing. I could set another day, but
even though I had been lucky the first time, a second time
would simply make you more cautious, and I would be unable to avoid letting you know my real intentions. Yes, things
were all right this way. I was made to realize fully last night
that getting you back through the mask and getting all the
others back through you was not the insipid thing one might
imagine from the impression the words alone make; when all
was said and done, getting you back was breaking down the
barriers of sex and bursting through my own vileness. Since
I was trying to get over the barrier and since my companion
was disposed to consent, there was no point in making a fuss.
You could not be so impudent as to haul out the old alibi of
not having realized what was going on. If I wanted to break

the fence myself, but didn't want to let my companion do so, that would be simple rape. But it would be amazing if the roadway between us were restored by such one-sided lechery. With such an act, the mask would have to disappear from the world, without leaving a trace that it had been alive. Moreover, if all I wanted was to rape, my real, scar-webbed face would have sufficed.

This was theoretically true, perhaps. But, having you with me at last, going down the stairs toward the underground passage chock-full of strangers, I felt stifled with unutterable anguish, bewilderment, and confusion, carried away by the overwhelming feeling of your presence. Isn't it generally rare to imagine by a sense of touch? I did not conceive of you as a glass doll or as abstract word symbols, but had a tactile sense of your presence as I got within touching distance of you. The side of my body next to you was as sensitive as if it had been overexposed to the sun, and each one of my pores panted for breath like dogs sweltering in the heat. And when I realized that you, a refined woman, were prepared to accept a stranger, I felt intolerably sad. I was being cuckolded by my own self, and at the same time I was a good-for-nothing who had been dismissed without reason. If that were the case, my shameful fantasies yesterday in which I had ignored my companion were far sounder. Wasn't even rape more wholesome than this? I began to feel enmity and seething hatred for this hunter-type face, wearing its sunglasses and its strange affected clothes and sporting a beard, making me realize again that the features of the mask were those of a stranger. At the same time I felt that you were a completely different person because you did not at once reject the face; and you gave me a feeling of oppressiveness, as if I were seeing poison smeared on jewels.

But the mask was different. The mask absorbed my anguish and seemed to have a capacity of turning it into nourishment, making the leaves and branches of my desires thick and luxuriant, like some jungle plant. Simply not having been rejected by you was to say that I had already got you, and I sank the fangs of my imagination into the nape of your neck, which rose smoothly from the collarless, buff-colored blouse. Since for me you were you, but for the mask you were simply a pleasing woman, there was no point in censuring its impoliteness. Yes, a vertiginous abyss lay between the mask and me. There was a difference between us, but it was only a few inches of facial surface, and for the rest we were the same. Think of the groove of a record. From such a simple device as that one can reproduce scores of tones. It is all the less surprising that man's heart should strike two opposing notes at the same time.

Of course, I should not have been surprised. Actually, you yourself were split into several parts. Just as I had a double existence, you did too. If I was another person wearing a stranger's mask, you were another person wearing the mask of yourself. Another wearing the mask of himself . . . a gruesome combination. . . . Although I intended to lay plans to bring about a second meeting, the results, to the contrary, would probably be a second good-bye. Perhaps I had made a slight miscalculation.

If I had suspected things would be like this, how much better to have pulled out at once. No, how much better, rather, simply to have got you to tell me the location of the stop as I had asked and let the rest of my plans go. Why in heaven's name was I shamelessly following around after the mask? Actually my confidence was not up to my explanation; my betrayed love had been drawn into a corner and changed to hate, my desire to reestablish the roadway had been frustrated and turned into a desire for revenge. Since I had come this far and had made quite sure of your infidelity, even though it had not been my motive to do so, the result was that my actions had fallen into step with the mask's. But just a minute. I have the feeling that, toward the beginning of these notes, I used the word "revenge" quite often. Yes, I did indeed. At that time, the main pretext for making the mask was to try to seek revenge on the arrogance of faces by deceiving you. But then it shifted to reestablishing relations with others, and the significance of seducing you changed to something mental, contemplative; furthermore, something physical was added, and there occurred an emotional explosion in the form of jealousy. Through this jealousy I was seized by a spasm of love as if I were parched with thirst, I was blocked by the barrier of sexual taboos, I became passionate, and then at last I again seemed to become a captive of my desire for revenge.

But there was something dissatisfying in this last desire for revenge, and I was worried. I had confirmed your unfaithfulness, true, but what sort of revenge should I take? Should I trust the evidence in your face and ask for your repentance, or should I press you for a divorce? Not at all; by doing anything like that, I should lose you. If a relationship with you were no more than my observing your unfaithfulness through the mask, that would be all right; I would go on watching my whole life long. And wouldn't I have ample vengeance by the very continuation of such perversion? For you would have to put up forever with a division of yourself that matched this split in me. Neither love nor hate . . . neither mask nor real face. . . . Perhaps I had found a temporary equilibrium in such depressing circumstances.

However, it was the triumphant mask's turn now to begin to lose its composure in the presence of my anxieties. As, some ten minutes later, I stirred my spoon around in my coffee in the restaurant at the end of the underground passage, the word of consent you casually uttered frightened away the self-confidence of the mask and seemed to drive it into two facing mirrors, talking with itself.

"My husband is away on business just now. . . ."

Well, what did you mean? You said nothing more, nor did the mask ask. Of course, if one put a common-sense interpretation on it, one could take it that you were justifying your answer to my invitation: that you need not return home to prepare supper and that it would make no difference if you ate out. But there was something courageous in the somber frigidity of your tone, as if you were standing firm, and your attitude seemed to have the effect of snapping a finger at the nose of the mask with its air of self-conceit. I wonder how we had ever been able to converse at all before this. Yes, the mask—surely it had read the line somewhere before—complimented you on the shape of your fingers and then asked about the cut on your right thumb that you had got making buttons. And after noting that your hand did not attempt to escape its gaze, it broached the subject of human relations, like some algebraic equation that does not include such divers items as name, occupation, and address. It was immediately after that, I think, that I began to explore your feelings. The mask did not try to question with whom of us the initiative for the seduction lay and manipulated you according to its own wishes, eagerly watchful. Having been outdistanced, I was simply dumb with amazement, like a child who has suddenly been pushed aside by its companion.

MARGINAL NOTE: *Oh yes, I remember at that time being overcome with panic lest my real self be discovered behind the mask.*

Surely, there was no proof at all that the mask had committed the seduction and that you were the one who had been seduced. Regardless of the wiles of the mask, which had gone about the matter with surprising adeptness, you had wanted to be seduced, hadn't you? Nevertheless, there was no possibility of doing things over at this point, and in order to spur itself on, the mask acted the seducer even more boldly.

However, that was beside the point, for the fact was that you were seduced. There is a saying that if you overcome one arm then you are revenged only one arm's worth; if you overcome both arms then you are revenged two arm's worth. All during the time we were in the restaurant the mask tried its utmost not to bring up again the subject of your husband. Thus, it felt it could even bring up the subject of the scar webs with composure, and though it might convince itself that the story concerned some one else, it was still a horrible thing. It was an annoying situation, because when you showed no disposition at all to mention your husband, I became blindly angry. Indeed, it was ignoring him—that is, me. Perhaps it was bitter contempt for him. I was very distressed, for I could not say positively whether it would have been better to get you to discuss him or not. Your bringing "him" up, however disagreeable, would have functioned as a check to the mask. I could only hope, as the seducer, that you would go on being the accomplice you were.

I was worried by the curious way you had of smiling with

only your lower lip . . . I was worried by your staring through me, beyond me into the distance . . . I was reproachful at your refusing the beer I had offered . . . yet I was opposed to your drinking too much . . . it was as if boiling water had been poured over me as I lay soaking in ice. While my left eye looked longingly at you, as at some spoils of war, at your fingers that were crumbling bread—at your soft, sleek fingers, except for the cut from your button work—what I saw with my right eye made me writhe in pain. I was a cuckold present at his wife's adultery. This was a triangular relationship with one actor playing two parts. If one were to make a drawing of "me," "the mask, that is, the other me," and "you," it would be a non-Euclidean triangular relationship, existing on a single straight line.

When we finished dinner, time suddenly began to jell around us. Perhaps it was the weight of the ceiling. The disproportionately massive concrete pillars standing in the middle suggested great heaviness. In addition, the underground restaurant was windowless. These was no place for the sun and its twenty-four-hour cycle to stray in here. There was only a timeless, artificial illumination. Time measured in units of tens of thousands of years flowed along right outside the wall in subterranean water courses and through the layers of earth, slicing vertically straight down. But your "husband," who was urging our time on, would never return as long as we waited like this. Oh time, suspend your flight, be a vessel containing only us. And we shall cross the street together as we are and reach our new home.

However, neither my mask nor I actually knew what you were thinking. You had put up no resistance to my transparent tactics of inviting you first to coffee and then to dinner—you were so completely without resistance that I wondered if you had not expected things to happen as they did—then you accepted, and the mask was completely op-

timistic that things were going as planned. But your resolute
attitude, as if you had poured mortar into the nooks and
crannies of your conscience, at once cast the mask into the
bedevilment of suspicion again. Of course, it was not only
your abruptness. If you were curt in accepting my invitation,
that would be proof that you were more than aware of the
sexual barrier and I could easily handle you, but you were
tender and showed a delicate consideration for me. You were
straightforward and natural, not the slightest bit bashful. In
short, you were quite yourself, not a bit different from your
usual self.

On the other hand, this lack of change perturbed the mask.
Where in God's name were you concealing the excitement of
anticipation, the inner flashings, dazzling glances, the breathing, of someone awaiting seduction?

The waiter cleared the table with obvious incivility. Ripples
formed on the surface of the water in our glasses doubtless
from the tremor of a subway train. The mask was flustered
and chattered meaninglessly, trying to insert here and there
sexually suggestive words, but you showed not even the reaction of refusal, not to mention consent. As I surreptitiously
watched the mask's confusion, I inwardly offered sarcastic
congratulations, but unfortunately I was unable to convince
myself of your unfaithfulness.

However, after this had been going on about twenty minutes—I wonder if you remember—the mask, coming out of
his paralysis, stretched out his foot and accidentally touched
your ankle with the tip of his shoe. An almost imperceptible
expression of agitation passed over your face. Your gaze was
fixed in the void. A shadow formed on your forehead and your
lips trembled. But like the generosity of a morning sky gradually suffused with light, you quite calmly ignored his blunder.
Inside, the mask was filled with laughter. The laughter, without outlet, became as if charged with electricity. The mask

had apparently succeeded in bringing down its prey. I needn't have worried so much. As I concentrated on the sensation of you which was transmitted by the tip of my toe, even the mask shut its mouth and recovered its pleasure in silent conversation.

Actually, it was really quite dangerous to attempt small talk. On the subject of garden plants, for example, our two conversations were in strange agreement; the subject of childless couples accidentally came up; without my being aware of it, technical chemical terms cropped up among my figures of speech; if I relaxed my attention there would be enough evidence to give the mask away. It would seem that man befouls his daily life with his own excretions far more than a dog does.

But for me your conduct was a brutal shock. Your self-possession while being seduced was a part of you I should never have imagined, although I could see that the mask was fascinated. It was a severe shock. Moreover, the foot that was touching your ankle was definitely my foot. But if I did not concentrate with all my strength I had no more than an indirect impression of things, as if they were out-of-focus, faraway, imaginary events. If my face were different from me, then so was my body. I had foreseen this, but when confronted with the fact, the thought was nonetheless painful. If I felt this way about your ankle, how would I be able to keep my senses when I touched your whole body? Could I resist the impulse to rip off my mask on the spot? Could this surrealist triangle of ours, which was already straining us to the limit, maintain itself against even greater pressure?

How hard I strove to endure the penance in the cheap hotel room. Without taking off my mask, without strangling you, I had to go on witnessing your being violated. I was as if bound hand and foot, with my head stuck in a bag with openings only for the eyes. I felt like shrieking. It was too easy! It was much too easy! Five hours had not yet gone by since I had met you. How easy it was! If only you had shown at least a modicum of resistance. Well, how long should you have resisted to satisfy me? Six hours? Seven? Eight? I was being stupid and ridiculous. Your licentiousness would be the same, if you held back for five, fifty, or five hundred hours.

Well, why didn't I have the courage to put an end to this festering triangle? Because of a desire for revenge? Perhaps. But I think there was a different motive. Had it been simply desire for revenge, would it not have been more effective to tear the mask from my face on the spot? But I was afraid. Of course, the behavior of the mask, which was demolishing my calm everyday life, was cruel, but returning to the faceless, enclosed days was even more terrifying. Fear strengthened fear, and like a bird that has lost its feet and is unable to alight upon the ground, I would have to keep endlessly hovering. But that was not the end of it. If I really could not endure the situation, the mask, alive as it was, might well kill you. Your fornication would be difficult to deny, which gave me an alibi.

But I did not kill you. Why? I wonder. Because I did not want to lose you? No, precisely not wanting to lose you was reason enough for killing you. It would be senseless to seek rationality in jealousy. Just look at yourself. You who had rejected me so positively, who had rebelled against my face, now lay broken beneath the mask! It was too bad that the lights had been turned off, for I could not satisfy myself with my own eyes—your chin where maturity and immaturity existed strangely together, the grey wart in your armpit, the scar from your appendectomy, the tuft of frizzled hair mixed with something white, the chestnut-colored lips between your spread legs—all of them were about to be possessed, violated. I should like to see every last detail with my own eyes in the full light of day. You had seen and rejected the scar webs, seen and accepted the mask; surely you have no objection to being seen yourself. But light did not suit my purposes either. I would not have been able to take off my glasses, and I carried all kinds of physical marks, like the scar on my hip I had got when we went skiing together long ago—and perhaps some I didn't know about but you did. I concentrated on capturing you in every way other than sight: legs, arms, palms, fingers, tongue, nose, ears. I did not miss a single signal that was emitted from your body: your breathing, sighing, the working of your joints, the flexing of your muscles, the secretions of your skin, the vibrations of your vocal cords, the groaning of your viscera.

I could not get used to being a man condemned to death. As all the juices were being wrung from my body and I was drying up, I had to continue to put up with this immorality, this struggle. In my anguish, the thought of death lost its usual solemnity, and homicide seemed no more than a slight barbarism. What in God's name were you thinking? What made me decide to be so patient—perhaps it was rather strange—was the dignity you maintained even while you were being violated. No, dignity seems a curious term for it. It was not at all a question of rape, nor was it a one-sided lawbreaking by the mask. Since you did not once make any pretense of refusing me, I must consider rather that we were partners in crime. It is comical when a partner in crime maintains dignity with his accomplice—it might be more precise to say a very assured partner in crime. Yet no matter how desperately the mask struggled, it was not ultimately able to be a fornicator, to say nothing of a rapist. You were literally inviolable. This did not change the fact that you were immoral and unfaithful. It also did not change the fact that you had stirred up my fierce jealousy, like boiling tar in a cauldron, like smoke from chimneys just after rain, like the water of hot springs seething up together with mud. The unexpected event that, by your attitude of inviolability, you did not in the ultimate sense submit to the mask, completely amazed and overwhelmed me.

It would seem that I had not yet fully grasped the significance of your assurance in the act of fornication with a stranger. There was apparently no lust involved. If there were, you would have been more obviously flirtatious. But, quite as if you were performing some ceremony, you never lost your seriousness from beginning to end. I do not really understand. What was happening inside you? I did not have a clue. Moreover, my sense of defeat, firmly rooted at that time, has unfortunately remained as an indelible blot to the very end —at least until this moment I write this. This insidious disease of self-persecution was worse than my fits of jealousy. Although I had deliberately put on the mask, opened up the roadway to you, and beckoned you in, you had passed me by and hastened along somewhere else. And I was left alone with my loneliness, quite the same as before I had donned the mask.

Ah, I do not understand you. I could not think that just because there was temptation you would respond, paying no attention to who the partner was, like a shameless streetwalker. But there was no proof against this. Had I been unaware of the natural-born harlot in you? If you were a real harlot, you would satisfy your violator, neither spurring him on when he was inadequate nor making him feel mistreated. What in God's name were you? Although the mask had frantically tried to break down the barrier, you had slipped through it without touching. Like the wind ... or a spirit.

I do not understand you. Putting you to any further tests would be nothing more than my own destruction.

THE following morning—well, it was already close to noon—we hardly spoke to each other until we left the hotel. Between spells of wakefulness, worried lest my mask might have come off, and snatches of sleep, when I dreamed repeatedly that I was rushing to leave for somewhere but had lost my ticket, fatigue pierced my forehead like a stake. However, thanks to the mask, signs of fatigue or shame showed on my face no more than on yours. But, also thanks to the mask, I could neither wash my face nor shave. My swollen features were agonizingly painful. Compressed by the unyielding mask, the ends of my beard, which had begun to grow, were obstructed and had begun to push back in. I wanted as quickly as I possibly could to get away from you and return to my hideaway.

As I lit my last cigarette, my real face, which had constantly been forced into bad roles, had begun speaking, touching on your guilty conscience, and I started involuntarily as you hesitatingly offered me a blue-green button. It was not the one I had picked up for you; it was one it had taken you half a month to do. At the time I was simply angry at your zealousness, but when I considered it again, I felt I understood you. Silver edged lines, as if scratched into a thick lacquered base with a nail, flickered in a lovely tangled skein. It was as if your voiceless cries were shut up within it. I thought the button was like a lonely cat raised by a doting old woman. Perhaps it was naïveté. But when I considered that it was a real challenge to "him," who had not even once glanced at your button, I realized this was a bold, determined act. I had intended to blame you but on the contrary was blamed myself; perhaps I was gradually getting used to my own defeatism. Who the deuce ever thought up the stupid proposition that women were anything to get carried away about? I wonder.

Outside, everything was shimmering in a light like plated chromium. The only reality was the odor of your perspiration that lingered in my nostrils. Back in my room, after hasty attention to my face, I threw myself onto the bed and did not awake until dawn had begun to break. I calculate that I had slept close to seventeen hours. My face was burning as if someone had been working on it with a file. I opened the window and, as I watched the sky, which was beginning to turn a clear blue, I held compresses of moistened towels to my face. At length the heavens became the very color of the button I had received from you, the color of the sea against which is outlined the vanishing stern of a ship. I felt unduly melancholy, and squeezing the flesh of my arms and my breast until it hurt, I involuntarily groaned in pain. What barren purity! Nothing could continue to exist in such a blue. I wished that yesterday and the day before could be eradicated. Actually, I suppose my plans had had some degree of success, but who in heaven's name was going to reap the harvest? And what harvest? If anybody, you would reap, you, a shameless harlot, who had cut through the mask like some great, solid shadow. But what existed here and now was only the blue of the sky and the pain of my face. . . . The mask, that should be the victor, lay stupidly on the table, like an obscene picture that has drained all one's desire; I wondered if I should start using it for target practice with my air pistol. And after that, what if I were to hack it utterly to pieces?

However, as I stood musing, the blue faded away, and the streets began to show their daytime face. My sentimental grumbling too fell away like an old scab, and whether I wished it or not, I was again brought back to the inescapable reality of the scar webs. Even though, with the mask, I could not at this point dream dreams like the flashings of holiday fireworks, to give it up and bury myself alive in a windowless cell would be even more unthinkable. After yesterday, I was still vacillating, but I had ascertained the precise center of gravity of this three-cornered relationship, and it was altogether possible to acquire command of the mask by adroitly keeping my equilibrium. No matter how violent my passing emotions, there was definitely a point to plans that one had spent time refining.

I hurried through dinner and dashed out of my hideaway. Since I had to return to the role of my real self who was coming back from a week's business trip, today I should have to put on the bandages, which I had not worn for some time. As I was leaving, I was startled at my reflection in the windowpane. I was terrifying! I had come to have a new and better opinion on the feeling of release that the mask provided. If I were to return straight home just as I was—it was a stimulating thought to me—I should produce a considerable effect on you in whom the sensations of last night were most surely still alive. It would definitely be worth trying. Providing I could stand it. Unfortunately I did not have the confidence. The sensations of the preceding night were still alive in me too. Perhaps I should have accused you, gone into a frenzy, and exposed everything in a fit of anger. No matter how agonizing, I wanted to leave this three-cornered relationship alone for the time being. I would meet you as "myself" after composing myself and accustoming myself to the ordinary world for a while.

But was the world really ordinary? I wonder. The gate to the Institute was still closed. When I entered through the side door, the guard, who was admiring a flowerpot as he brushed his teeth, was startled into speechlessness for an instant. I restrained him from dashing to the entryway and simply asked for the key. The smell of chemicals was familiar as an old coat. But the deserted Institute building—was it the odor? the sound of my footsteps?—was like some ghostly precinct inhabited only by tree spirits. To restore my relation with the present, I turned my attendance tab up and hastily changed into my white work smock. The report of the experiment-in-progress that had been assigned to the Group C assistants was written on the blackboard. The results were excellent. I was interested in them but in nothing more. In this building people showed a spirit of competition, were driven by desire for fame, were prey to jealousies, maneuvered to get the start on others by secretly sending for foreign publications, were disturbed by private matters, and became frantic about experiments and budgets, yet I felt this was a life worth living. I had the feeling, however, that it was not actually I who was devoting myself so assiduously to this work, but someone else who resembled me, and that this me was merely another tree spirit. I had not bargained for that at all. For a given technique there are the laws of that technique, and they cannot be influenced by anyone. Or if one did not maintain human relationships on all kinds of levels—like water fleas with other water fleas, jellyfish with other jellyfish, parasites with other parasites, pigs with other pigs, chimpanzees with other chimpanzees, field mice with other field mice—then would not chemistry and physics be meaningless too? Of course not! Human relationships are merely trivial appendages of human endeavor. If they are not, the only thing left to do is to give up this makeshift masked play and commit suicide.

A scar on a section of skin, bothersome to no one, could have no effect on my work. This work, no matter what anyone said, was mine. Whether I were a transparent man, a noseless man, a hippopotamus-faced man, so long as I could think, so long as I could manipulate my instruments, I should always fix my compass on this work.

Suddenly I thought of you. They say that women fix their compasses on love. I doubt the veracity of this, but women apparently can be happy with love alone. Well, then, I wonder if you are happy now. Suddenly I called to you aloud and longed to hear your voice answering me. I took the receiver off the hook and dialed the number but hung up on the second ring. In my heart I was not ready yet. I was still afraid.

After a while, the office workers gradually began to come in, greeting me one by one with surprised, sympathetic words. The building—and I too—at length took on its human aspect. I had been too anxious. Being here was not particularly good, but it was not especially disagreeable. If I could make my work at the Institute a roadway to others, supplementing my deficiencies with my mask, and get used to the double life, then by putting them together I could become a complete man. No, a mask was no substitute for a real face. It gave to a real face the unreal privilege of free passage through the barriers of sexual taboos, and so, far from becoming a complete man, I would doubtless lead the fragmented lives of several different men. Anyway, I would get used to a double life. I would adopt the habit, quite nonchalantly, of changing my clothes to suit different times and places. Just the way a single groove in a record can produce a number of different sounds at the same time.

In the afternoon, there was a trivial incident. In a corner of the laboratory a group of four or five men had put their heads together, and as I casually approached, one of the younger men in the middle hastily tried to conceal something. When I questioned them, I found that it was really nothing to hide: it was a petition about what to do concerning the problem of Korean immigration and emigration. In addition, although I did not censure him, he began to apologize profusely, while the other men watched us with distaste.

Was it that a faceless man is not competent to sign his name on behalf of Koreans? Of course, the assistant bore me no ill will; perhaps he was rather being respectful out of a feeling of pity for me. If men from the very beginning had not had faces, the problem of racial differences would never have arisen, whether one were Japanese, Korean, Russian, Italian, or Polynesian. But still, why did this so magnanimous young man make such a distinction between me who had no face and Koreans who had a different kind of face? When man evolved from the monkey, he did not do so by his use of tools, as is usually claimed, but because he had come to distinguish himself from monkeys by his face.

However, I asked to sign the petition. Everyone held his breath in expectation. But there was a lingering feeling of distaste. Why did I have to do something so meaningless? This invisible wall called "face" stood barring my way. Could you call this an ordinary world?

Suddenly I was aware of an unbearable fatigue, and, producing some suitable excuse, I returned home earlier than usual. I still was not completely confident of regaining the feeling of my real face, and even if I waited longer, there might well be no great improvement. Since I was wearing the bandage covering, as long as I did not talk I need have no fear that my agitation would be discernible; and, moreover, the agitation would not be mine alone. Would it not rather be far more painful for me to pretend not to see your agitation? I said to myself over and over again that even if I did encounter obvious confusion on your part, I should not be provoked by it and lose control of myself.

But even though you had not seen me for a week, you smiled at me just as before I left, without showing the slightest sign of embarrassment in your acts or in your expression; and

I could only stand for a moment dumfounded at this lack of concern. It was as if you had been kept in cold storage for a week. Had I become for you, I wonder, such a meaningless entity that you did not even feel the need to conceal your secrets? Or was this extraordinary shamelessness, this devil's heart in saint's clothing, your true character? Well, at last becoming rather ill-tempered, I demanded an account of the time I had been away; but without the slightest change of expression as you busied yourself with my clothes, you started in talking about the enlargement of the house next door, which was a violation of the building code, and of the war of letters that was raging between us and its owner; then you kept up a chatter in an innocent tone, like some child playing alone with his blocks, about domestic matters: a rumpus in the neighborhood over children who had not been able to sleep because of barking dogs, the branches of the trees in the garden that hung over into the street, should you close the window when the television set was on, should we buy a new washer because the old one made noise. . . . Were you the same person as the one last night who, like some fountain, profusely overflowed with the feelings of a mature woman? I could not believe it. Although I had fought bitterly against the division of my self into the mask and the face, for which I had had to prepare myself well, you endured the instantaneous split with composure and showed not the slightest regret. What did this mean, for heaven's sake? It was too unfair! How would it affect you, I mused, if I told you everything I knew? If I had had the button in my hands at that moment I should have thrust it in your face without a word.

But in the end, I could only keep silent like a fish. To show you the trick of the mask was nothing but disarming myself. If I could pull you down to my level, it might be all right to disarm. But the sacrifice was too great. Even though I might tear the mask off of your hypocrisy, you had a thousand layers of masks, and one after another a new one would appear; but my mask was only a single ply, and under that there remained not even a layer of ordinary face.

Our house, which I had not been in for a week, completely soaked up my daily life like a sponge; the walls, the ceilings, the floor matting seemed secure and solid; but for someone who had had the experience of the mask I could not help but perceive, however disagreeable it might be, that this solidity was merely a kind of sexual barrier that had become custom. And just as the existence of the barrier was merely a promise rather than a reality, I who had taken off the mask found my existence also shallow and illusory. And I thought of the mask —of the other world that I touched upon through the mask —as having a far greater reality. This feeling did not concern the house alone but also you. Although twenty-four hours had not yet passed since my desperate feeling of defeat, comparable only to death, incorrigibly I was already beginning to feel a withering hunger for the reality of you that I had been able to discover through my sense of touch. I began to tremble. They say that when a mole fails to touch anything with the ends of its whiskers, it develops a neurosis; I too required something to touch and was apparently already beginning to develop withdrawal symptoms, just as a drug addict whose source has been cut off still yearns for narcotics though he realizes they are a virulent poison.

I had exhausted my patience. I wanted to swim back to firm land quickly any way I could. I thought this was our house, but it was only a temporary shelter; and the mask itself —it was far from being a temporary face, for it had cured me of my seasickness while I was wearing it—seemed to be real land. I decided to go out as soon as we had finished supper, on the pretext of having suddenly remembered an urgent experiment, that I could not leave half done. I said that I should perhaps be staying away for the night. Although this was quite unprecedented, you did not seem to disapprove, nor did your face with its vaguely commiserating expression show any suspicion. There was no need to be concerned, whatever the excuse, if a faceless monster was going to spend the night out.

After I had arrived in the vicinity of my hideaway, I telephoned you, not being able to wait any longer.

"Has ... 'he' ... come back?"

"Yes, but he said something about going right out to work again."

"I'm glad you answered the telephone. If he had answered I should have hung up at once."

I spoke casually, trying to make my recklessness plausible, but after saying nothing for a while, you said in a thin voice: "I feel sorry for him."

These words pierced me, spreading rapidly throughout my body like pure alcohol. Perhaps these were your first feelings about the real me. But I could not think about such things now. If I could not get my hands on something quickly—anything, a log, a drum—I was apparently going to drown. Surely, if "he" really existed, this rendezvous would be a bit too reckless. He might come back at any time, for any reason. Even if he did not return, it was very possible he might telephone. It would be all right during the day, but what justification could you give for leaving the house at such an hour as this? I thought that you would naturally be reluctant; however, you consented with no hesitation at all. You too, struggling no less than I, were thrashing about in the waves searching for something to cling to. After all you were a shameless person too. You were prudish, hypocritical, shameless, impulsive, wanton, and lascivious, I thought, grinding my teeth under my bandages. I smiled a tight, cynical smile. Finally a shudder stopped the gnashing and froze the smile on my face.

What kind of a person were you, for God's sake?

What kind of a person were you, you who had gone through

the barrier of taboos unopposed and unabashed, who had
seduced the seducer, plunged him into self-contempt, you
who had never been violated? Yes, you had not once tried to
ask the given name, family name, or occupation of the mask.
As if you had seen through to the real person behind it. The
freedom of the mask and its alibi completely faded away be-
for this behavior of yours. If there is a God, may he appoint
you a hunter of masks. I would most certainly be hunted
down by you.

A VOICE called to me from the bottom of
the emergency stairway. It was the superintendent's daughter.
She was demanding the yoyo. For an instant, I was going to
answer, and then, seized with panic, I nearly ran away. It was
not I who had made the agreement with the girl but the mask.
At length I got control of myself and in my confusion realized
that what I could do was pretend not to understand. I could
only assume that she had mistaken me for someone else.

But the girl did not appear to notice my theatricals and
simply repeated her demands for the yoyo. Or was she perhaps
thinking that since the "mask" and the "bandage" were
brothers, an agreement made with one would automatically
include the other? No, such wishful thinking was successfully
demolished by the girl's next words.

"Don't worry.... We're playing secrets."

Indeed, had she seen through me from the beginning? Yet how could I have been seen through? Where had I made my mistake? Could she have peeped in through a crack in the door as I was putting on my mask?

But the girl only shook her head right and left, repeating that she did not understand why I did not understand. Was my mask something that could not deceive the eyes of a retarded girl? No, I suppose that she had been able to see through me precisely because she was retarded. Just as my mask would not fool a dog. An uninhibited intuition is often far more keen than the analytical eyes of an adult. There could not be such apparent deficiencies in a mask that had successfully deceived you who were closest to me.

No, the significance of this experience was not a simple thing, like seeking an alibi. Suddenly I could not control the shiver that rose gradually in me at the profound realization of this "uninhibited intuition." Such intuition suggested that my whole year's experience could be completely destroyed with a single blow. Wasn't it a sign that the girl had seen directly through to my real self without being taken in by the outward appearance of the mask or bandage? Such eyes actually existed. What I was doing must surely be funny to a girl like this.

Suddenly, the passions of the mask, my hatred for the scars, began to seem unbearably hollow, and the triangle with its roaring spin began gradually to lose momentum, like a carrousel whose motor has been switched off.

While the girl waited by the door, I got the yoyo. "It's a game of secrets," the girl whispered softly once more. She ran down the stairs, wrapping the string around her finger, childlike, unable to hide the smile that appeared in the corners of her lips. For no reason, tears welled up in my eyes. I washed my face, removed the ointment, and put on the mask after spreading it with adhesive material; but quite some space had already come between it and my face. Never mind. I was quietly sad, like the surface of a tranquil lake under a cloud-filled sky, but I said again and again to myself that it would be well if I believed the child's eyes with complete confidence. Wouldn't anybody first have to return to this kind of intuition if he sincerely wanted to face others?

AND that night when I came home from my second meeting with you, I decided to begin writing these notes.

Actually, had I waited a little longer, I should have torn the mask from my face in the middle of the act. I could not stand seeing you unsuspectingly seduced by a mask that the superintendent's daughter had seen through so simply. Moreover, I too was tired. The mask was no longer a means by which to get you back, but only a hidden camera through which to watch your betrayal of me. I had made the mask for the purpose of recovering myself. But it had willfully escaped from me and, taking great pleasure in its evasion, had become defiant; the next time I would bar its way. Moreover, among you and the mask and me, you alone had escaped intact. What would happen if I were to let such a situation go on? From now on, "I" would try to kill the mask at every opportunity, and the mask, being the mask, by every means would forever try to contain my revenge. It would strike back, for example, with a plan to kill you.

When all was said and done, if I did not wish to make matters worse, there was nothing to do but liquidate this three-cornered relationship by a three-party agreement, which included you with us. Then I began writing these notes—at first, the mask had a terrible contempt for my determination, but since nothing resulted, it ridiculed me in silence—and close to two months have gone by since then. In the meantime we have met over ten times, and each time I was desperate when I thought of our approaching separation. The expression is not gratuitous; for me it really was a harrowing experience. How many times I lost my confidence and gave up these notes. I prayed for the fairy-tale miracle of awakening one morning to find the mask stuck firmly on my face, to discover it had become my real face. I even tried going to bed with it on. But the miracle, of course, did not happen.

At such times, what cheered me most was to watch the girl quietly playing with her yoyo in the shadow of the emergency stairs, unseen by anyone but me. She was burdened with a great misfortune that she could not perceive as misfortune. She did not know how much luckier she was than the rest of mankind aware of unhappiness. Perhaps this attitude of hers, her having no fear of losing, was instinctive. I wish that I, like the girl, could bear losing.

I happened on a curious photograph of a mask in the morning paper. It was a mask used by a primitive people. Over the whole surface, traces of impressed rope formed a geometric pattern, and a centipede-like nose began in the middle of the face and rose above the head, while from the jaw were suspended a number of oddly shaped, meaningless objects. The image was not clear, but I stared at it in fascination for a long time. The face of a tattooed man imposed itself over the picture, and then the veiled heads of Arabian girls; I was reminded of the story I had once heard of the women in *The Tale of Genji* who thought that revealing the face was the same as exposing the privates. I did not hear it from just anybody, I heard it from you. The mask had got the story from you at one or another of our meetings. What was your purpose, for heaven's sake, in telling such a tale? They thought their hair was the only thing to show men, and they covered their faces with their sleeves in death. I mused about those women who hid with their faces, trying to penetrate your design, and this faceless period of history was unexpectedly brought home to me, unrolled like a picture scroll. In ancient times the face was not something one exposed to light; by bringing the face into full daylight, civilization was able to fix the core of man in it. Suppose the face did not simply exist but was made. I had planned to make a mask, but actually I had not made a mask at all. The mask had become my real face, and thought itself in fact real. No, that's enough . . . such things are of little consequence at this point. The mask too apparently intended to come to terms, and so shall I get on with the conclusion? But later, if I could, I should like to hear your confession too. . . . I don't know where we go from here, but there appears to be time left to talk things over together.

Yesterday I gave you a map to lead you to this hideaway for our last meeting. The appointed hour is gradually approaching. I wonder if I haven't left something out. It is too late if I have. The mask was loath to part from you. Since the button you gave me is rightly the mask's, let it be buried with him.

You must have finished reading by now. I have placed the key under the ashtray at the head of the bed and want you to open the closet. To the left of the rubber boots in the front lie the corpse of the mask and the button. I leave it all up to you. I shall have returned home a step ahead of you. I pray with all my heart that you will come back with your usual expression, as if nothing has happened. . . .

A record for me alone,
appended to the Grey Notebook,
written on the back of the last
page and to be read backwards
toward the beginning of the notebook.

. . . I kept on waiting. I simply went on waiting, emotionlessly, like barley sprouts that, having been repeatedly trampled on the whole winter long, only await the signal to raise their heads. . . .

I thought of you reading through the three notebooks in the hideaway apartment with no room even to stretch your legs, an apartment born with an old face. Like some protozoan organism with but a single fiber of nerve, I continued to float quietly in lightless, colorless, empty expectation.

But curiously, all I could think of was this image of you. Why was I incapable of tracing the place in these notes at which your inner nature was depicted? Far from that, I had come to the point where, like some scene observed through dirty glass, I could not locate any particular passage in these notes, which I had read and reread time and time again until I should have been able to recite any phrase. My heart was cold, salty, and limp, like a piece of half-dried squid. Was it because I had given up, thinking it would be unavailing no matter how much I tried to start all over again? Yes, this state of blankness was one I had experienced on finishing a series of experiments. And the more involved these experiments, the more profound the blank that followed.

Thus, this bold wager put me in a situation where everything was up to you, no matter what the dice turned up. Of course, I knew very well that exposing the true character of the mask would probably hurt and humiliate you. But you had wounded me by your betrayal, and we were about even on these two points. There was no object in being defiant; I had absolutely no intention of accusing you, no matter what reaction you showed to the notes. Tentatively, the situation had deteriorated even further from what it had been before the advent of the mask. Our relationship had come to be locked in a column of ice, but as one solution, I was amply prepared to be receptive to your reactions.

No, I could not go so far as to call this a solution, yet at least it was saving the situation. Bitter regret, irritation, defeatism, imprecation, self-tormenting sentimentalism—all such bitterness I wrapped away, and for good or for bad I heaved a sigh of resignation as if I had accomplished something by this. It was not that I had no desire for things to turn out right. I had raised the white flag by not taking off my mask when I was in bed with you but waiting to tell you about it in these notes. Whatever the result, it would surely be much better than this extraordinary three-sided relationship—this self-intoxication with jealousy that continued to grow like a cancer.

I could not say that I had reaped no harvest at all. My efforts did seem to have put me in a better position than before, but such an experience could not be wiped away, leaving no mark at all. At least I had made a big catch simply by realizing that my real face was merely an incomplete mask. I was perhaps being too optimistic, but this knowledge gave me great strength. Even if I were to be enclosed forever in this unmelting column of ice, I would discover sufficient human

life in it to get along without ever again going through the
useless struggle I had been locked in until now. However, I
had better think things through carefully again after I have
returned with your surrender in hand. At this point, there is
nothing to do but wait....

I collapsed limply on the matting of the living room, like
some marionette whose strings have been cut, trying not to
resist the flow of time. A rectangular piece of whitish sky, cut
out between the window frame and the eaves of the house
next door, seemed quite like the extension of a jail wall. Without taking my eyes from it, I persuaded myself that this was so.
I was not the only one who had been shut in; considering the
whole world a jail was quite in keeping with my feelings at the
time. Even more, I imagined that everyone was frantically
trying to escape from the world. The real face becoming useless, like a vestigial tail, was an unexpected fetter, and apparently one from which not a single person had succeeded
in escaping. But ... I was different. I alone—it had lasted but
a moment—had experienced life beyond the wall. Unable to
stand the overconcentrated air there, I had come running
back; still, I had had the experience. As long as I could not
deny existence beyond the wall, my real face, which was
merely an incomplete copy of the mask, could never over-
whelm me. Since you have heard my confession, you can
surely have no objection to these points at least, but....

But the concrete wall that cut off the sky gradually lost its
luminosity, and as it dissolved into the darkness, I was overcome with an uncontrollable irritation at my efforts to defy
the passage of time. For God's sake, how far have you got in
your reading? I should have some idea if I knew the average
number of pages you read per hour, but.... Suppose you did
a page a minute: that would make sixty. Then since four
hours and twenty minutes have gone by, you should be reaching the end pretty soon. Of course, you would be distracted

and bored at times. You will probably just have to grit your teeth and put up with it, as if you were seasick. But no matter what the delays, you can't need more than another hour. I suddenly jumped up and then remembered that there was no reason to, except that I did not feel like sleeping. I turned on the light and put the kettle on the gas burner. On my way back from the kitchen, I unexpectedly caught your odor—the smell of your cosmetics, coming from the dressing table at the entrance to the bedroom.

I was overcome by a paroxysm of nausea, as if I had had the inside of my throat painted with iodine. It was apparently an immediate reaction of the scar webs that had been laid bare. But at this point, was I qualified, I wondered, to look down on another's cosmetic equipment, I who had already once taken the main role in a masked play? I must be more generous. Once and for all, I should have to graduate immediately from this childish state in which I clung to make-up and wigs. Then I decided to concentrate all my attention on the psychology of make-up, seeking a cure for my deep abhorrence of cosmetics. Make-up—making a face—is indeed a denial of the real face, but a gallant effort to get a little closer to others by transforming the expression. But when a woman's make-up obtains the desired effect, is she jealous of it? Women do not particularly seem to be. It is a very curious thing. Why do deeply jealous women not show the slightest reaction to others who have imitated their faces? Is it a lack of imagination, or a spirit of self-sacrifice? Or is it that they have an excess of self and imagination, and that the distinction between self and others has ceased to exist? All this was pretty wide of the mark and apparently quite incapable of curing my abhorrence of make-up. (Of course, it is different now. I'll continue in the light of my present feeling. The fact that women get along without being jealous of their own make-up is perhaps the result of instinctively perceiving the drop in

value of their own face. It is because they instinctively realize
that the virtues of their real faces are merely left-overs from
a period when hereditary property was one's security; and unfortunately they are without property. Isn't this attitude far
more realistic, far more consonant with reason, than that of
men who cling to the authority of the real face? Of course,
women condemn make-up for children. I wonder if they do
not have some misgiving about it. If they do, the responsibility probably lies in the conservatism of secondary education
rather than in women's lack of confidence. If one were to
press the effectiveness of secondary education to its logical
conclusion, naturally men too would accept cosmetics freely.
No, let's stop. . . . At this point, no matter how many different
possibilities I claim, they can after all be only a prisoner's
lament. In a nutshell, the mask was probably just not competent to cure my latent phobia for make-up.)

For distraction I turned on the television set. As luck would
have it, it was just the time for the foreign news, and a report
was in progress on the Negro riots in America. Having talked
about the wretched black people in torn shirts who were being
marched away by white police officers, the announcer continued matter-of-factly:

—The racial disturbances in New York are a cause for
concern at the beginning of this long, black summer.
They have materialized just as predicted by competent
sources. Harlem streets are overflowing with more than
five hundred helmeted police, Negro and white. One is
reminded of the summer of 1943. In some churches, opposition meetings are being held along with Sunday serv-
ices. The contempt and mistrust that exist between
police and colored citizens. . . .

The words gave me an intolerable feeling of pain and depression, as if a sharp fishbone had thrust itself between my

teeth. Of course, I had almost nothing in common with the Negroes, except for being an object of prejudice. The Negroes were comrades bound in the same cause, but I was quite alone. Even though the Negro question might be a grave social problem, my own case could never go beyond the limits of the personal. However, what gave me such a stifling feeling as I watched the riot scenes stemmed from an association of ideas whereby I saw thousands of men and women, like me without faces, gathering together. Could we, the faceless, arise resolutely against prejudice like the Negroes? It would be impossible. Disgusted with each other's ugliness, we would probably begin to battle among ourselves. If we did not do that, the only thing for one like us would be to start running full speed until he disappeared from sight. No, if all this were true, I could still have borne it. However, I was apparently quite fascinated with the riots. On the slightest pretext, groups of us monsters might make unprovoked attacks on the faces of honest citizens. Out of malice? Or would it be some ploy to profit by increasing our ranks with every ordinary face we smashed? Both were definitely strong motives, but I seemed to be stimulated by a desire to be buried as a soldier in the riot's storm. Surely the soldier enjoys an anonymous existence. Even without a face he would have no difficulty in accomplishing his mission, and he would be provided with an excellent *raison d'être*. Faceless battalions would be ideal groups of soldiers. Unflinchingly rushing on to destruction for the sake of destruction, they would make splendid fighting units.

This was perhaps quite true, but I was still as alone as before. I with an air pistol concealed in my pocket, I who had not even attempted to shoot down a bird. Disgusted, I switched off the television set and looked at my watch; the appointed hour had already gone by.

Naturally, I was upset. I listened for sounds outside, checking my watch every few minutes. I had an unbearable feeling

like flood waters beginning to rise. There! Footsteps! But
when the neighbor's dog began to bark, I realized that it was
someone else. But now? No, surely. The sounds were too
heavy for you. For some time I listened to the noises of autos
stopping and the opening and closing of doors, but unfortunately they came from the direction of the lane in back. I
grew more and more distressed. What in God's name was
holding you up? Had you met mishap? A traffic accident? A
rapist's attack? If you had, at least you could have telephoned
... even you who liked rape.... No, I must not say that. Even
jokingly there are things you say and things you don't. Our
experience had a thin, supersensitive skin that could never be
touched by such expressions.

How would it be, since I was so worried, if I went to meet
you? Let's not jump the gun. If I left now, we would miss
each other on the road. Even if you had finished reading, it
might well be taking you more time than I had calculated to
collect your thoughts and decide how best to answer me.
Then there was also the business of burying the mask, which
I entrusted to you. Even though you left the notebooks as
evidence, you may have decided to smash the button and cut
the mask into bits in order to do away with every last vestige
of this nightmare, and this may have taken more time than I
anticipated. Whichever it was, from now on it was only a
question of time. Perhaps you were already on the way home.
In three more minutes you would be at the door, ringing your
usual two short buzzes. Yes, only two more minutes ... one
more....

It didn't work. Let's begin again from the beginning Five
minutes more ... four ... three ... two ... one ... As I kept
repeating these sequences, nine o'clock came round, then ten,
and before I knew it it was almost eleven. Like a steel pipe
that has split open under strain, my senses vibrated with the
commotion in the distant streets, moaning and answering

back in timid whispers. What other possibilities could there be, in heaven's name? Where else could you go besides returning here? But there was no answer. Naturally. There could be no answer. As long as you were careful and did not misread the notes. . . .

Then suddenly I let out a curse. Hastily wrapping the bandages around my face, I locked up and hurried out. What was I fiddling around for anyway? I should have made up my mind much sooner! Perhaps it was already too late! Late? How could it be too late? I did not know myself what I meant by that, but my premonitions, darker than the inside of a monster's throat, spewed out ominous vapor.

The premonitions were absolutely correct. It was a little before midnight when I arrived at the apartment. The light in the room was out and there was no sign of anyone. Cursing the self-complacency with which I had gone on mindlessly waiting until it was so late, I mounted the emergency stairs and opened the door, a bitter taste in my mouth. My heart was pounding like a hammer. After making sure there was no sound in the room, I carefully turned on the light and looked around. You were not there. Your corpse was not there either. The room looked exactly as I had left it. The three notebooks lay on the table, and even the sheet of paper I had put there, with instructions for you to open to the first page of the first notebook, lay untouched under the ink bottle I had weighted it down with. Then you had not been in the room after all. The mystery was growing. Although the burden of my responsibility was lighter, the fact remained that it would be even more of a disaster if you had gone off without reading at all than if you had disappeared after having read. I looked in the closet. Neither the button nor the mask showed the slightest sign of having been touched.

But . . . just a minute. That smell. . . . Yes! The smell, faintly colored with the odor of mold and dust, was unmistakably yours. Then you had been here. Yet the fact that the note I had left was in the same place as before seemed to indicate that you had ignored the notebooks. . . . What in the deuce did it mean when you had taken the pains to come this far?

As I carelessly perused the note, I gave a start. The paper was just like what I had used, but the writing was different. It was a letter addressed to me, written in your hand on the back of my own note. You had apparently disappeared after having read the notebooks. The worst had apparently come to pass, just as I had feared.

No, I should not use such words as "the worst" so glibly. The contents of your letter far exceeded any of my expectations and took me completely by surprise. No matter how much I had been afraid, perplexed, worried, distressed, and upset, such feelings meant nothing now. With a dash of the pen, as in a puzzle where a flea is transformed into an elephant, the outcome had been changed into something different from what I had planned. The mask's determination, its thoughts, its struggle with my real face, and the petition to you that I had tried to get across through the notes—all had been made ino an absurd burlesque. It was a terrible thing. Who could imagine that one could be so ridiculed, so humiliated by oneself?

MY WIFE'S LETTER

IT WAS NOT the mask that died among the boots, but you. The girl with the yoyo was not the only one to know about your masked play. From the very first instant, when, elated with pride, you talked about the distortion of the magnetic field, I too saw through you completely. Please don't insult me any more by asking how I did it. Of course, I was flustered, confused, and frightened to death. Under any circumstances, it was an unimaginably drastic way of acting, so different from your ordinary self. It was hallucinatory, seeing you so full of self-confidence. Even you knew very well that I had seen through you. You knew and yet demanded that we go on with the play in silence. I considered it a dreadful thing at first, but I soon changed my mind, thinking that perhaps you were acting out of sympathy for me. Then, though the things you did seemed a little embarrassing, they began to present the appearance of a delicate and suave invitation to a dance. And as I watched you become amazingly serious and go on pretending to be deceived, my heart began to fill with a feeling of gratitude, and so I followed after you meekly.

But you went from one misunderstanding to the next, didn't you? You write that I rejected you, but that's not true. Didn't you reject yourself all by yourself? I felt that I could understand your wanting to. In view of the accident and all, I had more than half resigned myself to sharing your suffering. For that very reason, your mask seemed quite good to me. In a happy frame of mind, I reflected that love strips the mask from each of us, and we must endeavor for those we love to put the mask on so that it can be taken off again. For if there is no mask to start with, there is no pleasure in removing it, is there? Do you understand what I mean?

I think you do. After all, don't even you have your doubts? Is what you think to be the mask in reality your real face, or is what you think to be your real face really a mask? Yes, you do understand. Anyone who is seduced is seduced realizing this.

But the mask did not return. At first you were apparently trying to get your own self back by means of the mask, but before you knew it you had come to think of it only as your magician's cloak for escaping from yourself. So it was not a mask, but somewhat the same as another real face, wasn't it? You finally revealed your true colors. It was not the mask, but you yourself. It is meaningful to put a mask on, precisely because one makes others realize it is a mask. Even with cosmetics, which you abominate so, we never try to conceal the fact that it is make-up. After all, it was not that the mask was bad, but that you were too unaware of how to treat it. Even though you put the mask on, you could not do a thing while you were wearing it. Good or bad, you could not do a thing. All you could manage was to wander through the streets and write long, never-ending confessions, like a snake with its tail in its mouth. It was all the same to you whether you burned your face or didn't, whether you put on a mask or didn't. You were incapable of calling the mask back. Since the mask will not come back, there is no reason for me to return either.

Nevertheless, these notes were a terrible confession. I felt as if I had been forced onto an operating table, although I was not sick, and hacked up indiscriminately with a hundred different knives and scissors, even the uses of which were incomprehensible. With this in mind, please read through what you have written once again. Surely even you will be able to hear my cries of pain. If I had the time, I should like to explain the significance of those cries one by one. But it would be dreadful if I were so careless as to let you return while I was still here. It really would be dreadful. While you spoke of the face as being some kind of roadway between fellow human beings, you were like a snail that thinks only of its own doorway. You were showing off. Even though you had forced me into a compound where I had already been, you set up a fuss as if I had scaled a prison wall, as if I had absconded with money. And so, when you began to focus on my face you were flustered and confused, and without a word you at once nailed up the door of the mask. Indeed, as you said, perhaps death filled the world. I wonder if scattering the seeds of death is not the deed of men who think only of themselves, as you do.

You don't need me. What you really need is a mirror. Because any stranger is for you simply a mirror in which to reflect yourself. I don't ever again want to return to such a desert of mirrors. My insides have almost burst with your ridicule. I shall never be able to get over it, never.

(And then came about two and a half lines of erasures, obliterated to the point of illegibility.)

WHAT a surprise attack. To imagine that you perceived that my mask was a mask and nevertheless went on pretending to be deceived. A swarm of shame, centipede-legged, streamed out, choosing the parts of me most subject to goose flesh—my armpits, my back, my sides. Indeed, my nerves, feeling the humiliation, seemed to be at the very surface of my skin. I became flacid as a drowned man with the hives of my shame. It was stupid of me, however normal it may have been, to say that I had not wanted to be a clown and unaware of it; but these very lines have become those of a clown. To imagine that you had seen through everything! It was as if I were putting on a play in which I was the only actor, thinking I was invisible, believing in a fake spell. I was completely oblivious to the fact that I had been seen by a spectator. My swarming shame plowed my skin. Sea urchin spines sprouted in the turned-up furrows. Soon I should be obliged to join the ranks of spiny creatures. . . .

I stood swaying in blank amazement. When I saw my shadow teetering with me, I realized that it was not my imagination but that I actually was swaying. I had made a terrible blunder. I had taken the wrong bus someplace. How far back would I have to go to change for one in the right direction, for God's sake? As I stood wavering, I tried to retrace the route of my memories with the help of a stained, illegible map.

The jealousy-filled night when I decided to write these

notes. The afternoon of the seduction when I first spoke to you. The time I thought I was becoming a lecher. The faintly smiling dawn when I had at last completed the mask. The evening with its promise of rain when I began making the mask. And then the long period of bandages and scar webs that had led to all this. Still not enough? Though I had come this far, if I had taken the wrong route, I should have to find another point of departure in yet another direction. I wonder whether I was really stagnant water within, despite the outside container, as you imply.

There is no reason for me to accept this assertion of yours. I absolutely cannot agree with the opinion that someone who plants the seeds of death is a selfish person thinking only of himself. The expression "selfish person" is an extremely happy and interesting one, I think, but however you consider it you lend it too much significance when you think of it as anything more than a result. Thinking only of oneself is forever a result, never a cause. Because—I wrote this in my notes—what contemporary society needs is essentially abstract human relationships, so that even faceless people like me can earn their wages with no interference. Naturally, human relations are concrete. One's fellow man is increasingly treated as useless and at best continues a piecemeal existence in books and in solitary islands of family groups. No matter how much television dramas go on singing the cloying praises of the family, it is the outside world, full of enemies and lechers, that passes on a man's worth, pays his wages, and guarantees him the right to live. The smell of poison and death clings to any stranger, and people have become allergic to outsiders without realizing it. Loneliness is terrible, of course, but being betrayed by the mask of one's fellow man is much worse. We are awkward at espousing the illusions of our fellow men, but we do not want to be so stupid as to drop out of step. Our habitual, daily routines appear merely as common, everyday

battles. People strive to protect themselves against the en-
croachments of others, dropping a Venetian blind over their
faces and fastening it tight. And if things go well they dream
up impossible desires—just as my mask tried to do—wanting
to escape from themselves, to be invisible beings. No stranger
is so tractable that one can know him just by wanting to. Was
it not rather you who were seriously afflicted with this oblivi-
ousness to strangers, you who were possessed with the idea
that you could make the conquest of a stranger by thinking
only of yourself?

Of course, it serves no purpose to cling to such trivial
thoughts at this point. The essential thing is the truth, not
arguments or complaints. There are two indications that your
sniping at me was fatal. One is the cruel revelation that while
you had seen through the real character of the mask, you had
nonetheless gone on pretending to be deceived. The other is
the merciless chastisement of claiming that I tediously talked
on and on about alibis, anonymity, pure goals, and the destroying of taboos. In actual fact I did not perform a single real
act but simply went round in circles writing these notes.

My mask, which I had expected to be a shield of steel, was
broken more easily than glass. I cannot refute you on that. As
you said, I had come to feel that the mask was closer to being
a new face for me than a mask. If I still intended to persist
in believing that my real face was an incomplete copy of the
mask, then I had gone to a lot of trouble to make a fake mask.

Perhaps this was so. Abruptly I recalled the primitive mask
I had seen some days before in the newspaper. Certainly that
must be a real mask. Perhaps one could only call something
which completely got away from the real face a mask. The
popping, bug-like eyes, the great mouth filled with fangs, the
nose set with shiny buttons. . . . Down the sides of the nose a
number of tendrils had swirled out over the whole face, and
the entire circumference was stuck with long bird feathers,

like a quiver for arrows. The more I had looked at it, the more weirdly strange, the more unreal it had appeared. As I had stared at it, wanting to put it on myself, I had gradually begun to grasp its meaning. It was the expression of a poignant aspiration to go beyond man, an effort to consort with the gods. What a horrible imagination! It was a violent compression of will in an attempt to combat a natural taboo. Perhaps I should have made a mask like that. If I had, from the very beginning I should have been able to dispense with my feeling of deceiving others.

Not at all. Since I had spoken rashly, I had been subjected to your sarcasm when you spoke of complicated scissors and knives of incomprehensible uses. If it was all right to be a monster, weren't my scar webs enough without the mask? Gods change, and so do men. Man has gone through periods of covering up his face, like the ladies in *The Tale of Genji* or veiled Arabian women, and at last we have arrived at the period of the real face. Of course, I do not claim that this is progress. It may be thought of as man's victory over the gods; but at the same time it may be a sign of his allegiance to them. We never know what tomorrow will bring. Surprisingly, it is not altogether impossible that the future may see a period of rejecting the face again. But the present age belongs to man rather than to the gods. There was a reason why my mask was identical with my real face.

No, that's enough. Enough of reasoning. If I searched, I could certainly find as many pretexts as I wanted. But no matter how many objections I marshalled, I should not be able to reverse the two facts that you pointed out to me. I should have gradually come round to the second one: that my mask had complained without ultimately doing anything. Enough of this coat of shame. It would be all right if it were only a question of clowns and fiascos, but since the experience had turned out to be worthless I was too wretched and embarrassed even to justify it. It would be meaningless to call it desperation. I had had a perfect alibi, unrestricted freedom, yet I had gained nothing. In addition, I had been ridiculous to destroy my own alibi by writing up such a detailed report. I was like some wretched creature in ideal sexual prime, but without a penis.

Yes, perhaps I should write about the movie. I think it was around the first of February. I did not name the movie in my notes, but rather than being unrelated to what I was writing about, it was much too pertinent. I had the feeling it would be ludicrous to mention it when I was making the mask, and I deliberately avoided it. However, as things have come to this pass, there is no purpose in being superstitious. Or perhaps the situation has changed; anyway, my impressions of it have completely altered. Surely it was not simply cruelty. The film was eccentric and did not create much of a sensation, but I think you will recall the title, *One Side of Love*.

A SLENDER, neat-looking, modestly dressed girl was gliding along in a quiet, stark setting. She had a transparent, sprite-like profile. As the picture showed her walking from right to left, she revealed only the left side of herself to us. She walked along almost rubbing against the concrete building in the background with her right shoulder, which we could not see. She seemed dazzled by the world, and this fitted her grief-stricken profile, strengthening even more the impression of her loveliness.

At the curb, on the same side of the street, three young men who looked like delinquents lolled against a railing, each with one foot propped against it, awaiting the arrival of a victim. Seeing the girl, one of them whistled at her. The girl showed no reaction, as if she lacked sense-organs to receive external stimuli. Another of the boys, provoked, left his place and approached her. With an experienced gesture he grasped the girl's left arm from behind and tried to pull her back, muttering something obscene. The girl, as if resigned, stopped walking and slowly turned and looked in the direction of the young man. The right side of her face, which she revealed for the first time, was pitifully disfigured with keloid ridges and distortions, and was completely transformed. (No full explanation was given, but the name "Hiroshima" was constantly repeated in the following dialogue.) Startled, the young man stood in dumb amazement, while the girl, turning once more her beautiful, fairy-like profile, walked on as if nothing had happened.

She went down several streets, and every time she came to a crossing or other place that did not offer adequate cover on her right side, it was an obvious ordeal—I was about ready to jump out of my seat in sympathy for her—and finally, after several blocks, she came to a barracks-like structure surrounded with barbed wire. The building was strange. It was as if we had suddenly been taken back twenty years; soldiers in war-time uniform were roaming around the courtyard. Some, with empty expressions as if they had returned from the grave, were giving orders or complying with them; still others would repeatedly advance three steps, then freeze, and salute; among them the most impressive was an old soldier, who compulsively kept repeating the Imperial Military Rescript.

Singly the words were distorted and the meaning lost, but the general idea and the tone were clearly there.

It was a mental institution for old soldiers. The patients continued to live faithfully in the past, in an eddy of time that had stopped twenty years before, unaware that the war had been lost. The girl's bearing as she walked through this depressing setting was amazingly lighthearted and insouciant. She and the men exchanged no words, but evident between them was a feeling of sympathy, as among fellow men who have been deprived of time. At length the girl, while being thanked by one of the orderlies, began to do the washing in a corner inside the building. This was an act of charity that the girl had chosen to perform once a week. When she looked up, she could see, between some buildings, a sun-drenched lot where children were innocently playing baseball.

Then the scene changed to a view of the girl's life at home. Her house was a small, suburban dwelling where the family made pressed tin toys, a prosaic, bleak place. But when the right and left sides of the girl's face appeared alternately in this simple setting, a delicate change came about and the cheap foot presses lined up in the workroom began to moan disconsolately. As this daily life was shown in conscientious, over-long detail, everything expressed an unutterable sense of grief for the future of this girl that would never come, and for the half of her face whose beauty would never be rewarded. On the other hand, we could understand how sympathy could be unbearable to her. And so we were not particularly surprised when in a fit of despair one day she was seized with the desire to apply sulphuric acid to the good side of her face and make it as ugly as the other. Of course, if she had done so, it would not have made sense. But she could think of no other way, and no one had the right to blame her.

Then, again on a different day, the girl suddenly turned

to her brother and said: "It doesn't look as if there'll be war for a long time, does it?"

Yet, in the girl's tone there was not the slightest note of wishing others ill. She apparently intended to suggest nothing like revenge on those who were unblemished. She seemed to nurture only the naïve hope that, if there were war, standards of value would be instantly reversed and people's interest would concentrate far more on the stomach than the face, on life itself rather than outer appearances. The brother apparently understood her feeling very well, and matching her tone, said quite casually: "No, not for some time, I suppose. But as far as tomorrow is concerned, even the weather report isn't very reliable, you know."

"Yes, I suppose so. If you could know what was going to happen tomorrow so easily, there wouldn't be much use for fortunetellers, would there?"

"True enough. Even with wars, you usually realize they've begun only after they've started."

"That's right, isn't it? Accidents, too. If you knew you were going to have one before it happened, you wouldn't have it."

It was pathetic and unbearable to hear them talking about war as if they were waiting for a letter from someone.

But in the town there was nothing that announced a resurgence of stomachs or of life. The camera traveled the streets for the benefit of the girl, but all it could catch was distorted gluttony and prodigal wastage of life. A deep sea of exhaust gases . . . numberless construction sites . . . groaning bins for garbage disposal . . . clanging fire engines . . . the frantic eyes of crowds at amusement places and bargain counters . . . a police box ringing and ringing . . . and the continuous bawling of television commercials. . . .

At length, the girl felt that she could not stand waiting any longer. Then she who had seldom asked for anything earnestly began to coax her brother to take her somewhere, somewhere far away—just once in her life. The brother realized immediately that the stress fell on *life* rather than on *once*. Since there was no way of helping and since he did not feel he could let her be more lonely than she was, he resigned himself to agreeing; the only way of expressing his love for her was to share her unhappiness.

Thus, several weeks later, the brother and sister went to the seashore. In a room of a country inn facing the darkening sea, the girl, hiding the injured right side of her face in the shadows and wanting to show even her brother only her beautiful side, looked happier than she ever had before, as she tied a ribbon in her hair. When the sister said that the sea was expressionless, the brother answered that that was not true at all, that it was the best of talkers. But this was their only difference of opinion, and as each vibrated to the other like a lover, the slightest word became doubly meaningful. The girl tried to pretend she was smoking a cigarette. At last their excitement gave way to a comfortable feeling of fatigue, and each of them lay down on their beds that stood side by side. In the meantime, from the window they had left open to see the moon, they watched the golden globe fall into the sea, spreading out along the horizon between sky and water; the girl spoke, but her brother no longer answered.

The girl watched the ridge of the moon gradually arch like a golden whale; for some time she waited for something to happen, but then at once reflected that this was a trip for the purpose of ending her waiting. Placing her hand on her brother's shoulder, she shook him to awaken him, whispering: "Won't you kiss me?"

The brother was too upset to go on pretending to be asleep. Looking through half-closed eyes at his sister's transparent, porcelain-like profile, he could neither scold her, nor, of course, could he consent. But the girl was not discouraged. "You can never tell . . . there might be a war tomorrow," she continued, whispering entreatingly, supplicatingly, as she brought her lips closer and closer to her brother's, her breath coming in gasps.

Thus the desperate destruction of a taboo began with a mad, incomplete fusion between the two discordant hammers of anger and desire. Love and hate . . . serenity and murderous intent . . . fusion and rejection . . . caressing and beating . . . tossed between conflicting passions, a high-speed plunge from which there was no return. But if this is shameful, who today can avoid being implicated?

Day was gradually breaking in the semicircle of sky, when the girl, listening for the breathing of her sleeping brother, softly arose and began to put on her clothes. Beside her brother's pillow she placed two envelopes she had previously prepared and quietly left the room. The moment the door closed the brother, who was supposed to be sleeping, opened his eyes wide. A senseless groan came from his half-open lips and a line of tears ran down his cheeks. Leaving the bed, he went to the window and looked out, gritting his teeth savagely. At last he saw the girl, like a white bird, running with little steps toward the black, heaving sea. Again and again the white bird was thrown back by the waves until at last it rode upon them, appearing and disappearing as it swam toward the open sea.

His knees had begun to ache unbearably on the hard floor when a single line of red lights appeared in the distance. His eyes were distracted by them for an instant, and when he looked again, the white spot of his sister had completely vanished, never to be seen again.

It seems to be proverbial that the story of the ugly duckling ends with the swan's song. This is typical opportunism. How would you feel if you were the swan? No matter what song others sang for the girl, she did die, she was unmistakably defeated. I don't want to be like the swan. I don't want that. If I die, there is no one to think of me as a swan, and furthermore I have a chance of winning. Well, when I first saw the movie I turned my face away in anger, but it is different now. I cannot escape a new sense of envy for the girl.

Anyway, she did act. She tried splendidly to break down an especially difficult sexual taboo, and even death, since she chose it herself, was far better than doing nothing. Thus she made even utterly unrelated strangers feel sorry for her and realize that they too were accomplices in her death.

All right, I too would give just one more chance to my mask, which fortunately had continued in existence. I would rescue all my past efforts from the void by breaking the present situation with some act—anything. Fortunately, my change of clothes and the air pistol were as I had left them. I unwrapped the bandages and put on the mask. There was an instantaneous change in my psychological make-up. For example, I did not even feel the forty years of my face. Looking into the mirror, I felt a certain nostalgia, as if I were meeting an old friend. The unique intoxication and self-confidence of the mask which I had quite forgotten began to be recharged with a hum. Let's not jump to hasty conclusions. The mask might not be absolutely right, but it was not completely wrong. In any situation the right solution isn't the only one.

Eagerly, as if protected by armor, I went out into the night streets. As I had expected, there was no one abroad at such an hour, and the sky lowered over the roof tops like a sick dog. A humid wind pierced my throat, and the feel of rain was in the air. I opened the directory in a nearby telephone booth, thinking of looking up two or three places where you might have taken refuge. Your parents' house, a schoolmate's, a cousin's.

But none of these produced any results. I could make nothing of the terribly vague answers I got, which I could believe or doubt as I liked. Since I had anticipated this situation to some extent, I was not altogether disheartened. Wouldn't it be better to go out and find you myself? There was still a little time before the last train, and if time were short I could get to the station fast by taxi.

Gradually anger welled up within me. I could understand your vexation, but after all wasn't it merely a question of your pride and your pretense of being humiliated at having been forced to associate with a clown? I did not intend to treat your pride as unimportant, but I could not help but wonder if it was exacerbated enough to make you break off all relations as you had done. I should like to ask you: when the boy kissed his sister in the film, what side did he kiss her on? You probably could not answer. For you did not cooperate with me as much as the boy did with his sister. Even though you recognized the necessity of the mask, it was only a domesticated mask that would never transgress the taboo. So, this time, you had better be careful. The mask that descends on you this time will be a wild animal. Since you have seen through it already, the mask will concentrate on its lawlessness, unweakened and unblinded by jealousy. You have dug your own grave by yourself. I have never had the experience of having anything in writing produce such results as these notes did.

Suddenly I heard the sharp clicking of a woman's heels. Only the mask remained; I had vanished. Instantaneously and without thinking, I concealed myself in a lane directly at hand, and releasing the safety catch of my pistol, I held my breath. What was I doing this for? Was it only play acting to test myself, or was I plotting something in earnest? I probably will not be able to answer the question myself until the final, decisive instant, until the woman comes into my range of attack.

But think a minute. I wonder if I shall become a swan with an act like this. Can I make people feel guilty for me? It is useless to think. What is amply clear, at least, is that I shall be lonely and isolated, that I shall only become a lecher. There will be no other reward outside of being freed from the crime of being ridiculous. Perhaps that's the difference between movies and actuality. Anyway, I shall have to go through with this, for doing so is the only way to conquer the face. Of course, I do know that the responsibility is not the mask's alone, and that the problem lies rather within me. Yet it is not only in me, but in everybody; I am not alone in this problem. True, indeed, but let's not shift the blame. I shall hate people. I shall never admit the necessity of justifying myself to anyone!

The footsteps are coming closer.

So nothing will ever be written down again. Perhaps the act of writing is necessary only when nothing happens.

A Note About the Author

Kobo Abe was born in Tokyo, but grew up in Mukden, Manchuria, where his father, a doctor, was on the staff of the medical school. At the end of World War II he returned to Japan. In 1948 he received a medical degree from Tokyo Imperial University, but he has never practiced medicine. In that same year he published his first book, *The Road Sign at the End of the Street*, and three years later he received the most important Japanese literary award, the Akutagawa Prize, for his novella *The Crime of Mr. S. Karuma*. In 1960 his novel *The Woman in the Dunes* won the Yomiuri Prize for Literature; subsequently this book was made into a film, which won the Jury Prize at the Cannes Film Festival, and it became the first of Mr. Abe's novels to be published in translation in the United States. Among his other major works which have been translated into English and other languages are *The Box Man, The Ruined Map, The Face of Another,* and *Inter Ice Age 4.* Today, Kobo Abe directs his own theater company in Tokyo, for which he creates several new plays each year. The company toured the United States in the summer of 1979, presenting performances in several cities. Mr. Abe lives in Tokyo with his wife, the artist and stage designer Machi Abe.

E. DALE SAUNDERS, translator of Kobo Abé's *The Woman in the Dunes* (1964), received his A.B. from Western Reserve University (1941), his M.A. from Harvard (1948), and his Ph.D from the University of Paris (1952). He is an associate professor of Japanese studies at the University of Pennsylvania, having previously taught at International Christian University, Tokyo, and at Harvard University. Among his publications are *Mudra: A Study of Symbolic Gestures in Japanese Buddhist Art* (1960) and *Buddhism in Japan* (1964).